The Fantasy Girl

Allan Taylor

The Fantasy Girl
Copyright ©2017 Allan Taylor

ISBN 978-1506-903-96-5 PRINT
ISBN 978-1506-903-97-2 EBOOK

LCCN 2017933581

March 2017

Published and Distributed by
First Edition Design Publishing, Inc.
P.O. Box 20217, Sarasota, FL 34276-3217
www.firsteditiondesignpublishing.com

1

The nightmares are the worst part. I can be in a deep sleep or the middle of some other dream, and then all of a sudden I'm back in the fucking Humvee again. It's so clear, it's almost like I'm wide awake, that same narrow street with the bombed-out buildings on both sides hemming us in. We were going fast with everybody quiet and on edge, the stink of our sweat mixing with the smell of the Humvee's exhaust, all of us wondering what the fuck we were heading into. Some guys were probably praying to themselves. I can feel the dryness in my throat again, and I'm craving a drink. I know what's coming, but I can't move; it's like I'm frozen.

Then we go over the bomb again. The noise comes close to shattering my eardrums, but the concussion from the blast is worse, rattling my brain around in my head as once again I'm airborne, landing hard on my back in the street with the pain going through my body like a powerful electric shock. I can hear somebody screaming and feel the heat from the flames. I'm struggling to remain conscious as I force my body to crawl toward the sound of the screaming. And then there's nothing, and I'm awake, soaked with sweat and shaking, my body sprawled across the bed. I lie there without moving, staring at the ceiling and waiting for my heart rate to go down. Instinctively, I feel around to make sure I'm all in one piece even though I know it was only a dream. I lie there like that in the darkness, sometimes for an hour or more, not moving, waiting for the images to recede. Finally, when I can get up the strength, I drag myself into the bathroom and throw up, as if my body, like my head, is trying to purge it all away. Then, I go into the kitchen and make myself a pot of coffee, and sit there and wait for dawn to come.

2

Becoming a cop hadn't exactly been a lifelong dream of mine. I grew up on the Cape, the oldest of four kids, and, like in many families, as the oldest I had it the toughest. I could never please my father, who worked two jobs to put food on the table for us and always seemed angry at the world in general, and me in particular. My father had grown up the hard way with a father who'd beat him, and I guess that was the only way he knew how to discipline a kid, especially a boy, which quickly led me to stay away from him as much as I could. I started getting into fights in middle school, and fighting at school got me in trouble, which got me into even more trouble at home. My mother tried to keep bad reports from the school away from my father, but that didn't always work and on those occasions there'd be hell to pay. I finally dropped out of high school the summer after my junior year to join the Army and get away. My father's parting words to me had been maybe the Army could make something out of me because he couldn't. My mother had simply cried.

Even though I'd dropped out of high school, getting into the Army hadn't been all that hard back then with Iraq and Afghanistan both pretty hot and not exactly a lot of guys rushing down to their local recruiter to sign up. In its infinite wisdom, the Army decided to make me a military policeman, which turned out to have its advantages when they sent me to Iraq, where I spent a lot of my time guarding the Green Zone and running VIPs back and forth to the airport, which was pretty much a tit job compared to what a lot of guys wound up doing over there.

On the whole, though, Iraq turned out to be even worse than I'd expected, especially outside the wire. It was hot, filthy, boring, and really fucking dangerous. You never knew who the enemy was, and every day you lived in constant fear of being shot at or blown to pieces by an IED. They strapped bombs onto women and even onto little kids, they packed them in cars, and sometimes they just left them on the side of the road under some object that might draw your attention, like a copy of Playboy or something. There were bomb blasts constantly, and practically every day you rode by a place where there were dead and maimed bodies from a recent detonation littered all over the street. They even planted bombs under the people who'd been blown up, so cleaning up after a bomb blast was tricky and took a long time with the dead just left lying out in the open. The smell of burnt flesh was awful, and it was something you never got used to.

And it was a pretty lonely existence. The women who served in the U. S. military over there were mostly either ugly or gay, or both, although that didn't stop about a zillion horny guys from hitting on them just about every time they turned around no matter how ugly they were. Anytime any of those women had ever wanted to get laid, she could've easily had a couple battalions of hard dicks to choose from. And the Arab women, who were mostly covered up from head to toe anyway, didn't hold much appeal, and nobody'd wanted some Arab woman's crazy brothers coming after him with Kalashnikovs because he'd fucked their sister. So, you pretty much had to take care of your needs yourself. Of course, it wasn't like I'd ever been a great ladies' man or anything back in high school; back then, I think a lot of the girls had probably stayed away from me intentionally.

But like I said, as unpleasant as it was my time in Iraq, for the most part, wasn't as bad as a lot of people's. I had pretty regular hours, slept on a cot and shat in a real toilet, the food was decent, alcohol was plentiful, and we had the internet and movies. Sometimes we even had live entertainment from an American or Australian band that was over there because they weren't good enough to play anywhere else. To help while away the time, I picked up body building thinking it would help me keep in shape. After a while, though, I started to really get into it and wound up going to the gym in the Green Zone five or six days a week in my off time. I began reading a lot about body building online and learned how to work on specific muscle groups to refine my overall look. I couldn't see myself entering body building competitions when I got back to the States in a skimpy thong with oil all over me, and most of the guys who did that kind of thing were more bulked up than I wanted to be anyway. But I liked the look and the feeling it gave me, and I thought it might improve my chances with the ladies once I got back to the real world.

I managed to get my high school GED while I was over there and made it to sergeant before my tour ended. And I was fortunate to get out of there alive and not come home in a body bag, although I came pretty fucking close. We were playing backup, which was the worst part of our unit's job. Whenever somebody in our division got their subpubic appendage caught in the ringer somewhere, there was always another unit assigned to be on call to come pull them out. But every once in a while, that other unit wasn't enough and they needed more backup, and our unit rotated with a bunch of others to serve that function. Fortunately, we weren't on call very often, but when we were there was always the possibility we could wind up in some pretty scary shit. If the call came in, which could be anytime day or night, we had to scramble and get there by the most direct route, usually riding into some shit show with little or no idea what the fuck was going on. And that was what we were doing the night we got hit. Somebody had set up an ambush and must've figured out in advance the way help would most likely come. So, heading to the rescue in one of the older version Humvees that had no armor plating in the floor, we wound up driving right over a bomb they'd planted in the middle of the street.

There were five of us crammed into the Humvee, and I was up top manning the M60. The explosion lifted the thing up like a toy and deposited it in the middle of the street on its side, where it burst into flames. The two guys in the front didn't have a chance and were dead on impact. I got thrown out onto the street, fracturing my collarbone, cracking my hip and a couple vertebrae in my back, and giving me a pretty severe concussion. I remember lying there in the street in some pretty serious pain, but that's all the memory I have of what happened until I woke sometime later on a table in a med unit with bright lights glaring down at me from the ceiling and two male nurses standing over me. I had burns on my hands and a number of other parts of my body, my head felt like somebody'd used it as a soccer ball, and I was in a lot of pain just about everywhere. But because my injuries were non-life threatening and treatable in country, I didn't get an early trip home, although when I was able to go back to my unit after about three weeks of bed rest, they put me on light duty for the rest of my tour. When I finally got my ass out of there and made it home, I was eligible to re-enlist and they tried to entice me into staying in, but I knew reenlistment meant going back to Iraq, maybe multiple times, and that didn't seem very attractive. I'd been lucky the first go-around, and I wasn't interested in having my number come up a second time. I wound up spending my last three months in the Army at Fort Bragg in North Carolina painting rocks until I was discharged.

When I got out, it took me a while to get readjusted, coming back to a world that on one hand was familiar but at the same time wasn't. All the stuff I'd thought about for months on end, the sights, the smells, the food, the women, the freedom, it was all there, but it was like Iraq was on some far away planet people only knew vaguely about and didn't want to let intrude into their otherwise comfortable lives. Young soldiers were getting the shit blown out of them every day, not to mention all the Iraqi civilians, and nobody seemed to really understand what it was like or cared. They just wanted to live their own lives and not think about it. It made me angry, like I wanted to shake them all and tell them to wake the fuck up. Here I was, where I'd dreamed for months of being again, but somehow it was all wrong and I didn't fit in, and I began to feel isolated and alone. And then the nightmares started.

After a bunch of those, and the feeling I was starting to fall into a deep hole, I decided I'd better try to get some help and see if there was something they could do for me. I didn't know where to go so I figured I'd try the VA, which was at least free, and I figured they'd be the ones who'd probably know the most about returning vets. What a fucking joke although I have to admit people warned me. I went there a total of four times and each time it was the same: you spent literally hours sitting around waiting to be seen, first by a receptionist just to check you in and go over your paperwork, and then by somebody you explained your problem to, and then by somebody in the psych unit who told you your reactions were common among returning vets, and they'd probably recede over time. Finally, on the fourth visit they must've figured I wasn't going to go away so they assigned me to a therapist who was supposed to evaluate me.

She was Asian, probably in her mid-twenties, petite and extremely attractive with dark skin that stood out against her white lab coat, beautiful long black hair and a soft smile. She wasn't Chinese or Japanese, but maybe Thai or Malaysian. When we shook hands, her hand felt tiny in mine and exquisitely feminine. With a large three ring binder in one arm, she led me into a small office that was mostly empty except for a gray metal desk set and a single hard plastic chair. She started out by asking me why I'd come, and I told her about the nightmares. She then proceeded to ask me questions for about forty minutes, about my childhood, my parents, school, why I joined the Army, and about Iraq, taking non-stop notes in the binder as I talked. I watched her as we were going back and forth, thinking about how beautiful she was and what it would be like to be in bed with her. It wasn't until we'd been talking for about thirty minutes that I was finally able to tell her about the Humvee getting blown up and all that shit. She nodded blankly, scribbling away as I described it all, obviously unable to really relate to anything I was saying.

Finally, at the end she told me nightmares were fairly common among returning combat vets, and as time went on I might develop some mild depression and perhaps at times feelings of isolation. She also told me to watch out for periods of anxiety and possibly moments of extreme anger. Like everybody else I'd seen, she said hopefully these symptoms would all recede over time and there wasn't a lot they could do to speed up the process, that I needed to heal like I'd suffered an actual physical wound. She also warned me to stay away from drugs and alcohol. I asked her about medication, and she told me there wasn't anything they could give me that was really going to help. She told me if I wanted to pursue a disability claim, I'd probably need a supporting opinion from somebody from the outside, and if it met the requirements they'd classify my symptoms as a disorder and I'd be eligible to receive disability payments although the process would probably take a while, maybe as long as a year. Yeah, like I really wanted to hire somebody to prove I was mentally disabled so I could get thirty bucks a month from the government and probably never get a job other than maybe working a pizza oven.

The whole thing was pretty superficial, like she was talking about somebody else's problems and not mine, and I really had trouble relating to this woman other than having horny thoughts about her. Hopefully she couldn't read my mind although I'm sure I probably wasn't the first horny interviewee just back from Iraq or Afghanistan she'd had to deal with. In the end, I thanked her and we shook hands again, and I walked out and didn't go back.

As far as the rest of my life was concerned, after I was discharged my choices were either to go back to school or get a job. School didn't hold much appeal, even with the government paying for it, and I had second thoughts about trying to get a job as a cop, but that was the only training I had. I finally decided I'd try to find something with some small town police department, figuring working as a city cop, which would've paid more, might've been too much for me considering my mental state at that particular point in time. I managed to get an entry level job on the police force of a small town in New Hampshire called Lakeville, where they didn't exactly have a lot of qualified candidates beating down the door. But I quickly found I couldn't stand New Hampshire, or Cow Hampshire as some people called it, and those miserable long, depressing winters.

Needing to get out of New Hampshire, the Cape had seemed like an obvious choice since I'd grown up there, and by a stroke of luck I managed to hook up with the police department in the town of New Salisbury. Of course, being a small town cop on the Cape wasn't a whole lot different from being a small town cop in New Hampshire; it was boring and the pay sucked, but at least I knew the Cape and the winters there weren't as bad, and I was able to support myself on what New Salisbury was paying me living in a tiny one bedroom cottage on the property of an elderly couple who were tickled to have a cop as a tenant to protect them from God knows what.

When I moved back to the Cape and took the job with New Salisbury, I figured at some point I should try to reconnect with my parents, who were now fairly close by. I hadn't had any contact with them since the day I'd walked out the door, which had obviously been my choice, but a lot of time had gone by, and I knew if I was ever going to have a relationship with them it was going to be up to me to take the first step, and the last thing I wanted was to run into my mother somewhere by accident. It took me about a month after I started work in New Salisbury to finally get up the courage to call them. There was no way I was going to just show up on their doorstep; I was afraid that might've been too much for all of us to handle. So, one evening after I knew they were probably finished with dinner, I dialed their number. It rang a couple of times, and then my father picked up. "Hi, Dad," I said, "it's Brian."

There was a long silence on the other end of the line, and then finally he said, "We don't know anybody by that name," and hung up. And that had been pretty much it.

3

July 19, 2012 Now, four years later, I was still working for New Salisbury and sitting on the desk in front of me was the first murder file I'd ever seen. It was a collection of manila folders bound together so you could flip through them like a book. Each folder had a clip inside so that the endless amounts of paperwork generated in a murder case could be fastened into the appropriate folder, and in the back were a couple of large envelopes to hold photographs, lab results, and technical stuff like that. Handwritten with a black marker across the front cover of the file was the victim's name—Valerie Jean Gray—and stapled to the inside of the cover was a five-by-seven color photograph of the victim, her high school graduation picture taken only a couple months before. She was in her cap and gown, looking slightly to the left of the camera and trying to look serious and smile at the same time. Her long blond hair was neatly arranged on her shoulders, and her blue eyes were sparkling in the photographer's lights. It wasn't a great picture, but you could see she looked older than somebody who was just graduating from high school, and even in the stupid graduation cap you could see how beautiful she was.

The fact that this was the first murder file I'd ever seen was hardly surprising given there weren't exactly a lot of murders in small Cape Cod towns like New Salisbury, and local cops like us usually weren't set up to handle a real murder case like this anyway. Valerie Jean Gray's file belonged to the Massachusetts State Police, who were officially in charge of investigating her homicide. The official case file was kept on the State Police's database, but it seemed like the people on the investigative side still liked to use a hard copy, and, expecting they'd need our help from time to time, they'd made a hard copy of the file for us as well. As new paperwork was generated, they'd email it to us to print out and put into our copy of the file. Some genius on our end had to keep track of all this complicated stuff and be the contact person when they needed something, and I said I'd do it. Out of eleven cops on the payroll besides the chief, I was the only one who'd volunteered.

The first we'd heard about a body being found was a phone call from the state cops the day they fished her out. They'd told whoever took the call that a woman's body with no identification on it had been found floating in Vineyard Sound down off the Elizabeth Islands by a guy out in his boat striper fishing. They'd described the victim as a woman about five-foot-seven, probably in her early twenties with blond hair, and asked if we'd had any reports of someone with that description having gone missing, which we hadn't. It wasn't until the next day when the two State Police detectives assigned to the case had shown up on our doorstep that we'd found out the identity of the victim and that it'd apparently been a homicide.

The two detectives were James Cavanaugh and Vincent Balzano. Cavanaugh fit the profile of a stereotypical Irish cop with thin lips, a pasty complexion, and not much of a personality. He was of average height and build with lousy teeth, receding red hair, and a heavy South Boston accent, which, on those rare occasions when he said anything, was grating to listen to. He carried a soft-covered notebook with him everywhere he went and was constantly writing things down, and when he wasn't doing that he liked to crack his knuckles.

Balzano was about five-foot-seven, overweight, with a swarthy Mediterranean complexion. He had thick black hair cut short, bushy eyebrows, a crumpled nose that looked like it had been broken a couple times, and a dark five o'clock shadow. His natural facial expression made him look like he was sneering at you, which seemed to fit his personality perfectly. Both of them looked like they got their suits at the Salvation Army. Neither was particularly impressive, or likable.

When they'd showed up that first day, they'd met with the Chief, Tom Mullally, who'd been a cop in town for almost forty years. Mullally wasn't the brightest bulb on the old holiday tree, but you don't have to be all that smart to make it as a small town Cape Cod cop. Now over sixty, he was expecting to retire in a year or two and move to Florida. He had a big red nose and a generous gut hanging over his belt, largely the product of a life-long love affair with doughnuts. His hair was completely white and if you'd put a beard and a red suit on him, he would've made a perfect shopping mall Santa Claus. He couldn't read without his glasses, which he hated to wear, and he didn't have much of a sense of humor. Most of the guys in the department thought he was a real pain in the ass to work for, but I'd managed to get along with him okay.

After a couple of quick phone calls, Mullally had been able to tell the two visitors that the victim had just graduated from the local high school a few weeks before and had lived alone with her mother. She'd had no police record, and, as previously indicated, hadn't been reported missing. Mullally had given them the mother's address and directions to the high school so they could talk with the school authorities, and that was about all the information we'd been able to provide to them at that point. Now, three days later, I was going back over what had made it into the file since their last visit because the Chief and I were scheduled to meet with them again that morning and one of us needed to be up to date on what was in the file. I knew Mullally expected that would be me as he wasn't particularly strong on paperwork.

Going through the file that morning didn't take all that long because there wasn't a whole lot in it yet, mainly just background stuff. The medical examiner had issued his report the day after the body had been found in which he'd concluded that Valerie Jean Gray had most likely died as a result of head trauma. The severity of the injury indicated she had been struck with considerable force on the right side of her head by a smooth object, most likely something metal. The jaw on the opposite side of her face was also broken, suggesting she'd first been struck in the jaw and then the fatal blow had been delivered to the other side of her head. Her body had been found floating in Vineyard Sound partially wrapped in a large sheet of plastic that had been tied around her with a piece of boat line. Evidently, one end of the boat line had at one time been attached to something else, but at some point the line had snapped, leading the medical examiner to conclude that someone likely had killed her with a blow to the head, wrapped her body in the plastic sheet and tied it with the boat line, and then disposed of the body in the Sound with the line attached to some heavy object that was supposed to anchor the body to the bottom. This arrangement had apparently failed when the line had snapped after some period, probably because of the weight of the body once water had gotten into it and the force of the current, allowing the body to float to the surface where it had eventually been discovered.

The medical examiner's best estimate was that the victim had been dead for approximately seven to ten days before she was found. Because of the length of time she'd been in the water, it was impossible to tell anything about the circumstances of her death other than the blow to her head. When she was pulled out, she was fully clothed, barefoot, with one of her earrings missing. No trace of drugs or alcohol had been found in her system, although the medical examiner noted that because of the length of time she'd been in the water this finding couldn't be considered definitive and the possibility that she'd had drugs or alcohol in her system at the time of her death couldn't be ruled out. It had also been impossible to tell whether she'd had intercourse in the period immediately prior to her death, although the fact she was found fully clothed and there were no obvious signs of a struggle on her body indicated it was unlikely she'd been sexually assaulted before she was killed. The medical examiner had at least been able to determine she wasn't pregnant. Her cell phone was still in the rear pocket of her jeans, but after all that time in the salt water the phone was, not surprisingly, useless.

Cavanaugh and Balzano had interviewed the victim's mother, who, according to their report, was disabled from work and on welfare, and, by their observation, had an alcohol problem. They'd been able to elicit from her that she hadn't reported her daughter missing because she'd thought the young woman had taken off somewhere. The car her daughter had been driving the night she'd disappeared had been found the next day parked on the street across from the local bus station with the keys under the seat. According to the mother, her daughter didn't have a car of her own; the car she was driving that night had belonged to a friend who lived several houses up the street and had frequently loaned the car to her daughter. The mother had expected her daughter would show up at some point, or she'd hear from her, the thought of possible foul play apparently never having entered her mind.

The mother said her daughter had worked part-time at a local diner while in high school to help them make ends meet, and was working there for the summer when she'd disappeared. She'd been hoping to attend the University of Massachusetts in the fall but was going to need a complete financial aid package for that to happen, and she'd apparently been continuing to investigate her options on that front when she'd disappeared. The mother believed her daughter had had boyfriends from time to time but didn't know who any of them were as her daughter had never brought any of them home or talked about any of them. She said she'd named her daughter after her own favorite TV star when she was growing up, Valerie Harper. She said she'd always called her daughter Valerie, and didn't like it when people called her Val, which the young woman had apparently preferred. The two state cops had gone through the young woman's room and had taken her laptop, and somebody at the State Police lab was apparently going through it, although nothing of interest had turned up from that source so far. They'd also apparently taken a few other odds and ends from her room, but the inventory wasn't included with the report.

After talking with the mother, the two state cops had then interviewed the friend who'd loaned her car to the victim the night she'd disappeared. The friend's name was Virginia Rongoni, who described herself as having been the victim's best friend since grammar school. Apparently, when Ms. Rongoni had heard on the news that the body of an unidentified young woman with blond hair had been pulled out of the Sound, she'd immediately called the state cops,

11

and they were then able to identify the victim by using her dental records. The two of them had graduated from high school together the past spring, and Ms. Rongoni had a summer job working as a counselor at the day camp run by the town's Rec Center. The two young women had apparently been planning to go to UMass in the fall and room together if the victim had somehow been able to come up with the money.

According to Ms. Rongoni, she'd been devastated by the loss of her friend. She confirmed she'd loaned her car to her friend on the night in question, which she'd apparently done on numerous other occasions. Typically, when she'd borrowed Ms. Rongoni's car like this, the victim would then leave the car in her friend's driveway after she'd finished with it and walk home. When Ms. Rongoni didn't find her car in the driveway the next morning, she'd checked with the victim's mother and found out her friend apparently hadn't come home the night before. When there was still no sign of the victim by later in the day, she'd called a friend with a car and the two of them had gone looking for the victim and the missing car. They'd apparently driven around for quite a while before they'd found the car parked on the street across from the town's bus station with the keys under the seat. Ms. Rongoni said at that point, they hadn't felt it was their responsibility to report the young woman's disappearance to the police where her mother hadn't done so, figuring like her mother their friend had probably just taken off somewhere, maybe on a bus, and they'd likely hear from her soon, although Ms. Rongoni admitted the whole thing had seemed strange given her friend had never done anything like that before or even talked about it. She said she'd been hoping to hear from her at any time, although she said as time went on she became more and more concerned. Finally, when she'd heard on the news they'd found a young woman's body in the Sound, she'd immediately become fearful it was her friend and at that point had called the State Police, although she had no idea why anyone would've wanted to harm the young woman.

Ms. Rongoni described the victim as having been extremely attractive with guys hitting on her all the time. She'd apparently had a Facebook page for a short while but had shut it down when she saw how much attention it was attracting. According to Ms. Rongoni, the victim had never shown much interest in any of the boys at the high school, gravitating mostly toward older guys. Over the past year, she'd had a relationship with a guy named Bobby Frank, who'd graduated from the high school a couple of years earlier and worked locally as a mechanic. According to Ms. Rongoni, Frank had a motorcycle, and Ms. Rongoni referred to her friend's relationship with Frank as her "motorcycle period." They'd apparently broken up the previous winter when the victim had begun applying to colleges.

Ms. Rongoni said after that, her friend had started borrowing her car to go out at night, although she didn't know where her friend had gone or who she might've been seeing as her friend had never confided to her what she'd needed the car for on those occasions. Then, after graduation, she'd apparently hooked up with one of the ballplayers on the town's Cape Cod League baseball team, a guy named Sean McGruder, who was from South Carolina and attended the state university there. Young McGruder was living for the summer on his father's motor yacht, which was tied up in the harbor in town after the old man had apparently had it brought up from South Carolina so the kid would have a place to live for the summer while he was playing ball. Tough life. Ms. Rongoni said she believed her friend had been going to meet up with McGruder on his boat on the night she'd disappeared.

The State Police had Ms. Rongoni's car dusted for fingerprints but apparently no unidentified prints had been found, although it was noted this wasn't all that surprising given the amount of time that had elapsed between the victim's disappearance and when the car was finally dusted, especially considering the amount the car had been used during that period. There had been a video cam running in the parking lot of the bus station on the night in question, but there was nothing on the tape from that night that was out of the ordinary, although the camera's field of vision didn't extend across the street to where Ms. Rongoni's car had been found.

Balzano and Cavanaugh had also gone to the high school, where they'd met with the principal and had looked at the young woman's academic record. She'd been a good but not an exceptional student with no record of any trouble. Not a lot of activities, but it was known she was working part-time to help support her mother. The principal had referred to her as an "attractive girl" from a single-parent family, who, other than Ms. Rongoni, had mostly kept her distance from the other students, and, as the principal described it, had seemed more interested in the world outside of school. She hadn't gone to the prom in either her junior or senior year, which the principal assumed was by choice as he thought she likely would've been a prom queen candidate if she'd chosen to go. His understanding was she'd been accepted into college in the fall and was applying for financial aid. That was about it as far as the file was concerned; obviously, nobody'd come up with any kind of smoking gun yet. Finished going through the file, I flipped back to the photograph stapled to the inside of the front cover again and looked at it for a moment, and then closed the file.

4

July 19, 2012 The New Salisbury police station was a nondescript, single-story brick structure on the town's main street. The interior layout was pretty basic: a large, open common area when you walked in with a few desks scattered around, the Chief's office, a bathroom, a locked storage area, and two small holding cells in a locked area in the back that were rarely used. That morning, Cavanaugh and Balzano met with Mullally and me in the Chief's office, which was the only place in the stationhouse where you could hold a closed-door meeting. I'd shaken hands with the two state cops when they'd come to our office the day after the body had been found, but this was the first time I was going to be able to hear firsthand what was going on. I had to bring an extra chair in from the common area and with the four of us wedged into the Chief's tiny office, it was pretty cramped, and sitting there next to Cavanaugh I thought I was going to pass out from his cheap aftershave.

After we'd all sat down and Cavanaugh had his notebook out on his lap, Balzano, who I was soon to learn did most of the talking for the two of them, got things started. "So, what do you think about what we've got so far? Any thoughts, reactions, anything stick out at you?" He looked first at Mullally and then at me.

Mullally screwed up his face like he was trying to think of something to say that wouldn't sound stupid, so I jumped in to try to save him. "Doesn't seem like there's a whole lot to go on so far," I offered tentatively.

Balzano gave me a patronizing smile. "Well, it's only been a couple of days," he said. "These things don't usually get solved overnight. But we didn't know whether you guys might've spotted anything interesting from what's turned up so far."

I looked at Mullally and we both shook our heads. "No," Mullally said, "nothing so far."

Balzano nodded. "Okay, well, I'm not all that surprised. You guys ever have a case like this before?"

"You mean a homicide?" Mullally asked. "No, there hasn't been one here in town since I've been here. There have obviously been murders on the Cape over the years, and I've talked with a few of the cops who've worked on some of those cases, but, no, we've never had any firsthand experience with this kind of thing. Totally new to us."

Balzano nodded, and he and Cavanaugh briefly exchanged glances. "Well, you'll probably learn a lot before this is over," Balzano said. "At least I hope you will." He turned to me. "Yeah, you're right, we don't have a lot to go on yet, but, like I said, it's early. Unfortunately, though, we've got a corpse that was in the water a long time, and when you get a corpse that's been outside for an extended period, say, in the woods or in the water like this one, those can be some of the toughest ones to solve. In most cases, the corpse is usually one of your main sources of information: exactly how the victim died and when, whether sex or drugs were involved, maybe even a sample of the perpetrator's DNA, that kind of thing. Unfortunately, this corpse doesn't tell us much of anything."

"Looks like someone took her for a boat ride, hit her over the head and dumped her in the Sound," I said.

"Maybe," Balzano replied, "but you have to wonder why the car she was driving that night wound up parked over by the bus station."

"Maybe she met the perpetrator there and took off with him," I said. "From there, they wound up on his boat."

"But why meet across the street and leave the car there instead of in the parking lot?" Balzano said. "It looks like somebody may have known there was a video cam going in the lot and wanted to avoid being seen."

"Well, most people around here know you can't leave a car in that lot overnight," I said. "There're signs up. The bus company will have your car towed." Out of the corner of my eye, I saw Mullally nodding in agreement. "So, if somebody'd wanted to leave their car there late at night, they would've had to leave it on the street if they didn't want it to get towed."

Balzano nodded. "Okay, that might explain why the car was out on the street, but it doesn't explain why the car wound up over there in the first place. We checked the bus schedule and there are no buses that go through there after 8:00 o'clock at night. The first bus in the morning is at 6:00 am, a commuter bus to Boston. The terminal opens a little before that. We're looking into the possibility she may've spent the night somewhere and then driven over and gotten on a bus in the morning. If she did that and bought a ticket with a credit card either at the bus station or online, there'll be a record of it but not if she paid cash at the station. We've got somebody at the bus station showing her picture around but nothing's turned up so far. The problem is the amount of time that's passed since she disappeared. People forget fast. But then if she actually did get on a bus and took off somewhere, you'd think she would've then had to come back at some point for her body to have wound up in the Sound. That part of it's a little screwy."

"Maybe she met somebody on the bus, maybe on the return trip," I said. "They got off together, took his car, and left hers."

Balzano shrugged. "I guess that's possible, but it's still a little tough to imagine. And you also have to wonder why she'd leave the keys under the seat presumably for her friend, but not let her friend know where she'd left the car."

"Maybe she didn't get a chance," I said. Balzano shrugged again.

"You think this was done by somebody from around here?" Mullally asked. "We don't get many violent crimes in this neck of the woods. Maybe an occasional domestic violence call, but that's about it. And, like I said, we haven't had a murder in this town since I've been here."

"Well, with the little we know right now, Chief, just about anything's possible," Balzano replied. "We're running a database search on everybody whose prior behavior might fit this crime but it's a longshot, especially where we don't know much about the actual circumstances of the victim's death. At the same time, though, we think it's more likely she met up with somebody she knew that night, which would probably be somebody from around here. The medical examiner found no evidence of a struggle or that she'd been sexually assaulted before she was killed, and if it'd been a stranger, you'd think that's what he would've been after with her looks. And it's hard to see this as a robbery."

Mullally frowned. "Well, like I said, having a murderer around who's somebody local would be something brand new for us, at least as far as we know. Drugs and break-ins are mostly what we get around here. Drugs've become a big problem on the Cape and the break-ins have gone up as a result."

Balzano nodded. "Yeah, we know about the drug problem on the Cape. The whole southeastern part of the state's the same."

"You think drugs could've had anything to do with this?" I asked.

Balzano shrugged. "We don't have anything that points in that direction right now, but we've got a long way to go, and, like I said, almost anything's possible. And there're certainly plenty of murders in the drug business. It's a dangerous business, and if the drug problem gets any worse around here you're going to see a lot more violent crimes, I can promise you that. You guys find out anything more about the victim?"

Mullally shook his head. "We don't really know anything more about her at this point. Pretty girl, just graduated from high school and hoping to go to college, lived with her mother, never been in any kind of trouble we know of. Doesn't seem to be any reason why somebody would've wanted to kill her. That's why it seems more likely to have been some stranger, probably with sex on his mind. Started to beat her up to get at her and wound up killing her."

Balzano nodded. "Well, like I said, we can't rule that out, but you guys probably know that statistically there're relatively few murders where the victim didn't know the perpetrator. Where the victim's a woman, it's usually somebody she's been in a relationship with, either a husband or a boyfriend, or somebody who got rejected by her. This young woman was apparently extremely good looking and probably had had multiple relationships and who knows how many other admirers, although I agree those looks also could have easily attracted some weirdo passing through. Like I said, we're doing a database search on similar crimes, but our main focus in the first instance is going to be on the people she knew around here and we may be looking to you for some help on that."

"Well, we've got two guys we know she'd had relationships with," I said. "The old boyfriend with the motorcycle and the one she was seeing when she disappeared, the ballplayer from South Carolina with the boat in the harbor. He was the one she was supposedly going to see that night. You guys talk with him yet? There's nothing in the file about it."

"Yeah, well, that's a slightly complicated situation," Balzano said. Out of the corner of my eye, I saw Mullally give him a puzzled look. "The guy's supposed to be a big deal college athlete, and his old man's a lawyer down in South Carolina who we understand is pretty well connected politically. So we thought we'd try to gather as much information as we could from other sources first before we talk with junior, and let him have a lawyer present if he wants when we sit down with him. With his old man being a big shot lawyer, we don't want to screw this up and then down the road have the whole thing get thrown out on some technicality. There's no question he's somebody we've got to take a close look at, but the fact the car she was driving that night was found over by the bus station sort of suggests either she never met up with him, or if she did, she then went somewhere else afterward. Also, keep in mind there haven't been a lot of Cape Cod League ballplayers who've committed murder as far as we know."

"Well, he's got a boat," I said.

"Yeah," Balzano replied, "and so do a lot of other people around here."

"What about the guy with the motorcycle?" I asked. "The old boyfriend?"

"This somebody from around here?" Mullally asked.

"His name's Bobby Frank," Balzano said. "I think you know him."

17

Mullally frowned. "Yeah, we know him. He's a knucklehead. Multiple drug arrests. What the hell was she doing with him?"

"She was going out with him before she met up with the baseball player," I said. "Sorry, Chief, I didn't recognize his name in the file, otherwise I would've mentioned it to you."

"No reason for you to have known him, Brian," Mullally replied. "I don't think you were ever involved when we've nailed him before. Guy's a shithead. Hard to imagine why a nice girl like her would've been hanging around with somebody like him. I'd think he'd be somebody you'd want to take a close look at, too."

"No accounting for some people's taste," Balzano said. "Yeah, we know about the priors. We've talked with him already, although it's not in the file yet. He's got an alibi of sorts, says he was home sick for a couple of days around the time the victim disappeared. He lives at home with his mother and she took care of him. He never went anywhere the whole time according to both of them, including to a doctor. We checked with the garage where he works and they verified he called in sick and missed three days of work. According to the guy who runs the garage, he still wasn't feeling well when he came back to work."

"Doesn't sound like much of an alibi," I said. "Practically anybody's mother would lie for them in that situation."

"I know the mother," Mullally said, "and I can't see her making a very good witness. You guys talked to her, what'd you think?"

Balzano smiled. "A little rough around the edges."

"That's a polite way of putting it," Mullally said. "She works around here someplace, I don't know what she does, but I know she likes her booze. Big woman, loud, especially when she's had a few. And I wouldn't be surprised if she's one of junior's biggest customers." Out of the corner of my eye I could see Cavanaugh making notes.

"Maybe the victim dumped him and he was pissed," I said. "Anger got the better of him. Or maybe it had something to do with drugs."

"Maybe," Balzano replied, nodding, "but right now unfortunately that's all speculation."

"He have a boat?" I asked.

"No, but like I said, there're a lot of boats around here," Balzano replied.

"Have to be a fairly good-sized boat to drop her down by the Elizabeths," I said.

"Whoever it was could've dropped her almost anywhere," Balzano replied. "She was in the water a long time. Could've drifted a long way in the tide and the current before she was spotted. May not have even been a boat, she might've been dropped off a bridge for all we know. At this point, we're not ruling anything out. That's the problem with this case, there're too many possibilities. We've got two former boyfriends and who knows how many other guys a girl that attractive might've gone out with. Her friend said she was going out at night somewhere before the baseball player came along that she didn't want to talk about, and we've obviously got to follow up on that as well. You never know where these things are going to lead in the end."

"It's still hard to imagine why somebody would've wanted to kill her," Mullally said. "That's why I still think it's more likely it was some stranger looking for sex."

"Trying to figure out a motive in these things is pretty much a waste of time," Balzano replied. "Most of the time you don't find out what the real motive was until you catch the perpetrator. What you need to focus on is who might've had the opportunity and the means, and right now that could've been just about anybody."

I shrugged and looked at Mullally . He looked at the two state cops. "Well, looks like you've got your work cut out for you," he said.

"Yeah, some of them are easy, and some of them aren't," Balzano said. "You take what you get. Like I said, statistically this was most likely done by somebody she knew, but whoever it was, amateurs almost always make mistakes and whoever did this has already made one very big mistake which was trying to dispose of the body the way they did. If they'd done a better job, she'd still be on the bottom of the Sound and just another missing teenager, and we probably wouldn't be sitting here. I can practically guarantee we'll find more mistakes in this before it's over."

"How can we help at this point?" Mullally asked. "I probably don't need to tell you this thing's already caused quite a commotion in town here and a lot of people are going to be pestering us about when it's going to get solved. And it's getting a lot of media attention, which isn't making things around here any easier."

"We understand, Chief," Balzano said. "Our biggest problem right now is we've got a lot going on. Like just about every other agency in the Commonwealth, the State Police are under-funded and everybody's really stretched. We work mostly in Fall River and New Bedford, where there're a lot of street gangs and the murder rate's a lot higher than around here. We don't get over this way very often, and we've got a lot of cases going on besides this one and not enough hours in the day. So, like I said, we may have to lean on you guys from time to time to help us out. The first couple weeks are critical. If you don't come up with a legitimate suspect in the first couple weeks, these things can drag on for a long time. Some of them unfortunately never get solved. But this is a small town, and we're hoping that's going to work in our favor."

"Just out of curiosity," I asked, "what percentage of them don't get solved?"

Balzano shrugged. "Maybe twenty percent, something like that." Out of the corner of my eye, I saw Cavanaugh nod slightly. "But there're extenuating circumstances in a lot of those cases. Like, for instance, in a lot of them we pretty much know who did it but we just can't prove it. It's obviously really frustrating when that happens."

"Twenty percent seems like a pretty high number," I said.

"Depends on how you look at it. But this case isn't going to be one of those, so don't even think about it," Balzano said.

Mullally nodded. "Good. Okay, tell us what you need."

"Well, for right now, just keep your eyes and ears open," Balzano replied. "If you think of anything or anything comes to your attention, just let us know, no matter how trivial it may seem. Otherwise, when we need something, we'll let you know. And keep track of what we send you. That way, we won't have to explain stuff to you as we go along."

"Well, whatever you need, just contact Brian here," Mullally said nodding at me. "He'll be coordinating at this end. He'll know how to get hold of me day or night. Like I said, we obviously want to get this solved as quickly as possible."

"I'm sure you do, Chief," Balzano replied, "and so do we. Well, thanks for your hospitality." Cavanaugh flipped his notebook shut, put his pen in his shirt pocket, and they both started to get up.

Mullally stayed seated behind his desk. "There's one more thing I need to talk with you about," he said. Balzano and Cavanaugh sat back down. "Like I said, the media's been all over us on this," Mullally went on. "The day it was released that this was a homicide, we had news trucks from two Boston TV stations camped out in our parking lot practically before we knew it. They finally left that night after it was obvious we weren't going to tell them anything, but I got a call about an hour ago from one of the stations saying their lead news anchor, some woman named Carmen Belafontaine, is coming down here to do a piece on the case. I told them I couldn't stop her from coming, but she shouldn't expect any interviews with either us or any town officials, and they should direct any questions they have about the case to the State Police. Did I handle that right?"

Balzano nodded, smiling grimly. "Yeah, that's exactly right, just refer everything to us. We've got press relations people who handle that stuff and the media all know it. They probably called you just to find if you were going to be stupid enough to talk to them. That station loves this kind of thing—beautiful young girl has her head bashed in on sunny Cape Cod. I guess there're a lot of people out there that really suck this kind of thing up."

"Carmen Belafontaine's a pretty big deal, isn't she?" I asked. I'd seen her a few times on TV. She was supposedly from some island in the Caribbean, long black hair, sexy looks.

Balzano nodded. "Yeah, in the TV business she supposedly is, but she's no different from any of the other media people as far as we're concerned. No reason to treat her any differently from anybody else. Stay away from her and her people, and just refer them to us. She's gonna do her thing, so just stay the hell out of the way, and make sure the town officials know to do the same. Nothing good can ever come from talking to the press in the middle of an investigation like this. Especially somebody like her."

Mullally nodded. "Okay, that's all I needed to know. Thanks." He stood up and the three of us did as well, and we shook hands all around.

I walked the two state cops the out to the front door. When I came back inside, Mullally was standing in the doorway of his office and motioned for me to come back in and close the door again. "A real mess," he said after the door was closed and we'd sat back down. "Glad they're handling it. Ever have a case like this when you were in the service?"

"No, no murders or anything like that, and nothing that ever got any media attention."

"Well, it'll be a learning experience for both of us, no question. I want you to stay on top of it, keep track of the file and everything that's going on. I'll probably get calls from the selectmen from time to time wanting to know what's happening and I'll need you to keep me up to speed. Like they said, nothing to the media, just refer them to the State Police. No talking to anybody besides me including the other people around here. Anybody asks you anything, just tell 'em you can't talk about it. Understood?" I nodded. "This takes priority over anything else you're doing," he continued. "I don't care about patrols, paperwork, anything, you've got a pass on all that. If the state cops need anything, you jump. Okay?"

I nodded. "Mind if I do a little snooping around, see if anybody knows or has seen anything?"

Mullally furrowed his brow. "That's maybe not a bad idea. They told us to keep our eyes and ears open. If we can contribute something, that'll make us look good. But stay the hell out of the state cops' way, okay? What else?"

"I'm good, Chief."

"Just keep me informed."

"Will do," I said.

5

July 19, 2012 With a free pass to do some investigating on my own, I decided the first thing I'd do that afternoon would be to take a drive over to Valerie Jean Gray's mother's house. The town's coastline faces south along Vineyard Sound, and there are several large salt water inlets off the Sound that are called ponds. The house was situated on one of those ponds on a road that ran north to south along the western side of the pond down toward the Sound where it dead-ended at a marsh that then stretched about a hundred yards from where the road ended out to the Sound. Valerie Gray's mother's house was the next to last house on the street before the marsh. It was a small, one-story white cape with green shutters and trim that looked like it'd been built back in the 1950's and hadn't been painted since, with somebody having done an amateur patch job on the roof that made the place look even more run down. There was no garage, just an empty gravel spot for a car beside the house, and the little lawn area in front of the house was mostly just weeds. In a town that prided itself on having a lot of high end real estate, this place was obviously at the bottom end of the scale.

I pulled the cruiser into the gravel spot beside the house and got out. I could see out back the pond came up to about fifty feet from the house. There was no dock or any sign of a boat. The window shades inside the house were pulled down most of the way, and there was no sign of life anywhere. The front steps were made out of cinder blocks that had been cemented together. I climbed up to the front door and rang the doorbell. The house was quiet, and I couldn't hear the doorbell ring inside. I tried it again and still didn't hear anything, so I rapped on the door. About twenty seconds went by and I was about to bang on the door again when I heard somebody moving around inside. I could hear someone hook the chain on the inside of the door, and then the door opened as far as the chain would allow, which was about four inches. An older, heavy-set woman with long, straggly gray hair peeked out at me through the opening. She was wearing a dingy green bathrobe and an old pair of pink fuzzy slippers. Her face looked gray and was deeply lined, but I couldn't see her eyes because she was wearing sunglasses. I assumed this was Valerie Gray's mother.

She stood there looking me up and down. Finally, she said in a low, gravelly voice, "What do you want?"

"Good afternoon." I said, trying to sound professional, "I'm Officer Bonner. Are you Valerie Gray's mother?"

"If it's about my daughter, the police've been here already," she said, obviously irritated at my presence on her doorstep.

"Yes, I know," I said. "I'm just doing some follow-up work. Could I chat with you for a few minutes?"

She looked me up and down again, and then finally said, "Go ahead."

"Maybe it'd be better if we talked inside," I told her.

She stood there for another minute staring at me blankly as if pondering my request, and then finally closed the door and I heard her fumbling around inside with the chain. When the door opened again she was standing behind it as if she didn't want anybody passing by on the street to see her. I took my hat off as I stepped into the house, and she closed the door behind me. The house had a damp, musty smell to it. To the right was the entrance to the living room and a hallway led off to the left. I stepped into the living room and looked around. The interior was in the same condition as the outside with faded wallpaper that was peeling in spots along the baseboard, cracks in the ceiling, and ugly brown shag wall-to-wall carpeting that badly needed cleaning. The only items of furniture in the room were an old couch and a discolored old easy chair in fabrics that didn't match. There was a small folding TV table beside the chair and on it were a box of tissues together with what looked like some used ones, an empty plate and a fork, a couple small white plastic medicine bottles, and a half empty glass of what appeared to be water. The chair faced an old TV that sat on a low stand across the room. I could see there was a kitchen in the back of the house off the living room.

As I was looking around, she shuffled past me without glancing up, picked up the TV remote that was lying in the easy chair and sat down heavily. Then, she looked up at me and said in the same gravelly voice, "What do you want to talk about?" No invitation to sit down.

"Like I said, Ma'am, I'm doing some follow-up on your daughter's death," I said, feeling a little stupid standing there in the middle of the room holding my hat and looking down at her. "I know what you told the other officers who were here, and I'm not going to go over that again. I've just got a few more questions

I'd like to ask you, and then I'd like to look at your daughter's room if that's okay. I know the other officers looked at it when they were here, but it would be helpful if I could take a look at it, too."

"You can look at anything you want," she said. "What do you want to ask me?"

"I know the other officers asked about whether your daughter had had any boyfriends. I just wanted to follow up on that. Did she ever mention any male friends at all?"

She frowned. "They already asked me that."

I hesitated for a moment. "Let me ask it this way: did your daughter ever talk about going out with a guy with a motorcycle?"

She shook her head.

"Did anybody with a motorcycle ever stop by, maybe to pick her up or drop her off?"

She shook her head again.

"What about anybody who played on the town's Cape Cod League baseball team? She ever mention anybody like that?"

"No."

"Did she ever mention anybody with a boat? A big boat?"

"No."

"Any kind of a boat?"

She shook her head again.

"She ever mention anybody at all? Any male friends? Anybody she might've gone out with?"

"No, I already told the other officers all that," she said wearily. "I don't know why you're going over all this again."

"I know this is difficult," I said, "but we're trying to find out who may have been responsible for your daughter's death and anything you can tell us might be helpful. Did your daughter have any friends at all that you know of?"

"Gina Rongoni. That's the only friend I know."

"Any acquaintances maybe?"

"Gina Rongoni. That's all."

"Your daughter worked at the Shanty Diner?"

"That's right."

"Did she ever mention the names of anybody she knew there?"

"No."

"Sounds like she kept to herself a lot."

"I wouldn't know. She came and went as she pleased. Did her homework, worked at the diner and stayed out of trouble as far as I know."

"She was going to go to college in the fall?"

"That was what she was hoping, but she was going to have to get somebody to pay for it."

"How was she doing on that?"

"I wouldn't know."

"Doesn't sound like you two talked a lot."

"Look, Officer whatever your name is," she said sharply, "I don't have to sit here and listen to remarks like that from you. If you're done with your questions and you've got other business here, I'd appreciate it if you'd get that over with and get out."

I thought to myself, *she's just lost her daughter, which would be hard on anybody let alone somebody in her situation, so cut her some slack, for Christ's sake.* And I thought of my own mother, who was probably close to this woman's age. "I'm sorry, Ma'am," I said, "I apologize for having to do this, but we're just trying to make sure we haven't missed anything. Please forgive me. That's all the questions I have, and if I could just take a quick look at your daughter's room now, I'll be on my way."

She pointed with her thumb toward the hallway that ran toward the other end of the house. "Down the hall on the right."

"Thank you," I said. "I'll only be a couple minutes."

The hallway was covered with the same ugly brown carpeting as the living room. There were two doors off the hallway on the right, one of which was closed, and I assumed that was the bathroom. The other was the door to what had obviously been the victim's room. There was a second bedroom across the hall, which I assumed was the mother's, and I had no intention of going in there.

Valerie Jean Gray's bedroom was about eight feet by ten feet with a single window looking out onto the backyard and the pond. Pink was the predominant color—the walls, the curtains, the rug, the bedcover on the single bed, and the big stuffed dog sitting on top of it were all some shade of pink. There was no closet or dresser. In their place, somebody had put up a large storage unit on one of the walls that had shelves and baskets for clothes and a space for hang-up items.

The wall over the bed was devoted to pictures of rap artists that had been cut out of magazines and made into a collage. Hanging on the opposite wall was a bulletin board covered with photographs pinned to it, virtually all of them of the deceased starting when she was a little girl up through high school. She'd been cute when she was little but had turned into a striking young woman by the time she'd reached adolescence. There were a couple of her with Gina Rongoni, but otherwise there was nobody else in any of the pictures. Standing there in the middle of the room, I was reminded of the times in Iraq when I'd had to inventory the stuff of somebody who'd been killed in action and pack it all up to be shipped to the deceased's family. I had that same awkward feeling you get when you go through the things of somebody who's died, like you're invading their privacy. It makes you realize that once you die, you don't have any privacy any more.

In a corner of the room by the window was a small desk that looked like the kind you buy and put together. The desk had a shelf unit on it that held several spiral notebooks, a couple paperback books, one on writing style and the other a collection of poetry, and a paperback dictionary. I pulled the pair of latex gloves I'd brought with me out of my pocket and put them on, and then pulled the notebooks off the shelf one at a time and flipped through them. They looked like they were all just notes from various classes. Then, I thumbed quickly through the books but found nothing of interest there either. On the desk was a large plastic drink glass that had a big red rooster on it with the name "Gamecocks" printed in red underneath that was filled with pens and pencils. I picked up the glass and looked it, and as I did my eye caught a cream colored plastic pen with a pink top on it mixed in with the others in the glass. I pulled it out and looked at it. Printed on the pen in pink script was the name "The Beach Rose Inn" with an address in Hyannis Port, a phone number and a web address. It was the kind of pen you find in hotel rooms. I examined it for a moment and then slid it into the pocket of my shirt.

There weren't many places in the room to hide anything, and I was sure Balzano and Cavanaugh had done a thorough search when they'd been there, but I looked anyway, checking under the mattress, behind the clothes baskets and under the desk. Nothing. Having quickly run out of places to search, I pulled off the latex gloves and stuffed them back into my pocket, and went back down the hall to the living room where the TV was on loud with some stupid daytime game show. As I walked into the room, I saw the mother still sitting in her chair take one of the white plastic medicine bottles down from her lips and start to screw the cap back on. So that's where she keeps her booze, I thought to myself. As I walked back in, she calmly put the bottle back down on the table beside her and stared at the TV. "Are you done?" she asked without looking up at me.

"Yes, Ma'am," I said. "I may have to come back at some point, but that's it for right now. Thank you for your time, and I'm sorry for the inconvenience. I'll let myself out."

She didn't say anything but just nodded and continued to stare straight ahead at the TV. I left the way I'd come in. The whole thing was incredibly depressing.

6

July 20, 2012 My duty assignment the next day was patrolling, which meant driving around town in a cruiser watching out for traffic violators and being on call for emergencies, like if somebody's cat got stuck up a tree. Patrolling wasn't exactly my favorite duty because of the associations it sometimes triggered with the patrolling we did in Iraq, and when that happened I'd start to get stressed and fearful I was going to run into some unseen danger. I know it sounds stupid when I say driving around a town like New Salisbury actually made me think I was back in Iraq, but at times that was in fact the case. When it happened, which fortunately wasn't too often, I'd usually just pull over somewhere and get out of the car until my head cleared. Like most of the Cape, when the town filled up in the summer the traffic on the local roadways was pretty awful and that was often the worst time for me, not that I ever wanted to share those feelings with anybody.

One of our responsibilities in the summer when we were out patrolling was to drive by each of the schools at some point to make sure there hadn't been any vandalism while they were empty. This gave me an excuse to drive over to the high school to see if there might be somebody there who could give me some more information about Valerie Jean Gray and at the same time provide me with a welcome distraction. The high school was located outside the main part of town on a large tract of public land, which, in addition to the two-story, brick main building and the gym that had been built back in the 1980's, also afforded lots of room for athletic fields and a large parking lot. It was a beautiful summer day, a little on the warm side, the kind of day when everything seems to slow down a little. The trees were a lush green in the bright sunshine, and the vapor trail of a passing airliner left a pair of thin white lines across the otherwise cloudless sky. *Nice day for the beach*, I thought to myself as I pulled into the drive that led up to the school.

The big parking lot only had three cars in it. I kept going past the lot and pulled the cruiser into the circle in front of the building where I parked in front of the main door. Inside, the hall lights were off and the place was quiet. I took my sunglasses off and hooked them onto the pocket of my shirt, and started tentatively down the main hallway looking for some sign of life, my footsteps on the tile floor echoing down the empty corridor. The first doorway I passed was the principal's office, which was completely dark. As I continued to make my way down the darkened hallway, I heard a female voice call out from behind me, "Hello, Officer, can I help you?"

I turned around to find a woman probably in her early thirties walking down the hallway toward me. She was about five-foot-five with short hair done in a stylish cut with bold blond streaks. She was wearing pink designer jeans, sandals and a pair of large gold bangle earrings. Her white t-shirt was stretched tightly over an extremely nice looking pair of breasts. She looked to be about twenty pounds overweight, but overall she wasn't bad. She stuck out a hand with long pink nails and a bunch of bangle bracelets hanging from her wrist. "Hi, I'm Jen Cozen," she said. "I'm the school's guidance counselor. Are you looking for someone in particular?" *Nice smile,* I thought to myself, *and no wedding ring.*

I took off my hat as we shook hands. She smelled good. I flexed a little to try to show off my chest and arms in my short-sleeved uniform shirt. "Nice to meet you," I said. "I'm Brian Bonner. Looks like the principal's not in?" I asked, looking vaguely over her shoulder down the hallway toward the principal's darkened office.

"No, he just left for a couple weeks. His annual vacation. I'm the only one here right now other than the custodians. Is there something I can help you with?"

"I'm looking for some information about a student who graduated this spring, Valerie Gray?" I said, trying to maintain eye contact and not stare at the arresting contours of her t-shirt.

She furrowed her brow. "I assume this is part of the investigation into her death? There were a couple State Police officers in here a few days ago who met with the principal about her, and he asked me to put some information together for them. I still can't believe it. The whole thing is so shocking."

"Yes, it certainly is." I said. "We're all shocked. The State Police have asked us to help with the investigation, and I was hoping I might find somebody who could give us a little more background information."

"Well, I might be able to help you although I'm not sure how much. I had some limited contact with her because I work with all the juniors and seniors in my job as the guidance counselor. I also teach math, but I never had her in class.

If you'd like, you can come down to my office and I'll tell you what I know, which may not be a whole lot, but there's really nobody else here right now."

I smiled. "Thanks, that'd be great of you."

"Come on this way," she said, motioning down the hallway. As we walked toward the end of the hallway, she said, "I don't know whether you're aware, but there's going to be a memorial service for her in a couple weeks here at the school. One of her friends is organizing it."

"Sounds very nice," I said.

Her small office was down a flight of stairs in the building's below-ground level at the end of a long corridor of classrooms. There was an above ground window behind her desk that brought in natural light, and a bookshelf crammed with college catalogues and brochures that took up one whole wall. Along the opposite wall were a couple five-drawer filing cabinets, and hanging from the ceiling molding all around the office were a lot of small, colored pennants with the names of different colleges on them. Every flat surface in the room was covered with piles of papers, including a large pile on the only chair besides hers.

She looked at the chair, frowned, and said, "Oh, let me get that out of the way for you." She bent over and picked up the pile, and after glancing around for a place to put it, finally put it down on the floor in a corner of the room. "There we go," she said, gesturing for me to take a seat in the now empty chair. I sat down, and she went around the desk and sat down facing me. "You'll have to excuse my mess," she said, "but I'm transitioning from one year to the next, and I've got files on all the students, material on about a hundred colleges, financial aid forms, you name it. I've got to get it all updated and ready for the fall. There'll be a mob in here as soon as school starts. It seems to get more intense every year."

I nodded. "I imagine. From what I understand, Valerie Gray was planning to go to UMass?" *Try to keep eye contact,* I thought to myself again, *and don't stare at her boobs.*

"Yes, if she'd been able to get the financial aid she needed. I don't really know where she was on that. I hadn't talked with her about it since before graduation. She lived alone with her mother, and I understand they don't have a lot of money."

I nodded. "I know you didn't know her all that well, but let me ask you, can you give me at least some idea what she was like? Anything at all would be helpful."

She furrowed her brow. "What Val was like? Everybody called her Val by the way. Well, she was attractive. Very attractive, actually. Tall and quite striking looking. Very mature in both her looks and her demeanor. If you saw her, you'd never think she was in high school. She probably could've gotten into half the clubs in Boston without an I.D."

"Must've attracted a lot of male attention."

"Oh, God, yes. With a lot of the boys, it was actually pretty funny the way they'd stare at her with their mouths open when she walked down the hall in something form-fitting. Quite a figure. Most women would be jealous."

"Did she flaunt it a lot?"

"No, not really. Frankly, she didn't have to."

"Must've had a lot of boyfriends."

"Not in school, as far as I know. She seemed to pretty much look down her nose at the boys in school—the jocks, the brains, all of them. She could very well have had male friends outside of school, but I wouldn't know anything about that. She actually didn't have a lot of friends in school. Another girl in her class, Gina Rongoni, was probably her only close friend. She's the one who's organizing the memorial service. They were going to go to UMass together."

"No male friends you know of?"

She shook her head. "No."

"Ever see her with a male companion outside of school?"

"I don't think I ever saw her outside of school."

"Do you know what she was like as a student?"

"Well, as I said, I never had her in class but as the guidance counselor I know what her grades were. They were decent, mostly B's with a few C's thrown in and maybe an A or two. Not bad really considering she was also working part-time. Her SAT scores were pretty much in line with her grades, both in the 500's. She got two teachers to write college recommendations for her. One of them gave her a very positive review, more than I would've expected. The other one was more consistent with her academic record."

"Athletics?"

"Not that I know of. She probably didn't have the time. Or the interest for that matter. Frankly, it's kind of hard for me to imagine her on one of the teams with the other girls. It was like that was high school stuff, and she was beyond all that."

"Mature beyond her years, it sounds like."

"In many respects, that's right. If you think about it, though, low income, single parent family, having to work at an early age, she probably had to grow up in a hurry."

"Any problems you know of, like drugs or alcohol? Seeing as how she was so mature?"

"No, not that I know of. I gave a copy of her school record to the principal to give to the other officers who were here, and it didn't show any of those kinds of problems, at least not that the school was aware of."

I thought for a minute. "She looked older than her age, and she was extremely attractive. Anything unusual in her relationships with any of the male teachers? I know that's kind of a tough question."

She paused. "I need to be careful with that one and not say the wrong thing." She thought for a moment and then continued, "Well, a lot of them looked at her, that's for sure, but what man wouldn't? Male teachers have to be really careful you know, but they're only human. I looked at her too for that matter, just because she was so striking looking. There were more than a few times when I thought to myself, wow, if I looked like that I wouldn't be teaching, that's for sure." She smiled. "But that's probably more information than you were looking for."

I smiled back. "No, I understand. It gives me a flavor of what she was like. Do you know whether she ever came on to any of the male teachers or any of them ever came on to her?"

She looked away and thought for another minute. Then, she turned back to me. "Tell me, Officer, is this off the record?"

"Please call me Brian."

"Okay, Brian, so are you going to quote me on any of this?"

"You don't see me taking notes or a tape recorder or anything. I'm just looking to get some background information in what is a very serious case, and any help you can give us may be valuable. Your name will be kept out of it, I promise."

She nodded and paused again for a moment. "Okay, let's just say she had a fairly close relationship with one of the male teachers. I know he had her in a couple of his classes, and he's the one who wrote the glowing recommendation for her. We don't have faculty advisors for the students here, but I had the impression he was sort of her informal advisor. A lot of kids make friends with the teachers, especially by the time they're seniors, and sometimes they go to them for advice so it wasn't all that unusual. But it was a little different in Val's case because she was so aloof from everybody else in the school."

"Who's the teacher?"

"His name is Hunter Phillips. He teaches English. One of the classes he teaches is an elective for seniors on the romantic poets. It's not a big class because there aren't that many kids who're that interested in poetry, especially by their senior year, but I know Val took it. I saw it on her transcript when we sent it to UMass, and I was a little surprised."

"Any reason to think there might've been anything going on between the two of them besides poetry assignments?"

"No, nothing I can actually point to, but you never know, I guess. He's an older man, probably in his forties. Lived in England at some point and went to a university there, picked up a British accent I've always thought was phony. Comes on like an English poet, tweed jackets, that kind of thing. I guess some of the girls think he's to die for, and maybe Val was one of them. And with her looks and maturity, any kind of close relationship between the two of them probably could've had the potential for something more, but of course as you can tell I'm just speculating."

"He married?"

"No, divorced. Lives in town. I understand he has family money, teaches mostly for kicks. Must be nice."

"Sounds like quite a ladies man."

"Some people may think he is. Anyway, I think you can see why what I've told you is confidential. I have nothing to link the two of them together other than as just an attractive student and her male poetry teacher."

"Anything else about her you can think of?"

"No, not really. As I said, I didn't really know her that well, and my impression was she was a pretty private person. The times I met with her about college, she didn't say a whole lot. If you want to know the truth, I'm not sure she was all that excited about going to college. A lot of these kids, that's all they want to talk about, and I have trouble getting them out of my office, but she didn't seem all that excited about the whole thing. She was pretty hard to read, really. As I said, she was in many respects a very private person, and she was definitely that way with me. There're probably other people around here who knew her better than I did, like maybe some of the teachers who had her in class, but if you want to talk with any of them you'll have to either track them down one at a time or wait until the Fall when everybody's back."

"I'll give that some thought. Well, I should let you get back to work. Thanks for taking the time to talk with me, you've been a big help."

"That's nice of you to say, but after I brought you all the way down here I don't feel like I've actually told you very much."

"No, you really have. I think I have a much better idea of what she was like now. And if you think of anything later, anything at all, just give me a call. Call the police station, they'll know how to find me." I stood up.

She got up and came around the desk. "I certainly will. Here, let me at least show you out so you don't get lost."

As we walked back upstairs to the front door, I tried to come up with some excuse to come by and talk with her again that didn't sound strained, but I couldn't think of anything. She'd certainly been friendly enough, but not having had all that much experience trying to figure out what was going on in women's minds, I thought I might be reading too much into it.

We went out the front door and stood beside the cruiser in the warm sunshine. "Well, thanks again," I said, putting my hat and my sunglasses back on.

"Oh, you're more than welcome," she replied. "Anything for the police. And you've brightened up an otherwise very dull day. Now I'm going to have to think of something else, so I'll have an excuse to call you."

"It'd be my pleasure, Ma'am," I said. "We're here to serve 24/7. Just pick up the phone." We shook hands again, and she gave me another warm smile.

I got into the car and started it up, and we exchanged waves as I pulled away. I watched in the rearview mirror as she turned and went back inside. *Jesus,* I thought to myself, *maybe she'll actually call. Yeah, sure, Stupid, like in your dreams.*

I was still out cruising around later that afternoon when a radio call came in saying it looked like some kid had overdosed at home. The dispatcher gave the address, which was on the other side of town, and asked if anybody was in the area. One of my colleagues, who was closer, picked up and said he was on his way.

When I got back to the stationhouse about an hour or so later, the door to Mullally's office was open so I stuck my head in. He was sitting at his desk trying to read something with his glasses perched up on his forehead. Sensing my presence, he looked up.

"I heard on the radio there was an O.D.," I said.

He frowned. "Yeah, sixteen year old girl."

"What'd she take?"

"Painkillers. About half a bottle's worth."

"Jesus."

"Came within a few breaths of killing herself. EMTs probably saved her. If it'd taken another ten minutes to get her to the hospital, she may not have made it. Becoming a regular thing around here."

"Suicide attempt?"

"They don't think so. They think she was probably just trying to get high and took too much. She was apparently alone, but they don't know whether she may've been online with some of her friends. That's what a lot of 'em do now, they get online together and take stuff, and then rave to each other about how great they're supposedly feeling. Most of 'em are probably faking it but there are always one or two stupid enough to actually do it."

"Where'd she get it from?"

"Who knows. Plain brown plastic bottle on the floor beside her. No prescription, so it probably didn't come from the family medicine cabinet although these days you never know. It'll be a day or two before we can interview her. Maybe we can find out then where she got it."

"If she'll tell you."

"Yeah, if she'll tell us, which they rarely do if their parents have talked to a lawyer."

"Anybody talk to them yet?"

"Yeah. Like most of 'em, they're in denial. No idea their little girl had any kind of a problem, the usual shit."

"Really observant."

Mullally shrugged. "Most of 'em look the other way. Don't want to believe what's going on in front of their eyes."

"Wonder where she got the money if she didn't get the stuff out of the medicine cabinet."

"They find it somewhere. Most of 'em steal it from their parents. And remember the enterprising young lady who was offering herself around on the internet?"

"Yeah, pretty screwed up."

"And these aren't kids from the other side of the tracks either, they're from well-to-do, supposedly intelligent families."

"At least well-to-do anyway."

Mullally nodded, frowning. "Glad I'm close to retirement. I wouldn't want to spend my career dealing with this stuff."

Neither would I, I thought to myself as I walked out. We'd had to respond to a fair number of drug O.D.'s in Iraq, as if guys getting shot at or blown up all the time wasn't bad enough. And when it happened, there was no 911 for anybody to call, so some of them were already dead when we got there. In the military, despite their easy availability, possession of virtually any drug without a prescription was a serious criminal offense, especially in a combat zone, and if you O.D.'d and survived it was essentially an admission of guilt that usually led to a court martial and a dishonorable discharge, which meant you wouldn't be eligible for any kind of medical treatment or benefits when you got out. So, if combat drove you to use drugs and you got caught and booted out, you were on your own. At the same time, though, like I said, drugs were plentiful over there and a lot of guys took them to relax and blow off steam, although there was also a bunch of guys who just wanted to get totally fucked up and stay that way the whole time they were over there. I pretty much kept away from that stuff knowing all too well as an M.P. what the consequences were of getting caught.

There'd been more than a few occasions over the years when I'd thought about why, with all my adolescent problems, I hadn't done drugs when I was a kid. I certainly could've and I had plenty of friends who did, but I think it was the fear of my father that had kept me clean. I don't know what he would've done if I'd ever gotten caught, but things were bad enough and I probably hadn't wanted to find out. Since I'd gotten back from Iraq, I'd thought a lot about drugs as possibly a way to ease my fucked up brain, or at least numb it, but everybody at the VA had warned me drugs weren't going to solve my problems and as a cop I'd seen too many druggies to not want to become one myself and probably lose the only decent job I could ever get in the process. So here I was, still a virgin, maybe one of the only ones left on the planet.

Carmen Belafontaine's piece aired that night, and I watched it at a bar in town where I'd gone for a beer. It was the second story on the evening news after coverage of a five alarm fire in East Boston. Carmen and her team really knew how to juice up a story, artfully portraying the case as the brutal murder of a beautiful young woman on idyllic Cape Cod at the height of the summer season that had created near panic among vacationers and natives alike. It started with a panoramic view of one of the town's beaches on a beautiful summer day with Carmen's sultry voice doing the narration.

The Town of New Salisbury is one of the most picturesque spots on all of Cape Cod. Nestled along the shore of Vineyard Sound, it is one of the favorite vacation spots on the Cape for the wealthy and the well-to-do with stunning beaches and scenery, renowned boating and golf, and some of the most expensive real estate on Cape Cod. The screen switched to shots of the town's harbor with boats going in and out, and then to some shots of a couple high end beachfront homes. *But it is a community that is living in fear tonight following the most brutal crime in the Town's history, and perhaps recent the history of all of Cape Cod.* The scene switched to a helicopter view of the Elizabeth Islands. *Five days ago, the body of a young woman was discovered floating in Vineyard Sound off the Elizabeth Islands. The police have determined that the woman had been savagely beaten to death, with her body then dumped into the Sound....*

Val Gray's graduation photo then appeared on the screen. *The victim was Valerie Jean Gray, who had just graduated from New Salisbury High School in June and was heading off to college in the fall with a bright future ahead of her. A strikingly attractive young woman, Valerie had lived alone with her mother, who was partially disabled, and Valerie had worked part-time while in high school to help the family make ends meet. She mysteriously disappeared on the night of July 8th and was never seen again until her battered body was discovered seven days later floating in the Sound. There is apparently no sign she had been sexually assaulted before she was killed....*

The investigation into this terrible crime is being conducted by the State Police with the help of the New Salisbury Police Department. A shot of the New Salisbury police station then appeared on the screen. *So far, the police have remained close-mouthed about the case, declining to provide any information other than issuing a general statement that an intense investigation is ongoing, and it is hoped that the perpetrator will be apprehended soon. New Salisbury town officials also declined to be interviewed. It is believed that so far not many clues have surfaced, and there is concern that because the victim had been missing for so long before her body was discovered, the trail may have grown cold. If the police have a suspect or a motive for this brutal crime, for now they're playing it extremely close to the vest....*

The silence on the part of the authorities has certainly not helped to calm the fears in the local community that there is a psychopathic killer loose in their midst. Was it a stranger or someone she knew? An extremely attractive young woman like Valerie Gray with her lovely blond hair and blue eyes was sure to have attracted a lot of attention. The graduation photo appeared again on the screen. *Perhaps too much attention....*

We talked with a number of people in town who all expressed the same concern, especially the women we talked to. Carmen was then shown on the main street in town with a microphone in her hand interviewing an apparent passer-by, a not particularly attractive, heavyset woman who looked to be in her 40's wearing sunglasses and dressed as if she was on her way to the beach. Carmen was wearing a high-fashion designer outfit, heavy makeup and deep red lipstick, which looked totally out of place in the middle of the summer on Cape Cod but plainly marked her as a celebrity. She asked the woman, *"Are you concerned there's a killer here in town who may have already selected his next victim?"* She then stuck the microphone under the woman's nose. The woman responded, nodding vigorously, *"Yes, I certainly am. I think everybody is. I think everybody's going to be really concerned until they catch whoever did this. You don't come to the Cape in the summer for this."* Carmen pulled the microphone back and asked, *"Do you think the police are doing enough?"* and then stuck the microphone back in front of the woman again. *"I'm not really sure what the police are doing. It would be nice if they told us they've caught someone."* Nodding, Carmen then asked her, *"Do you feel safe?"* The woman responded, *"No, I don't. I certainly hope somebody does something about this soon. Otherwise, I think there're going to be a lot of cancellations around here. People aren't going to want to come to the Cape on vacation with a murderer roaming around."* Carmen pulled the microphone back. *"Do you think this killer will strike again?"* The woman shook her head. *"I don't know. Right now, I don't think anybody does."*

Carmen turned and faced the camera as it zoomed in on her. Her perfectly coiffed, long black hair fell naturally on her shoulders and her sensual face held a grim expression. *Just about everybody we've talked to has said the same thing. They're frightened, and they want this killer caught. And as every day goes by, fear continues to mount. The State Police have urged everyone to remain calm, and have asked that anyone who has any information they think might be helpful in solving this terrible crime to please call the hotline number on the State Police website. But patience is beginning to wear thin. The mood of the community tonight is that this person needs to be apprehended soon before he strikes again. Until then, this will be a town that will continue to live in fear. This is Carmen Belafontaine reporting from New Salisbury on Cape Cod.*

The station then went to a commercial break. I took a sip of my beer. *Well, that ought to make everybody really pleased,* I thought to myself. *One thing's for sure, we're going to find out how smart the state cops are.*

July 23, 2012 It was Monday morning, and I was sitting at one of the desks in the common area sipping my coffee when Mullally came out of his office and over to me. "I just got a call from the state cops," he said. "They're wanna' stop by and talk with us about something. They'll be here in a few minutes. Bring a chair in and we'll wait for 'em in my office."

I picked up a chair and followed him into his office with it and sat down. "Any idea what's up?" I asked him as he went around his desk and sat down heavily, leaving the door to the office open.

He shook his head. "Nope, they didn't say."

"Maybe they've come up with something."

He shrugged. "Maybe."

We sat there in silence for a couple minutes. Finally, Mullally picked up something on his desk and began to read it. I stared around at the blank walls, Mullally never having been one to decorate his office. The minutes continued to tick slowly by. Finally, Mullally put down what he was reading and got up and went out into the common area, leaving me sitting there alone. A few more minutes passed as I continued to sit there staring at the walls, wondering where this was going. Then, I heard Mullally speaking to someone. I turned around and watched him as he greeted Balzano and Cavanaugh as they came through the front door, and then led them into the office.

"Hi, Guys," I said as they came in, getting up to close the door behind them.

"How's it goin', Brian," Balzano replied flatly as they sat down.

Mullally went around his desk and flopped into his chair, and then, looking at Balzano and Cavanaugh expectantly, asked, "So, what's up?"

"We've got some information we wanted to share with you that isn't in the file yet," Balzano began, "and we wanted to talk with you some more about somebody we talked about the other day."

Mullally frowned. "Who's that?"

"Young Mr. Frank. But first let's talk about what we've come up with. Jim?" he said, looking at Cavanaugh.

"Yeah," Cavanaugh said, "you never know what you're gonna' find in these things. Anyway, it turns out Ms. Gray, who was supposedly struggling to help her mother make ends meet, left behind a bank account with a little over fifteen thousand dollars in it. How's that for a surprise?"

"No shit," I said.

"No shit," Cavanaugh replied. "When we searched her room, we found some pretty expensive clothes, not exactly the kind of stuff you'd expect a high school girl who couldn't afford college would be likely to have. Designer stuff, the kind of stuff the merchants here in town don't generally carry. And some nice jewelry, too. So, naturally after that we checked to see if she had a bank account somewhere and this account turned up with the balance in it. So we got the records for the account, and, up until last winter, she had something like three hundred dollars in it. Then, in about March she suddenly starts making deposits. Five hundred here, seven hundred there. All cash. At different branches, probably so she wouldn't draw attention to herself. So the question obviously is, where'd the money come from and what was she doing to earn it?"

"Good question," Mullally replied, frowning.

"And the answer is most likely drugs," Balzano said, "or at least that's our first guess unless you guys've got a better idea."

"And you think she may've been working for Bobby Frank?" Mullally asked.

"Well, he's the one drug connection we know of right now, but parts of it don't fit together all that well."

"How so?"

"Well, for openers she'd supposedly broken up with him before the money started showing up. Now that doesn't mean it's impossible, it's just something to take into consideration."

"She was looking for money for school," I said. "Maybe she went back to him for a job, maybe threw in some sexual favors. Maybe those times she borrowed her friend's car last spring she was out dealing for him. It'd explain why she didn't want to tell her friend why she needed the car."

Balzano nodded. "That's certainly a possibility, but the problem is the balance in her account is a lot of money for somebody selling for a small timer like Frank. That's one of the reasons why we wanted to talk with you guys about it. If she was making that much selling for him, he had to be making at least that much if not more for himself. He's not going to let his little salesgirl make more than him, which means there's a fair amount of money changing hands here, more than he's accustomed to having go through his hands based on our review of his priors, which looked like chicken shit compared to this. Especially over just a few months' time."

Mullally nodded. "You're right about the priors. The stuff we've gotten him on before is really small time crap, in the hundreds, maybe a thousand tops. That's why he's out walking around and not locked up."

"And then there's also the question of why he'd kill his number one salesgirl," Cavanaugh said.

"Maybe he was still pissed at her for dumping him," I said. "Or maybe he was asking for more than she was willing to give in the sex department. They had another falling out and he killed her. Passion got in the way of business. Or maybe she had her hand in the till and he caught her. That'd explain why she had so much money. She got greedy, and it blew up on her."

Balzano shrugged. "A lot of maybes."

"You search his house?" I asked.

"For what?"

"Evidence. Drugs, maybe the murder weapon?"

"Based on what we've got so far, which is essentially nothing, there's no way we'd get a warrant to search his house. What're you going to tell the judge, you want to search his house because he's an old boyfriend of hers and he's got a drug record? Good luck with that one. Anyway, we wanted to try it out on you guys, see if we were missing something, but it doesn't look like we are. So, I guess we've gotta' keep scratching around, see what other possibilities may be out there."

"There's got to be a connection there somewhere," I said.

"Maybe," Balzano replied. "We'll see. In the meantime, we're set up to interview McGruder this afternoon. We decided we shouldn't wait any longer."

"That should be interesting," I said.

"You never know," Balzano replied.

I went off duty at 4:00 that afternoon and headed straight to the gym I belonged to, which was two towns away. It wasn't all that convenient but I needed a gym specifically set up for body builders, and not one of those places that are mainly for soccer moms who're trying to lose weight, which is what most gyms are geared for these days. This gym fit the bill with a lot of heavy weights and there was a regular group of guys who lifted there who I'd gotten to know, which was helpful because a lot of times with heavy weights you need somebody to spot for you who knows what they're doing and can get the weight off you if you run into a problem. And they weren't a bad bunch of guys to hang out with, which was nice given I didn't exactly have a lot of friends in New Salisbury. I couldn't hit the gym as often as I would've liked, like in Iraq where I had a lot of down time, but I was able to get there enough to keep toned up, and it at least provided me with something of a social life and helped me relieve some stress.

My usual workout time was about an hour. I'd decided after I'd finished and gotten cleaned up and had something to eat, I was going to take in a ballgame that evening. The town's Cape Cod League team, the Midshipmen, was playing and I wanted to check out McGruder, at least from a distance. I'd gone to a lot of Cape Cod League games when I was a kid, although I wasn't all that big a baseball fan. I'd played Little League baseball and that was about it. But back then, going to Cape Cod League games had at least gotten me out of the house at night, and I could go meet up with my friends there and we could screw around together. A lot of the girls in my high school used to go to the games with their friends, too, but they didn't pay much attention to us. I figured they went mainly to watch the stud college ballplayers perform, after which they probably went home and laid awake all night fantasizing.

The Cape Cod League was a big deal in New Salisbury. The League was supposedly started in 1885, and New Salisbury was one of ten towns around the Cape that fielded a team. Each town was allotted a selection of college players drawn from around the country who wanted to come and play. The town thought it was a big deal that a number of players who'd played for the New Salisbury team over the years had made it to the big leagues, like the town actually had something to do with it. The Middies' ballfield was behind the old high school, which had become the middle school after the new high school was built. It was a few blocks off the main street in town, and you parked either in the school parking lot or on one of the side streets around the school. It was a nice field with a dozen large light towers positioned around it to provide illumination at night when most of the games were played, and the town spent a lot of money keeping the field in tip-top shape. It was supposed to be for the exclusive use of the Cape Cod League, and there were no trespassing signs all around it. One of the more exciting parts of our job when we were out patrolling was to keep an eye on the field and shoo away anybody we caught on it.

A nice day had turned into a nice evening, and there was a good crowd on hand. One of my colleagues, Bill Leonard, had drawn duty at the game for the evening, and I chatted with him for a few minutes before making my way over toward the temporary metal bleachers on the first base side of the field behind the home team's dugout. A lot of people who came to the games brought a beach chair or a blanket and watched from the grass in foul territory, and others liked to stand behind the backstop or along the chain-link fence that ran out from both sides of the backstop to the two dugouts. I hadn't brought anything to sit on, and I didn't feel like standing through the whole thing, especially after my workout, so I figured I'd watch McGruder from the stands.

The scoreboard said it was nothing to nothing in the top of the third inning. The stands were about half full. As I scanned the metal rows for a place to sit, I spotted none other than my friend the high school guidance counselor sitting alone on the top row of the stands. She was watching what was happening on the field, and it didn't look like she'd seen me. *Maybe she's with somebody who's gone to get a hot dog or take a piss or something,* I thought to myself. I made my way up through the gaps between the other spectators until I was almost to the top when she spotted me. She rolled her eyes and shook her head in feigned disbelief, and then gave me a big smile.

"Long time no see," I said, making my way over to where she was sitting. "Okay if I sit down?"

"Please do," she replied, smiling. I sat down leaving a little room between us, hoping my nervousness didn't show. "Looks like you finally got a night off from grilling school teachers and sticking bamboo sticks under their fingernails," she said.

"Yeah, I was tired and needed the night off," I said. I feigned looking over at her fingernails. "How're the nails doing?"

"I'm going to have to get a new manicure, you torturer."

"At least I didn't do your toes, too. You come here often?"

"Wow, what a great line. No, not very, although sometimes it seems like it. Not a lot to do in this town. At least it's a nice night."

"Baseball fan?"

"Yeah, sort of. I played softball in college, and I coach the girls' varsity. You?"

"Not really. Something to do." She nodded. I glanced around. "I suppose I should ask, are you here with somebody?"

She smiled and replied, "I am now."

We turned our attention to the field. It was still the top of the third inning. McGruder was way out in center field where I could barely see him. "Know any of the players?" I asked her.

"A couple. The hot prospects for the Middies are supposed to be the centerfielder and the catcher."

"McGruder's the centerfielder, right?"

"That's right. Not surprised you've heard of him, he's supposed to be a major league prospect, maybe the best player in the League this summer."

"University of South Carolina, y'all," I said. "Go, Gamecocks. They call 'em the Cocks for short, you know." She gave me a skeptical look. "No, really," I said, "they do."

"If you say so," she said, and turned her attention back to the field. *That was pretty crude,* I thought to myself. *Great beginning. Try to act mature, for Christ's sake.*

We watched in silence for a while. I don't care what anybody says, but baseball is boring and this game was no exception. Of course, I didn't give a shit about the game, I was there to watch McGruder. And he was something to watch. He stood out from the other players just by the way he carried himself, even just trotting out to his position in center field. He wasn't particularly big, maybe six feet tall, but strong. And fast. The first time he came to the plate, he singled to right field and stretched it into a double standing up. He had dark good looks, a couple days' stubble, and long dark hair that made him look like a minor rock star. When he made it to second base, there was a lot of squealing from what looked like a group of high school girls standing below us along the fence between the backstop and the dugout.

"Quite the stud," I said.

She nodded. "He certainly is. Oh, to be young again."

"I don't know, maybe he likes older women."

She looked at me. "And I'm in the older woman category? Wow, you really know how to make a girl feel good."

Oh, shit, I thought to myself, *I can't believe I said that.* "What I meant was," I said quickly, "I don't really see him as your type. He looks terribly superficial to me, and I see you with somebody a lot more mature."

She chuckled. "That's right, just keep digging yourself deeper."

"I'm actually trying to dig myself out, but I can see it's not working."

"I'm just giving you a hard time, although the truth does hurt sometimes."

"Sorry, my bad."

She looked at me and smiled. "Don't be silly. A guy who's in college? Are you kidding? And I couldn't agree with you more about the superficial part."

Okay, time to shut up, I thought to myself. So, we continued to watch in silence as the game dragged along. Finally, something half way interesting happened in the top of the sixth inning. The game was tied and the Middies had brought in a new pitcher, who looked a little wild when he was warming up and walked the first guy he faced on five pitches. Then, his first pitch to the next guy was a fastball that plunked the poor bastard right in the ribs. *Ouch,* I thought to myself, *that looked painful.* Of course, it was ridiculous to think the pitcher was actually throwing at the guy when what he obviously needed to do was just get the fucking ball over the plate. But needing to create a little drama, the batter, acting like his manhood had been called into question, dropped his bat, threw down his batting helmet, and yelled something at the pitcher, who of course yelled something back. The batter started toward the mound yapping away at the pitcher, who stood there staring at him and not moving like he was daring the batter to start something. At that moment, the Middies' catcher came out of his crouch from behind the plate and in a few quick strides was in front of the batter blocking the his way to the mound. The catcher was black and an imposing specimen, probably six foot three and easily weighing 220 pounds, and in his catching gear and his mask he looked downright scary. He got down into the batter's face with the cage of his mask and started to force the guy backward, his chest protector jammed up against the guy's chest.

The plate umpire, who was a short guy and looked to be in his 50's, pulled his mask off and gamely tried to get between the two of them, but he barely came up to the catcher's armpit and started to get forced backward with the batter. The ump took a couple steps back and tripped over the bat lying where the batter had dropped it, and went down on his ass on the ground. At that point, both benches started to empty onto the field and it looked like we might be in for a brawl. I glanced around for Bill Leonard, thinking what a night to pull game duty. Then, it suddenly dawned on me that if this stupid thing got out of hand, I might have to wade into it myself as law enforcement.

Suddenly, out of nowhere McGruder, who'd apparently sprinted all the way in from center field, grabbed the catcher from the side in a bear hug, pinning his arms against his body and stopping his progress. Scrambling to his feet and seeing the catcher was at least temporarily immobilized, the umpire got up on his toes in the batter's face forcing him to back off, which the batter was probably more than happy to do at that point, although he kept yapping away at the pitcher and pointing at him over the ump's shoulder. I watched McGruder as he kept the catcher in a bear hug and talked to him, gradually calming him down. By this time, the other umpires and the managers and coaches were herding the players who'd come out onto the field back to their benches. I breathed a mental sigh of relief.

"Well, that was exciting," I said as order was restored.

"I've never seen a brawl at one of these games before," she said. "It's usually pretty laid back."

"That catcher's a big dude," I said. "I would've thought he'd get thrown out for making contact with the umpire like that."

"I would've thought so, too. As I said, he's supposed to be one of the top prospects this summer, so maybe that's why they didn't toss him. His name's Ras Dowling. Goes to school somewhere down South. Auburn maybe?"

"Looks like he should be playing football. And he seems to have a bit of an attitude."

McGruder had trotted back to center field by now, Dowling was back behind the plate, which the ump had ceremoniously dusted off, and the next batter was stepping in. Boredom resumed, and it seemed like it took forever for the stupid thing to finally end with the Middies ultimately coming out on top. We stood up as people began to file out of the stands. My companion started down and then saw I was still standing there watching McGruder as he made his way over to the fence between the backstop and home plate where his high school fan club was waiting for him. He was all smiles and there were more squeals from the young ladies. The deal apparently was that the girls all wore bathing suit tops under their clothes so they could expose their backs and shoulders for him to autograph with a Sharpie. *Probably won't wash again until the next game,* I thought to myself. *Better not let Dad see it, though.*

As I watched this performance going on, I heard my companion say, "Do I detect a slight twinge of jealousy?"

I looked down at her standing on the row below me and smiled. "Not because of his magic spell over those young drama queens down there by the fence, that's for sure."

She sighed. "Are we going to stand here all night watching this, or are you going to buy me a drink?"

Jesus, I thought to myself, *when was the last time you got an invitation like that?* "Best idea I've heard all night," I said. "Lead on."

I followed her down, and we walked out to the parking lot together where there was a mini traffic jam with everybody trying to get out of the lot at the same time. We agreed to meet at a place about half a mile down the road called Harry's Roadhouse. As I sat there in my car waiting for the traffic to clear so I could back out, I saw McGruder and Dowling come out of the field together with their equipment bags heading for one of the cars and laughing like they'd just mooned the parking lot. *Probably heading back to McGruder's boat for some post-game fun,* I thought to myself. *Like beer, dope, and sex.*

About twenty minutes later, I was sitting across from the high school guidance counselor at one of the high tables in the bar at Harry's, where it seemed like a lot of the baseball crowd had beat feet after the last out. Harry's, which had probably been around since the Cape Cod Canal was dug, was a low slung, single story, wood frame place that looked a like a stiff wind could knock it over. Inside, the walls were made out of old boards that were covered with those metal signs from back in the 1940's and 50's that advertised products like Coca-Cola, Wonder Bread and different brands of cigarettes. The lighting and décor seemed to be left over from the same era, and there was a trapdoor in the floor at one end of the long bar I'd been told had been installed during Prohibition to bring booze up from where it was hidden in the basement. Somehow over the years the place had kept its allure, and there always seemed to be a decent crowd in there, even in the dead of winter. Our perky waitress had brought us each a beer, which tasted terrific after a long evening of mindless baseball.

"So," my companion said, "did you enjoy the game?"

"Don't take this personally, but no," I replied, taking a long sip.

"Oh, dear, I'm sorry. We could've left any time if you'd wanted to."

"I'm just not a baseball person," I said. "Maybe we're not compatible." I gave her a big smile hoping she didn't take me seriously.

"Well, we may have other areas of mutual interest. You never know."

"I hope so. I had a nice time other than the baseball."

"Yes, it was fun. Maybe we can do something else together sometime."

"That sounds great. Maybe sometime soon, I hope."

"Well, I think that can be arranged," she said. "It's not like my social calendar's all that full these days. So, why did you go if you don't like baseball?"

"Like I said, something to do."

"At least there was some excitement. Almost a brawl."

"Yeah, and it would've been an even more exciting if I'd had to wade into it in my official capacity," I said.

"Oh, God, I hadn't thought about that."

"Yeah, well I did."

"No wonder you weren't having much fun." She paused. "You seemed to be watching McGruder a lot. Quite something, isn't he?"

"Yeah, he's really something alright. Quite the ladies' man, too, it appears."

She smiled. "He certainly does have his fan club, at least among the high school girls."

"Yeah, it seems he has a thing for high school girls."

She frowned. "What makes you say that? I wouldn't think being in college he'd have much interest in those adolescent wannabe's down by the fence. You'd think he could do a lot better than that. Do you think he's been doing more than signing autographs for some of those girls?"

I paused and looked around the room, thinking for a moment. Then, I said, "I guess I can tell you this because other people besides the cops know about it. McGruder apparently had a thing going with Val Gray."

The look on her face was as if somebody had just walked into the bar naked. "You're kidding." She leaned across the table. "Is he a suspect?"

"I'm not allowed to talk about it."

"Of course he is, he's got to be if he was seeing her. Or at least a person of interest, as they say on TV. Wow." She frowned again. "No wonder you were paying so much attention to him. I can see where he could've found her attractive and she could've fallen for him, but it's hard to imagine why on earth he'd ever want to kill her. Star athlete, maybe future major leaguer, bonks Cape Cod high school girl over the head and dumps her in the Sound? Kind of a tough way to end a relationship, don't you think? So what would've been his motive?"

"Who knows at this point. Again, this is all public information. He's from a wealthy South Carolina family, his father's a big deal lawyer down there. He lives on the old man's cabin cruiser tied up in the harbor, which the old man had brought up here so junior could use it to live on for the summer. It's party central for the team, and, of course, it's a much sought after destination for the young ladies in town. So you can see how it could've happened. She's a real knockout, he's a stud athlete with tons of money who's going to be a big star and throws great parties, she's from the poor side of town. Bingo. Let the games begin."

She was still frowning. "Yes, I can see all that, but what still doesn't make sense is why he'd turn around and kill her. Was she pregnant?"

"No. Like I said, right now there's no obvious motive as far as he's concerned, but relationships can go bad in a hurry sometimes. A guy's in love and he gets jealous, or maybe she tells him to get lost, or she humiliates him somehow. All of a sudden, the guy loses it. It happens."

"He turns into a psychopath."

"I'm not sure I'd go that far. It's more like a moment of rage, and then it's over and he regrets it." There was a silence for a minute. Then, I said, "Can I ask you something?"

"Sure. Is it something to do with the case?"

"Possibly. Do you remember a student named Robert Frank? Graduated a few years ago, at least I think he graduated. Didn't go to college, lives around here."

"The name rings a faint bell, but that's about it. If he didn't go to college, and I didn't have him in class, I wouldn't remember him. Why do you ask?"

"Just some background."

"He a suspect?"

I shook my head. "I probably shouldn't have started down this road. We should change the subject. Like I said, I'm not supposed to be talking about this while the investigation's going on. Sorry."

"Oh, don't apologize," she said. "I understand. Let's talk about something else."

We chatted for a little while about TV shows we'd watched lately and which of the town's beaches we liked the best. Finally, I pointed to her empty beer glass and asked, "You want another one?"

"Yes," she replied, "but not tonight." She reached into her bag and pulled out a pen, and wrote her phone number on the napkin that had come with her beer and slid it across to me. "Call me, and I'll buy the next round," she said.

I stared at the napkin. "I will definitely take you up on that," I replied, stuffing the napkin into my pocket.

I flagged down our waitress and paid for the beers. We walked out to the parking lot together and stood beside her vintage Toyota Corolla. She pulled the keys out of her bag and unlocked the door. Then, she turned and put her fingers on my bicep and rubbed it gently. "Thanks for a nice evening," she said, smiling. "Call me, I mean it."

"My pleasure, Ma'am," I said. "I look forward to it."

She got into her car and backed out while I stood there watching. As she waved and pulled away, I thought to myself, *I wonder where this is all gonna' lead.*

My little cottage was really a tiny mother-in-law apartment attached to my landlords' garage. It was three cramped rooms: a living room and kitchen combination, a bedroom just large enough for a single bed, and a bathroom about the size of a restroom on a commercial jetliner. The place was furnished with an assortment of odds and ends that my elderly hosts had probably run out of room for in their own house years ago but hadn't wanted to throw away, all of it looking like it pre-dated 1980, including the stove and the little refrigerator, both of which were a lovely avocado. The only place to eat was on a folding TV table. Needless to say, it wasn't a place you'd want to have anybody over, but it was at least livable and within my budget, although at times somewhat depressing and not a place you'd want to stay very long. If you had a choice.

Fortunately, I didn't have a lot of stuff, and the military had taught me to keep things in order, so despite the size of the place, I was able to fit what constituted all of my worldly possessions into it without a lot of difficulty. I'd purchased a used 22 inch flat screen TV from one of my colleagues, which I'd set up on the dresser in the bedroom. I lay on the bed watching TV for a while, surfing back and forth through the limited number of channels my low-end cable package offered without finding anything that held my attention for very long, but I didn't really feel sleepy even after my workout, so finally around 11:30 I decided to go out, figuring I'd take a drive over to the harbor and see if anything was happening on McGruder's boat.

The town's harbor was a long, mostly man-made inlet stretching about a quarter of a mile from top to bottom and about 200 yards across at its widest point, emptying into the Sound at its southern end through a channel wide enough for a couple large boats to pass each other comfortably. Both sides of the harbor were lined with boatyards, restaurants, bars and summer houses all packed in together. There were about a hundred moorings in the harbor, and to get one you had to spend about ten years, or maybe even longer, on a waiting list. In the summer, when every mooring was occupied the boats were so tightly packed in it looked like you could practically walk across the harbor over them. A passenger ferry to Martha's Vineyard ran in and out of the harbor in the summer, and, with the town's bus station, where Gina Rongoni's car had been found, about a quarter of a mile from the harbor, you could hop on a bus in Boston, Providence, or wherever in the summer, get off at the bus station, drag your stuff to the ferry and take off to the Vineyard without having to worry about a car.

The Vineyard Sound Yacht Club sat on a point at the mouth of the harbor on the right hand side on exiting into the Sound. The old yacht club building, which had been there forever, had been a classic old structure that was wiped out in a hurricane back in the 1990's and what was rebuilt in its place was a rather non-descript, two-story white facility with a deck that extended around the building on three sides at the second floor level. There were parties and weddings at the Club on weekends all throughout the summer, and on any given Saturday night in July and August, the deck was usually crowded with inebriated partygoers.

To handle all the boat traffic the membership generated, the Club had two docks. The larger of the two docks, and the one that got the most use, was on the side of the Club facing inside the harbor. Most of the members kept their boats on moorings in the harbor, and the Club had a launch that ferried members back and forth from that dock to their boats with all their boat crap, although some people preferred to keep a dinghy tied up to a large float at the end of the dock so they could row or motor out to their boat on their own without having to wait for the launch. There was also a wooden shed next to the dock that held tools and equipment that members could use to work on their boats. The other dock was on the far side of the Club outside the harbor mouth extending directly out into the Sound. It was added when the new club building was built to help handle the boat traffic, which could be pretty busy on a weekend afternoon in the summer.

A short walk up the harbor from the Yacht Club was a docking area for large boats that wouldn't fit on a mooring and that they didn't want going any further up into the crowded harbor. Immediately inland from the large boat docking area was a small park with trees and a playground setup with swings and a slide for little kids, and inland from that was a parking lot and then the street. McGruder's boat was tied up at the large boat docking area, and what it must've cost to park the thing there for the entire summer was probably obscene. The boat was a huge cabin cruiser over sixty feet long painted all white with gleaming wood trim and looked to be outfitted with all the latest electronic gear, with lines for water and electricity running up onto it from the dock. A Confederate flag was painted on the hull near the bow, and the name of the boat was painted across the stern: Blockade Runner, Charleston S.C. All ready to be commissioned into the Confederate Navy if hostilities ever resumed.

I parked in the parking lot opposite the large boat docking area and walked about half way across the park to where I was about forty yards from the boat. There was another big yacht tied up about fifteen yards down from McGruder's and the lights on that boat were all out, but McGruder's was completely lit up both inside and out, and, although the drapes in the big main cabin were closed, I could hear the low pulsing of music coming from inside the cabin. *The neighbors must love this,* I thought to myself, *the way sound carries over the water at night.* I looked down toward the Yacht Club, which was completely dark, and I could just barely make out the Club's launch tied up in its usual place at the inner dock. I'd driven that launch six days a week for two summers while I was in high school, and it'd been a pretty shitty job. I had to dress up in khakis, a Club polo shirt and a stupid Club belt, and keep my hair cut; but the worst part had been having to put up with all those stuck up rich people who liked to order you around and were always mad at you because you didn't come get them fast enough. It'd been my first exposure to those kind of people and I hadn't particularly enjoyed it. The hours had really sucked, and I couldn't go home until the last boat had come in and I'd picked up everybody who was coming ashore, which on summer weekends might be as late as 9:00 pm. And then I had to scrub the fucking launch down before I could go home. I was always getting sunburned and the money wasn't all that great considering what I had to put up with.

The launch was a pretty standard yacht club launch, wide with a flat bottom, a few benches and high rails so nobody would fall overboard, and the controls in the middle on the port side. It took some practice to get used to driving the thing as you really had to know what you were doing maneuvering between the moorings and coming alongside expensive boats and holding the launch steady, sometimes in choppy water, while discharging and picking up passengers, some of whom were pretty old, together with all their crap. If I'd ever scratched somebody's boat, I probably would've gotten fired, never mind if I'd ever lost somebody overboard. But I managed to maintain a spotless record over the two summers I drove the launch, although there were more than a few people I would've loved to have seen go into the drink in their fancy clothes.

Standing there in the darkness looking at McGruder's boat, I was tempted to go over to the dock and see if I could peek in and observe what was going on inside, but I quickly reined myself in. Getting caught snooping around McGruder's boat in the middle of the night when I was off duty would definitely not have won me a lot of points with Mullally or with Cavanaugh and Balzano, who'd made it clear McGruder had to be handled with care. *So just cool your jets and walk away,* I thought to myself. But I stayed there in the darkness for a while watching the boat and trying to imagine what was probably going on inside. Eventually, I turned and went back to my car and drove home. It took me a long time to finally get to sleep.

8

July 24, 2012 When I got in the next morning, there was an email copy of the report of the state cops' interview with McGruder the day before waiting for me. As expected, McGruder's father had hired an expensive lawyer to come down from Boston to hold junior's hand for it. They'd held the interview in some lawyer's office in town; it'd apparently lasted a little over an hour.

McGruder admitted he'd been seeing the deceased for a period of time before her disappearance. He said he'd met her after one of the Middies' games early in the season. She'd been to his boat a number of times, and he admitted to having had sex with her on a number of those occasions. He acknowledged his boat was a popular gathering place for members of the team after games, and local females were frequently invited or simply showed up, although McGruder denied there were ever any high school girls there with the exception of the deceased, who he claimed he didn't know had just graduated from high school until after he'd been seeing her for a while. Beer was consumed on these occasions, and they usually ordered out for food to be delivered. His lawyer refused to let him answer any questions about drugs. He had no recollection of the police ever showing up for any reason, or of any of the neighbors ever complaining. Although guests frequently slept over on the boat, the deceased usually went home at the end of the evening whether there was a crowd over that night or not. He said he understood it was because she lived alone with her mother, who had some kind of a health problem and needed her daughter to be home.

The last time he'd seen the deceased was on his boat. He said he wasn't exactly sure it was the night she'd disappeared, but he assumed it was. There'd been no crowd over that night with the only other people on the boat having been Ras Dowling and another one of their teammates. It was hot that night, and they were all inside in the boat's main cabin taking advantage of the air-conditioning and having a couple beers while they watched a Red Sox game on

52

TV. It was a long game, and when it went into extra innings, the deceased, who was clearly bored, said she was going outside for a few minutes to see if it had cooled off at all. McGruder estimated this was sometime close to midnight, although he wasn't sure. She was gone for a short while, and then came back inside and said she was going to take off for a bit, and she might or might not be back. McGruder said he had the impression she may've gotten a text or a phone call from someone, although that was mostly a guess on his part. He said he didn't think anything of it, knowing she was probably going to go home soon anyway.

According to McGruder, shortly after that Dowling announced he was tired and was going to go home. Dowling had a car, and, like most of the players on the team, was living with a family in town for the summer. McGruder said he was tired as well and after Dowling had left and the game finally ended, he and his other teammate, who'd decided to sleep over, went to bed, figuring by then the deceased had undoubtedly gone home. He never saw or heard from her again.

When pressed on whether he thought it strange she'd taken off the way she had that night, or whether he'd been at all concerned about her safety, McGruder said he hadn't really given it any thought at the time, particularly where, as he'd previously indicated, she'd gone home alone late at night on numerous other occasions before. He said when he later heard she'd been murdered and her car had been found up by the bus station, the best he could figure was that she'd gone to meet up with somebody, or she'd run into somebody on the way home.

McGruder described his relationship with the deceased as having been "more than good friends" and "fairly serious," and he described her as having been "fun." When he was asked to describe her feelings for him, he professed not to know. He denied having had any intention of breaking up with her anytime soon, nor did he think she had any thoughts of breaking up with him. He had no knowledge of anybody else she might have been seeing during the time he knew her, although he couldn't swear she never saw anybody else during that time. He said he was mystified when he didn't hear from her over the next couple days, and repeatedly tried to call her on her cell phone without success. He was shocked when he heard her body had been found and she'd been murdered, and had no idea why anyone would've wanted to harm her. He was adamant his boat had never left the dock since it'd arrived from South Carolina because his father didn't want him using it other than to sleep on where he wasn't experienced enough to handle it by himself, and, anyway, he thought it would've been too much of a hassle to disconnect the electricity and the water once they'd been hooked up just to go out and cruise around the Sound for a couple hours. His lawyer suggested the harbormaster could probably verify that the boat hadn't been moved since it'd arrived, which the State Police later confirmed.

The lawyer had also arranged for the state cops to talk to McGruder's two teammates, who'd corroborated McGruder's story about the night she'd disappeared. The state cops also talked with the family Dowling was living with, who didn't know when he'd gotten home that night as they'd gone to bed long before midnight, and Dowling's room was over their garage and had a separate entrance.

As I read the report and thought about it, it occurred to me that while I at least knew something about McGruder, I didn't really know anything about Dowling, whose role in the case seemed to have gotten a major upgrade where apparently nobody could vouch for where he'd gone that night after he left McGruder's boat. So I Googled Dowling to see what I could find out about him, and there was more there than I'd expected. Raseem Dowling was from Alabama and had been a big deal three sport athlete in high school. His father had been a minor league baseball player and had apparently kept his son focused on baseball, which had probably pissed off most of the college football coaches in the Southeast. He'd been drafted by the Oakland Athletics after high school, but had decided to go to college instead and had been given a full ride scholarship to play baseball at Auburn, where he'd continued to be viewed as a big league prospect.

He'd had several run-ins with the law while in college, the most notable of which was his having been accused along with three other teammates of having raped a nineteen year old sophomore at the university, although the charges had been dropped when the victim had apparently decided not to testify. He'd also been arrested for assaulting a police officer following a fight outside a bar. In that one, the prosecutor must've been an Auburn alum because Dowling had been allowed to plead guilty to disorderly conduct and serve six months' probation in addition to being suspended from the team for four games.

I figured Mullally would probably want to read the report about the interview with McGruder himself, but I had to wait about an hour before he finally showed up. Mullally liked to keep irregular hours by design. Sometimes he came in early before the night shift ended, and sometimes he came in late but stayed into the next shift. Occasionally, he even showed up in the middle of the night. You never knew what his schedule was going to be from one day to the next, which was his little way of keeping everybody on their toes. When he finally arrived, I gave him a couple minutes to get settled in his office, and then I walked in with the report.

"Morning, Chief," I said. "Got something you're probably going to want to read." I handed him the report.

He frowned and glanced at the report, and then looked back up at me. "What's this?"

"Report of the state cops' interview with McGruder."

He nodded and reached into his shirt pocket for the case containing his glasses. He pulled them out and put them on, and then slid them down on his nose as he picked up the report. I stood there in silence while he read it.

When he was finished, he put the report down on his desk and looked up at me, his glasses still perched on his nose. "Okay, I read it. Looks like McGruder's got an alibi. Of sorts."

I nodded. "That's not the only reason I wanted you to read it."

He glanced back down at the report again, and then looked back up at me again. "Okay, what else?"

"McGruder's got an alibi, but all of a sudden maybe there's somebody else in the picture who doesn't."

"You mean Dowling?"

"Yeah."

"I saw that. You think he may have followed her?"

"I'm just saying he could have."

"His buddy's girlfriend?"

"Hey, maybe they had something going on the side. Or she dropped a couple hints. Or maybe he was hoping to get a piece of the action. She tells him to fuck off, and he whacks her. He would've known about her car, and he's got a record."

"What kind of a record?"

"Charged with rape in college, but the victim chose not to testify. And assault on a police officer. There may be more, that's just what I found on the internet."

Mullally looked down at the report again. "The state cops must know about all that stuff, too, wouldn't you think?"

"You'd think so."

"So we've got another possible suspect, and no evidence."

"I'm just trying to keep you up to speed."

He nodded. "And that's what I told you to do." He picked up the report and handed it back to me. "Put it in the file. Let's wait and see what the state cops do with it."

I nodded and walked out.

The Bobby Frank thing continued to intrigue me. The report in the file on the state cops' interview with him identified the garage where he worked, which was part of a national chain that sold tires and did repairs. The garage was situated just outside the main part of town where there was a group of strip malls. It was a big place with a long garage that had five bays where they worked on cars and a showroom for tires and automotive products at one end. When I pulled in, there were cars being worked on in four of the bays, but there didn't appear to be a lot activity going on. That was most likely because it was lunchtime, which was when I'd chosen to arrive, figuring it'd probably be easier to talk with Frank during his lunch break. I decided to avoid the showroom at least at first, so I parked the cruiser at the opposite end of the building, thinking I'd take a stroll around and see if I could find Frank eating lunch somewhere. I wandered around to the rear of the building where the property backed up onto some woods. There was a picnic table in a small grassy area shaded by the trees where five guys who looked like mechanics wearing dark blue t-shirts with the garage's name and logo on the front were sitting around eating lunch. Parked close by in the shade of the trees was a Triumph motorcycle with a metallic purple gas tank and fenders, and lots of chrome. A matching metallic purple motorcycle helmet was hanging by its strap over the bike's handlebars.

They stared at me as I walked up. Nobody said anything. "Hi," I said, trying to sound friendly, "sorry to interrupt. Who owns the bike?"

There was a pause. Then, one of them said, "That'd be me."

He looked like a member of some crappy band. He was tall and skinny with zero muscle tone and long, greasy black hair. He had a reasonably handsome face with a stubble of beard and an earring in his left ear, and was wearing a tight pair of soiled jeans and a belt with a large silver buckle that said "Triumph" on it. His left forearm was covered with what looked like some pretty expensive tattoo work that disappeared up the sleeve of his t-shirt.

I said to him, "We had a report last night that somebody on a motorcycle with loud pipes was drag racing up and down the main street around two o'clock in the morning, so we're checking out any motorcycles we spot in the area today. I've got no reason to think it was you, but I'd just like to chat with you for a couple minutes if you don't mind. It'll only take a minute."

He shrugged. "You can ask me whatever you want. Wasn't me."

He stood up and walked around the table, and followed me over to the motorcycle. As I bent down and feigned looking at the pipes on the bike, I asked him, "Who're you?"

"Robert Frank," he said. "Like I said, it wasn't me. I do all the work on this bike myself. Those pipes are legal, I make sure of it. I don't need no trouble."

I stood up, still looking at the bike. "You out last night after midnight?"

"No fuckin' way. I was home asleep. Today's a work day. You can ask my mother, I live with her."

I turned to him. "Let's take a walk over by the garage. I have something else I want to talk with you about."

"What the fuck now?"

"It won't take long."

"Yeah, right, that's what you guys always say."

"A couple minutes, that's all."

He sighed in disgust. "Yeah, sure. Whatever."

As we walked toward the garage and out of earshot of the guys at the picnic table, they turned their attention back to their lunch. When we were far enough away that I was sure they couldn't hear us, I stopped and said to him, "I want to talk with you about Val Gray."

He snorted and glanced back at his friends, and then turned back to me. "So, the thing with the bike's bullshit?"

I nodded. "I wanted to talk to you in private. Just a couple questions."

"I've been over this already with the state cops. You oughta' talk with them."

"I have."

"Great, well, go back and talk with them again, then."

"Look, friend, I'm doing you a favor. You want to do this the hard way, that can be arranged."

"This is my lunch hour. I only got thirty minutes."

"I just want to ask you a few questions. This isn't going to take that long."

He frowned and looked down at the ground. "Yeah, sure. Okay, what do you wanna' know that I didn't already tell the state cops? I'm just gonna' tell you the same thing I told them, which is I was home sick as a dog. It was coming out of me at both ends. My mother was with me the whole time. I was outta' work for three days, and I was scared they were going to fire me. I didn't have anything goin' on with her at that point anyway. We broke up a long time ago. I saw her a few times after that, but there was nothing between us anymore. For a while I was hoping maybe there might be, but she made it pretty clear there wasn't. That's my story. I got nothin' else to say."

"Why'd you break up?"

"You'd have to ask her." He looked away for a moment and then back at me. "I'm goin' along fine having a good time, thinking everything's cool like we're in love and everything. Then, all of a sudden she announces one day we're through. Doesn't want to have anything more to do with me. It was like somebody hit me over the head with a tire iron. I asked her why, what's the problem, I thought we were gettin' along great, and she starts screaming at me, said she wanted to get out of this freakin' shit-burg town and didn't want to be stuck in a place like this and be poor all her life married to some fucking garage mechanic. Like, this all happened overnight, I never saw it comin'. One day everything's fine, the next day I'm a piece of shit and she doesn't want to have anything to do with me. What the fuck was I supposed to do? So that was it."

"When was this?"

"End of February, maybe the beginning of March. She was talking about college at that point, and I'm not the college type. Maybe that was it, I don't know. She had some crazy ideas sometimes. One time she says to me, hey, why don't we hop on the bike and take off, ride across the country, maybe go to California or someplace. I thought she was nuts. I laughed at her and she got really pissed. Looking back now, maybe I should've, but she probably would've dumped me at some point anyway. Money was a big thing for her, and I probably wasn't ever going to have enough. It was like she wanted to live in a big mansion in California or something."

"She ever mention seeing anybody else?"

He shook his head. "Nope."

"What about after you broke up? You said you saw her a couple times after that?"

"Yeah. Purely platonic."

"Why'd you two get together?"

He shrugged. "Just to talk. The first time or two I thought maybe she wanted to get back together, but it turned out she didn't want any part of that, she just wanted to talk, and when she wanted something she was tough to say no to."

"Where'd you meet up with her?"

"Down by the beach."

"This during the day?"

"No, end of the day. She was in school, and then she was working and I was doin' this."

"You and her do drugs together?"

"Sometimes. Back in the day."

"What kind of stuff?"

"Mostly weed. Once in a while, we'd try somethin' else."

"How often?"

He shrugged. "Few times a week maybe. When we were in the mood."

"Where'd you get it?"

"Here and there."

I paused for a moment. "You get her involved in your business at some point?"

"My business? What business's that?"

"Dealing. You've been caught multiple times, remember?"

He shook his head. "No, she never did anything for me back then."

"What about more recently? After you broke up?"

He paused for a minute, and then shook his head again. "She never worked for me. I'm outta' that business anyway."

"Yeah, sure you are. What about her? She get into the business herself at some point?"

He frowned. "She may've, I don't know."

"You don't know. Those times you saw her after you broke up, that was just reminiscing about old times, is that it?"

"Look, why're you asking me all this shit? She's dead so who the fuck cares?"

"We're looking for whoever killed her. If she was involved with some bad people, that's something we'd like to know."

"I don't know who the fuck she was involved with."

"But you know she was involved with somebody."

"Like I said, she may've been, I don't know."

"Know of anybody who might've wanted to harm her?"

"No."

"Any suspicions at all?"

He shook his head. "No. Other than seeing her a couple times, I got no idea what she was up to after she dumped me."

"When was the last time you saw her?"

"A couple weeks before she went missing."

"Where?"

"Down by the beach."

"What'd you talk about?"

"The weather, that kinda' thing." He looked at his watch. "I've got seven minutes to finish my lunch. Are we done?"

"Just a couple more. That last time you saw her, anything unusual or different about her?"

"Like what?"

"I don't know, anything she might've said, what she might've been doing, that kind of thing."

"I dunno', maybe. It was like she was up to something."

"She give you any idea what?"

"No. It was just, like, afterward I was wondering who she'd latched onto this time. She was always using people."

"Anything more specific than that?"

"No."

"After you broke up, do you know if she was seeing anybody else?"

"The baseball player?"

"Anybody else you know of?"

"No. Is that it?"

"You ever on his boat?"

He looked at me incredulously, and then laughed. "Are you shitting me?"

"I take it the answer is no?"

"Yeah, it's no. Now can I go back and finish my lunch?"

"You ever see her with any male friends besides him?"

"No." He looked at his watch again.

"You own a boat?"

"Fuck, no, I don't like boats."

"Okay, we're done," I said.

"Great. Thanks for killing my lunch break for me." He turned and said, "See ya' round," over his shoulder as he sauntered back toward the picnic table. I watched him go. When he got back to the table, he sat back down and said, "Fucking cops," in a voice loud enough to be sure I heard him.

July 25, 2012 I doubted the state cops knew anything about Hunter Phillips or his connection with Valerie Gray, whatever that connection might've been. I took a look in our records but couldn't find anything on him, which wasn't exactly a surprise. I found his address and decided to drive out there and see what I could learn. One thing I wasn't prepared for, though, was his house. It was a huge place that looked like it had been built in the late nineteenth or early twentieth century sitting on about four acres of land overlooking Vineyard Sound. There were trees and a stone wall in front of the house so you couldn't see very much from the street, but once you went through a narrow opening in the stone wall that had probably been originally built for carriages, suddenly the huge, three-story house was directly in front of you. A crushed stone driveway led up to the house and formed a circle in front. In the middle of the circle was an enormous holly tree that looked like it was probably as old as the house.

I pulled around the holly tree and parked by the front door. The driveway was empty and I figured there was probably a garage out back somewhere. I got out of the cruiser and looked up at the house, wondering if Jay Gatsby had ever slept there. It was a classic old oceanfront mansion with clapboard siding painted antique yellow with white trim that looked to be in immaculate condition. The massive front door was made out of oak and had a large brass whale tail for a door knocker. There was also a doorbell button to the right of the door. I tried the doorbell a couple times but got no response, so I banged the knocker. Still nothing. I stepped back from the door and looked up at the house again, trying to see if there might be some sign of life anywhere. All quiet. I decided to take a stroll and see if there might be somebody around back.

I followed a landscaped stone pathway around to the back of the house, which faced the Sound with a stunning view of the Vineyard in the distance. Off the back of the house was a large stone patio with a collection of expensive-looking teak furniture neatly arranged, and flower beds all around. A couple of large oak trees shaded the patio from the afternoon sun. Beyond the patio, an enormous lawn broken up by a few fruit trees stretched about three hundred feet down to the water, where I could see what looked like an old boathouse and a dock.

Across the patio, I spotted a broad-shouldered guy on his knees in one of the flower beds with his back to me. He was wearing a floppy straw hat that was faded dark brown from the sun, bib overalls, a long-sleeved plaid shirt and gardening gloves. He had some kind of a gardening tool in his hand, and he was clawing away at the dirt. I figured he probably worked for whoever did the landscaping.

"Hello, excuse me," I called out.

His head jerked up, and I could tell I'd startled him. He turned and looked over his shoulder at me, and then got to his feet and pulled his gloves off. I saw he had gardening knee pads on. He was a big man, maybe six foot two with sparkling blue eyes, bushy eyebrows, and long reddish blond hair that curled around his ears. He had a handsome square jaw that was covered with what looked to be about three days' worth of stubble, and his face had that ruddy look of somebody who likes his booze. "Yes, can I help you, Officer?" he said with an accent that sounded a little like Sean Connery. He stood there looking at me like he owned the place and it suddenly dawned on me this must be Phillips.

I made my way across the patio to him. "Sorry to disturb you," I said, "but nobody answered when I tried the front door. I came around in case there might be somebody out back here. I'm Officer Brian Bonner."

"Well, that was a good guess. Couldn't hear the front door. Sorry about that. Hunter Phillips," he said, extending his hand. "What can I do for you?"

Shaking hands, I said, "We're investigating the death of Valerie Jean Gray. I know you teach at the high school, and I was wondering if I could ask you a few questions. Beautiful house, by the way," I said, looking up at it.

"Thank you," he said, following my gaze. "Been in the family for years. Family's originally from Connecticut. Greenwich. Used to come up here summers. House's mine now. Mostly a labor of love at this point."

I nodded, and then gazed down toward the water. "Looks like there's a dock and a boathouse down by the water. You have a boat?"

He looked down toward the boathouse and smiled. "Yes, I have a boat, of sorts. It's an old wooden speedboat, a Chris-Craft. Inboard engine. They were all the rage back in the 40's and 50's. Came with the house. I don't think it's been started up in thirty years, maybe longer. I doubt you could do anything with it now. Maybe if you had it overhauled."

"That's a shame," I said. "It'd probably be pretty cool to ride around in."

"Oh, I don't know, I think it might look a little strange in this day and age. Anyway, what would you like to know about Val Gray? Are you a detective?"

"No, I'm just doing some background work to help out."

He nodded. "I see."

"I understand you were one of her teachers?"

"Yes, that's right. I had her in two of my classes—English her junior year, and a poetry elective I teach to seniors. Lovely young woman. A tragedy, really. I certainly hope you find who did it. Here, please sit down," he said, gesturing toward a couple teak chairs in a shady spot. "Can I get you anything?"

"No, thanks, I'm fine."

He took a seat across from me. I had the view of the Sound and the Vineyard. He took off his funny hat and put the hat and his gloves on the table beside his chair and faced me. I could see better why the girls at the high school thought he was hot stuff. "So, what specifically can I tell you?" he asked. "Val wasn't the best student I ever had, but she enjoyed literature and poetry, although it wasn't always easy for her. But if you love a subject, you'll usually do well in it eventually. She worked pretty hard at it, and I believe I gave her an A minus her senior year."

"Sounds like you knew her fairly well."

"Yes, fairly well I think, although in many respects she was a very private person. I probably knew her about as well as any of the teachers. She seemed to use me as something of a sounding board from time to time."

"Sounds like you talked about more than just school work."

"Oh, yes. We talked about a lot of different things, mostly about her, what she was thinking, what she was going to do when she graduated, that sort of thing. She lived with her mother, you know. Didn't really have a father. He left when she was a small child and she never saw him afterward. I got the impression her mother wasn't very attentive to her and she was left pretty much on her own most of the time. Learned to survive by herself, I imagine. In addition to being her teacher, at times I felt like I was playing a little bit of an uncle role, although not really."

"Where did these conversations take place?"

"In school. She'd come see me in the classroom after school, and we'd talk. Or sometimes when we both had a free period during the day. The seniors are given some leeway during the day if they maintain a certain grade point average. She'd come find me, and we'd talk. Sometimes we talked about school work, and sometimes we talked about other things. It was up to her, whatever she wanted to come see me about."

"How often was this?"

"Oh, perhaps every other week or so, something like that. It varied quite a bit. We didn't have any set schedule. It was up to her."

"Can you think of any of the specific things you talked about besides school work?"

"Oh, yes. As I said, we talked a lot this past year about her going to college. She wasn't sure she wanted to go. I tried to encourage her."

"I guess money was a problem."

"Yes, but that wasn't the only issue. She wasn't really sure she wanted to go to college. She was in a hurry to get somewhere in her life. She wanted to go somewhere where there were bright lights and exciting things going on, and she didn't really see college as being one of those places. I think she was afraid it was going to be like high school all over again."

"Where did she think she wanted to go?"

"She talked about a number of different possibilities. New York, Los Angeles, she even talked about Las Vegas. As I said, somewhere where there were bright lights."

"Wasn't she a little young for Las Vegas and places like that?"

"Well, yes, you'd certainly think so. But she seemed very confident. And she looked much older than her age, although those things were hardly a sufficient reason for her to take off for one of those places as far as I was concerned."

"You encouraged her to go to college?"

"Oh, absolutely, if she was going to be able to find a way to go. You alluded to money being an issue for her as far as college was concerned, and at one point she even asked if she could borrow some money from me. Of course I told her no as firmly as I could."

"Did she tell you how much she wanted to borrow?"

"No, we never got that far. I made it clear the answer was no when she first broached the subject, and she never brought it up again after that."

"When was this?"

"Oh, quite a while ago. Maybe last fall."

"Did she want the money for college, or just so she could take off and go to New York or Las Vegas or someplace?"

"I took her at her word that it was for college. Anyway, it was moot because I wasn't going to loan her anything no matter what she wanted it for. Teachers don't loan money to students. I'd get terminated for something like that. I told her that."

"She must've wanted the money pretty badly if she asked to borrow it from you."

"Well, college costs a lot these days even at a state school. I was confident that she'd find the money somehow."

"Why was that?"

"Well, as I said, she was very resourceful. She had what people refer to these days as street smarts. She was a tough young woman, well versed in survival. And at times quite manipulative, something I think was part of her survival technique. I didn't just fall off a turnip truck you know, and while much of the time I think she was genuinely looking to me for advice, there were certainly times when I could plainly see she was trying to use me. Asking to borrow some money was one of those occasions. I think she felt most of the time she could sweet talk her way to get just about anything she wanted. Those eyelashes would start to flutter, that smile would come out, and all her femininity would be on display. She could easily blind you if you weren't careful. It was often hard to keep in mind she was just in high school."

"Did she ever say or do anything you thought was overly suggestive?"

"You mean flirtatious? At times the way she acted some people might've thought that. At those times, I tried to maintain strict formality, let her know on no uncertain terms that wasn't going to work with me."

"What else did you two talk about?"

"Let me think." He looked off into the distance for a moment and then back at me. "We talked occasionally about her social standing in school. She didn't have many friends at school, which I think was largely her choice. To tell you the truth, she really didn't have much positive to say about the people in the school, the students, the teachers, anyone. She was pretty down on just about everyone around her and on living here in this town. As I said, she wanted very much to leave and go somewhere else. And she was quite ambitious, and in a hurry to get on to the next phase of her life, which she thought was going to be very different. And, as I said, she was very resourceful, and I didn't doubt that once she'd made her mind up to do something like that she'd figure out a way to do it."

"You mentioned she was attractive."

"Yes, she was. Quite attractive. I'm sure you've heard that from everyone. I don't think I can ever remember a female student who was quite so striking looking in such a mature way."

"And shapely."

"Yes, she was that, too."

"I'm told she attracted a lot of male attention."

"That certainly doesn't surprise me," he said, "although I really wouldn't know anything about that."

"She never talked with you about any male friends?"

"No, not with me." He smiled. "Thankfully."

"Thankfully?"

"Oh, God yes. If she'd ever broached the subject, I don't think I would've had the foggiest idea of what to say. And, again, I don't think it would've been appropriate as one of her teachers to talk about such things."

"Did you ever see her hanging out with any of the boys in school?"

"No. She had one girlfriend I was aware of, and that was about the only person I ever saw her with."

"Was she friends with any of the other male faculty members?"

"I have no idea. I don't think I ever observed her talking with any of the other male faculty members outside of class, but those are just my observations."

"Ever have any contact with her outside of school yourself?"

"You mean bump into her on the street, that sort of thing? I don't think so, not that I can recall anyway."

"Did you know she worked at the Shanty Diner?"

"No. I knew she had a job after school some days, but that's all I knew. I've never been in the Shanty Diner myself."

"Ever see her around town with any male friends?"

"No, nothing comes to mind."

"How about with any adult men?"

"No, as I said, I don't think I ever saw her anywhere outside of school."

"Any idea why anyone would've wanted to harm her?"

"I can't imagine. She was a lovely young woman."

"You must've thought about it, though. You knew her pretty well it seems."

He paused. "I've thought about the loss, of course, but not about whoever may have done it. I don't know why one human being would kill another, really. I suppose that's why we have you people to protect us and solve things like that."

I thought to myself, *'you people'? Jesus, what a fucking snob. This guy's a real asshole.* I asked him, "No suggestions, you can't help us at all on who it could've been?"

"No, I'm sorry."

I thought for a moment. "Do you know whether she was ever involved in dealing drugs?"

He frowned. "No, I've no knowledge of anything like that. She always seemed like a perfectly normal person to me."

"She never talked with you about it?"

"Absolutely not."

"Are you aware there's a lot of drug use on the Cape?"

"That's what I've read, and the school administration has told us the same thing."

"But you never talked with her about any kind of drugs or her dealing drugs?"

"No, never. I frankly don't know what I'd say if a student ever broached the subject with me. Probably end the conversation right there."

I paused and looked around for a moment, and then back at him. "You live alone here?"

"For most of the year, yes. I sometimes have family come in the summer, but not right now."

"Did Valerie Gray ever come here?"

He gave me a surprised look and then frowned. "Dear God, no."

"Ever give her a ride anywhere?"

"No," he said strongly.

"When was the last time you saw her?"

"At graduation."

"Did you talk with her then?"

"Yes, she sought me out after the program was over. Wanted to give me a gift. A bottle of wine, and a lovely card. I was quite flattered. It was very thoughtful of her. I've not gotten many gifts from students over the years."

"You didn't see her again after that?"

"No."

"You wrote a very positive college recommendation for her."

Again, he looked surprised. "Yes. I thought highly of her. She worked hard in my class and I felt she deserved it."

"You didn't think your relationship with her might've influenced what you wrote?"

"Relationship? I don't know what exactly you mean by our having had a relationship. I was one of her teachers and someone she sought advice from. It's hardly uncommon. That was the extent of my interaction with her. Listen, perhaps you could tell me why you're asking me all these questions? Some of them seem to be getting rather personal."

"We're investigating a very serious crime, Mr. Phillips. It's not intended to be personal. We just have to look at it from every angle."

"Well, some of these questions make me begin to think perhaps I should talk with my lawyer."

"That's totally up to you, Mr. Phillips."

"Are you finished with your questions? I think I've told you everything I know. Unless you have something else, I'm afraid I have other things I need to do." He stood up, obviously angry.

I stood up with him. "Fine, Mr. Phillips, that's all. Thanks for your time. Sorry if I've inconvenienced you. I'll find my way out."

He nodded, and I turned and left him standing there. Then, I retraced my steps around to the front of the house, got into the car, and drove out.

I stopped for coffee on my way back to the stationhouse. When I finally got there, Mullally was waiting for me. He led me into his office and closed the door. "I got a call from a lawyer in Hyannis named George Prendergast," he said. "Said he represents somebody named Hunter Phillips and that you've been harassing his client. He said if it isn't stopped immediately, he's going to seek a restraining order. What the fuck is that all about?" Although Mullally could be prickly at times, he rarely got really angry, but I could see this was one of those rare occasions. When he got angry, he had a tendency to spit when he talked, and he was spraying saliva all over the place.

"I can't believe that asshole actually called his fucking lawyer," I said. "I just talked to the guy, for Christ's sake. I didn't harass him, that's bullshit. He's got a lot of money, and he probably calls his lawyer every time somebody's dog wanders into his yard, the fucking snob. I was just trying to get some more background on Valerie Gray."

"Who's Phillips?"

"High school English teacher."

"He's a high school teacher, and he's got money?"

"Family money. You should see his house. Fucking mansion, for Christ's sake. Teaches just for kicks. And quite the ladies' man. Had a personal relationship with Valerie Gray and gave her a rave recommendation for college, and I thought he might be worth checking out. Like you said, local stuff the state cops probably wouldn't know about but would want to know about if there was something there."

"What kind of a relationship?"

"He was one of her teachers, taught her poetry and was a kind of confidante. Seems they got together from time to time and talked about a lot of things besides school work."

"Like what?"

"According to him, like about her going to college. He says she wasn't sure she wanted to go. Says she was thinking about heading off to the big city, maybe Vegas or someplace. Wanted to get away from this place pretty badly."

"Vegas? Jesus."

"That's what he said. He also said she asked to borrow money from him, supposedly for college, but according to him, he turned her down."

"How'd you find out about this guy?"

"Somebody who doesn't want their name mentioned."

Mullally frowned. "Is this person reliable?"

"Another faculty member."

"And this guy spent time with her?"

"Just in school according to him."

"Any evidence to the contrary?"

"Not yet."

"He married?'

"Divorced."

"How old is he?"

"Probably in his forties. Big guy, smooth, phony British accent, you could see how a high school girl could easily become infatuated, especially if they were having little one-on-one get-togethers. And with her looks, it's easy to see where it probably would've been pretty tempting for him."

Mullally looked away for a moment, his wheels obviously spinning. Then he turned back to me. "Okay, they wanted to know if there's anybody around here who might've had an interest in this young woman, and this guy obviously did. But unless there's more there than what you've told me, we'd better not go any further with this right now with his lawyer all over us. We don't have any evidence on him, and it could blow up in our faces. We get sued and the selectmen'll be bullshit. They're upset enough now. Did you see that newswoman on television again last night?"

"Carmen Belafontaine?"

"The one that looks like she works for an undertaker. Or maybe just crawled out of a coffin."

"No, I didn't see it. What'd she say this time?"

"It was supposed to be an update on the case, but of course there was nothing to update because the State Police haven't released any information since the body was found, so what she was really doing was just bashing the shit out of us for not having arrested anybody yet. Tried to insinuate violent crimes against women don't get the attention they deserve, that kind of thing. Like we're just sitting around having a circle jerk."

I shook my head. "Nice."

"Anyway, let's not create any more problems right now. Stay away from this guy Phillips for the time being unless something else brings him back into the picture. And nothing to anybody about him including the state cops, at least not unless we've got something more to go on. Understood?"

"Got it, Chief."

"Anything more comes up on this guy, I want you to come see me right away. His lawyer says any communications with his client are from now on to go through him."

"Okay."

"And for Christ's sake, let's not stir things up any more than they already are."

"I hear you, Chief," I said.

After work, I finally got up the courage to dial the number on the napkin that the high school guidance counselor had given me and listened to it ring three times before she picked up. "Hello," she said dryly.

"Hello," I said, having practiced what I was going to say, "this is the Sean McGruder Fan Club. We're looking for new members and were wondering if you'd like to join the Club."

I heard her chuckle on the other end of the line. "I'd love to, but unfortunately my Sharpie ran dry."

"No problem, Ma'am. Sean always carries an extra with him, and he'd be happy to autograph any part of you you'd like. He even makes house calls. Can I sign you up?"

"Sounds like my lucky day. I can't imagine what I did to deserve this."

"Sean spotted you in the stands at the last home game. He spends most of his time during games watching the stands and evaluating the females in attendance, and that's why you're receiving this invitation. Congratulations."

At this point she was laughing. "Well, I'm very flattered although I think Sean may want to have his eyes checked. I'd like to find out more about the Club but unfortunately I'm pretty busy right now, sitting by the phone waiting for a call from the police."

"Really, the police? Are you in trouble, Ma'am?"

"Not in nearly as much trouble as a certain police officer was going to be in if I hadn't gotten a call from him soon."

"I was just trying to play it cool, that's all."

"Well, you're so cool you're freezing at this point. So, you're calling to invite me out?"

"You must be clairvoyant."

"Of course. So what are you proposing?"

"Well, I was thinking maybe tomorrow night, some cocktails, dinner, maybe a nice bottle of wine someplace in town."

"Maybe I should play it cool and take a day to think about it."

"That would be spiteful."

"Yes, it would be, but I'm too kind a person for that sort of thing, so I accept. Cocktails *and* a bottle of wine, though. Should I be concerned that you may have an ulterior motive?"

"Of course not."

"A woman can't be too careful these days, you know."

"But you're going to have police protection."

"I'm thinking it's actually the police I may need protection from."

That night I had one of my nightmares. After it was over, I laid there for a long time thinking about what a fucked up mess I was. But there was nothing I could do but keep going. I'd actually thought a few times in the past about blowing my brains out, but each time I couldn't see myself doing it. I guess somewhere inside me there was a voice telling me I still had a chance to put the first part of my life behind me and find a happy ending, although I may've been just kidding myself.

10

July 26, 2012 The evening turned out to be quite a bit more enjoyable than I'd anticipated. I'd made a reservation at the town's Italian restaurant, which was about the best I could afford on my puny salary. My date wore a form-fitting top that showed a lot of cleavage, and sitting there in the restaurant I had trouble trying to keep my eyes from wandering in that direction. I'd be sitting there trying to maintain eye contact with her, but after a few minutes my gaze would inevitably start to slide downward. She would've had to have been unconscious not to notice where my eyes kept wandering to, but she didn't seem to mind, letting her boobs just hang out there in front of me, which made me hornier and hornier as the evening went along. We started with cocktails and then killed a whole bottle of wine with dinner, so, not surprisingly, we were pretty loaded when we left. When we got to the car, I asked her if there was anyplace else she wanted to go although I couldn't think of a lot of options myself. She thought for a minute, and then said no, but we could go back to her place if I wanted. *In the movies*, I thought to myself, *an invitation like that from a woman is usually an invitation to go home with her and have sex, but this wasn't a movie, and it was our second date if you wanted to call it that, and she was a school teacher, for Christ's sake. So don't read anything into it, Stupid. Maybe you can get a cup of coffee out of it if you're lucky.*

She lived in a small single-story house on a residential street lined with large oak trees, hers being the smallest house on the street. I parked in front of the house and turned off the engine. As we unbuckled our seatbelts, I asked her, "How're you doing?"

She gave me a slightly silly grin. "Well, I'm a little shit-faced, but I'm able to walk if that's what you mean."

I chuckled. "Yeah, well, I kinda' knew that. What I meant was, did you have an okay time?"

"Oh, yes, it was lovely, thank you. How about you?"

72

"Very nice, thank you."

"Well, that's good."

I looked around outside. It was dark, and the closest street lamp was about fifty feet behind us. It was quiet, and nobody seemed to be around. "Quiet neighborhood," I said.

"Yeah, it's all full-time residences, no summer rentals. Mine's a rental, but it's year round. Most of the people who live on this street are old, so it's quiet."

"How long've you lived here?"

"This house? Three years."

"You must like it."

"It's what I can afford on a teacher's salary, but it's not bad."

"You should see the little place I live in. I can barely turn around in it."

"Hey, we're both on the town payroll, you know. Nobody ever said we were going to get rich being a teacher or a cop. You like being a cop?"

"It's okay. Being a small town cop can be pretty boring at times, but it has its good parts. It's not a lot of hard work, and everybody's always sucking up to you and giving you freebies, like free cups of coffee, free desserts, free gas, free golf balls, you name it. Jesus, if I ate one tenth of the free food I've been offered, I'd probably weigh about six hundred pounds. And I don't have a college degree, so considering the alternatives it's okay at least for now. How about you?"

"Teaching's okay. I'm really busy during the school year with coaching and being the school's guidance counselor and everything, but I get the summers off, which is nice on the Cape, but it's getting boring, too. And living in a small town like this is death if you're not married. I've got to make some major decisions in my life pretty soon. Women have it tough when they start approaching a certain age and don't have a family."

"Yeah, you even went out with me. Shows how desperate you are."

She grinned. "I could say the same about you." She paused and then turned to me with a serious look on her face. "Is it alright if I ask you a question? You don't have to answer if you don't want to. I don't want to seem like I'm prying."

"That's okay, go ahead, what would you like to know?" I thought to myself, *I can always lie.*

She smiled. "I know it's probably a dumb question, but are you carrying a gun? I know I probably shouldn't ask, but I'm curious. If I'm out of line, just tell me."

I chuckled. "You had me scared there for a minute. Actually, that's a perfectly fair question to ask a police officer. The answer is yes, but not really. We're technically on duty all the time. If we see a crime being committed, or about to be committed, we're supposed to act whether we're working or not, so we're supposed to keep our weapon with us at all times, but that's not as easy as it sounds. Mine's a Glock, and it's big and bulky, and when you're not in uniform you can't just walk around with it stuck in your belt. You probably wouldn't get a lot of dates that way, that's for sure. At the moment, mine is sitting locked in the glove box in front of you."

She glanced at the glove box, and then looked back at me. "I'm glad it's locked. I'm not a big fan of guns. Ever had to use it?"

"Other than at the range, no."

"How'd you become a cop?"

"I was a military policeman in the Army."

"Where were you in the Army?"

"A couple places in the States, and I did a tour in Iraq."

"Oh, wow, that must've been tough."

"It was pretty bad. A lot worse than it looked like on TV."

"Why'd you join the Army?"

"To get away from my father."

"Oh, dear, I'm sorry to hear that. You told me at dinner you grew up around here?"

"That's right."

"You must have friends in the area, then."

"Not really. I left to join the Army after my junior year in high school and didn't really stay in touch with anybody."

"No old girlfriends around?"

"Never had many girlfriends, to tell you the truth."

"I find that hard to believe."

I shook my head. "No, I'm actually pretty shy."

"You must've had friends in the Army. Anybody you still stay in touch with?"

"Nah. The people you meet in the Army are from all over. Texas, Florida, Kansas, places like that. You don't have a lot in common with them except the Army and what you're doing. Everybody pretty much has everybody else's back, that's how you learn to survive in a place like Iraq, and you hang around and get drunk together and stuff like that, but once you get out you still don't really have much in common and people usually just go back to their former lives. And it's not like you've got a lot of fond memories of your time together, or at least I don't."

"I guess a lot of people who went to Iraq are having problems now?"

"Yeah, I guess so."

"Was it tough for you coming back?"

"I have my days, but I've been told it goes away over time."

"Well, you should be proud of your service. We should all thank you."

I shrugged. "Somebody had to do it."

"Are your parents still around here?"

"Still in the same place."

"Do you see them very often?"

"No, I haven't seen them since I left."

"I'm sorry to hear that."

I shrugged. "It's not like I had a happy family life. Like I said, my father and I didn't get along. The only one I really miss is my baby brother."

"How old is he?"

"I was the oldest of four kids, and he was the youngest with two sisters in between us. He's almost sixteen now."

"What's his name?"

"Ian."

"You were close?"

"Yeah, kind of, although he was just a little kid then. I was kind of his hero."

"That's nice."

"Yeah, I was some hero alright."

"Well, I'd think he'd be very proud of you now with your military record and everything."

"Maybe."

"Have you thought about trying to connect with him?"

I paused. "Yeah, every once in a while."

"What's holding you back?"

"I don't know how he'd react if he heard from me. And I'm not sure my parents would be real happy about it if they found out."

"I teach kids his age, and I think you might find it very rewarding if you were to reconnect with him. And I think you could keep it just between the two of you. You should really think about it."

"Thanks, I will."

"A family is something we all need."

I shrugged. "I don't know. I've been on my own for quite a while now so I'm used to it. It's not exactly what I would've chosen, but you don't always get what you want in life. Leaving home and joining the Army got me out of a lousy situation and gave me some training, so at least I've got a job. And who knows what the future will bring."

She nodded. "So, what do you want it to bring?"

I thought for a minute. Finally, I said, "I don't know, I guess what most people want. To be happy, maybe have a little money, some friends, maybe a family someday."

"Doesn't sound unrealistic."

"I don't know, we'll have to see."

"Have you thought at all about going back to school?"

I shrugged. "Yeah, maybe someday, but I'm not ready for that right now. At least if I decide to do it at some point, the government will pretty much pay for it so it's definitely something to think about."

"I would think so with the government paying and not having to borrow the money."

There was a silence. I thought to myself, *why am I telling her all this?* I gazed around outside again. Still nobody around. *She probably wants to go in soon*, I thought. I looked back at her, and she turned toward me in her seat, and, before I could say anything, she said, "I've got another question for you."

"Okay. Hope it's as easy as the last one."

"It shouldn't be that difficult. Anyway, you know that case you're working on involving Val Gray? The police are supposed to solve mysteries like that, aren't they?"

"Yeah, they're supposed to try."

"Well, I've got another mystery for you to solve."

I gave her a puzzled look. "What's that?"

She looked down at her hands and then back up at me. "The mystery is when you're going to kiss me."

"Umm, that sounds good," I said, trying to hide my surprise, and paused for a moment. "How about now?"

She nodded. "That would work."

Okay, control yourself, I thought to myself. *You've been eyeballing her boobs all night, and you're pretty worked up. Just relax and take it slow and gentle, and don't spoil things.* I slowly moved my head until my lips were almost on hers, and then I kissed her lightly. My lips stayed there for a moment, and she began to press her mouth back on mine. Before I knew it, our mouths were pressing hard against each other. My hand slid down to her waist and I pulled her toward me. I felt her breasts against my chest. Her mouth felt really good against mine. I couldn't help myself as my hand slid up from her waist onto her partially exposed breast, and she squirmed as my hand pressed against her. I started to slide my fingers inside her top and her bra, and I could feel the fabric of her top starting to stretch.

She pulled her mouth off mine and whispered in my ear, "Please don't rip it. It cost a lot."

"I don't want to rip it, you look so good in it."

"I thought you'd like it."

"I've only been staring down it all night."

She grinned. "I know." She ran her hand over my chest and down my bicep. I bent my head down and began kissing the exposed portions of her breasts. "Oh, God," she said breathlessly after a minute of this, "we can't do that here."

"Yeah, what will the neighbors say."

"They'll probably say that teacher's having sex with some guy in a car out on the street. We'd better go inside." She started to reach for the door handle and saw me hesitate. "Is everything alright?" she asked.

I sat there frozen for a moment trying to think. *You're all worked up, but is this really such a great idea? This woman obviously is looking for more than just a roll in the hay, as in a serious relationship, and you're not exactly in the market for something like that right now.*

She reached over and put her hand on my leg. "Have you got something you want to tell me?"

I glanced down at her breasts again and shook my head. "No. No, I'm okay. Go ahead, lead on."

11

July 27, 2012 The luminous hands on my watch said it was 3:53 am and I was naked and hung over, and searching around her living room in the dark for my clothes. We'd just made it in the door when she'd grabbed me and started kissing me and pulling my clothes off. God, was she horny. We never even got to the bedroom. As soon as our clothes were mostly off, she dragged me down on top of her on the living room floor. I got her bra off and pressed my mouth onto her naked breasts. After about a minute of this, she pulled my head up so that my mouth was pressed hard onto hers, our tongues going feverishly back and forth. Finally, she pulled her mouth away and whispered in my ear as she slid her undies off, "Get inside me." She sensed me hesitate and whispered, "Do you have a condom?"

"No," I whispered back, thinking to myself how stupid not to have come prepared, although who would've thought?

"In my bag. On the chair over by the door."

I crawled over to the chair on my hands and knees and rummaged around in her bag, where I found a box of three. I ripped the box open, pulled out a condom, got the wrapper off, and got it on. Then, I crawled back and got on top of her. She grasped me and guided me into her. She moaned softly as I entered her, and began to roll her pelvis up and down. I could feel her nails digging into my back. She started to whisper, "Yes, yes," as her pelvic thrusts became more and more violent. Then, I felt her body tense as she cried out, "Oh, my God, oh, my God," and continued to thrust her body upward. Suddenly, I felt myself on the verge of exploding, and then I did as we jerked up and down together pressing our bodies against each other.

When it was finally over, we lay there for a couple minutes, both of us a little sweaty. Then, I slowly rolled off her. There was a silence for another minute as we lay there beside each other on the rug, and then she finally said softly, "I need to use the bathroom. Go get into bed."

At some point, we both fell asleep. I woke up a couple hours later with rug burns, a hangover, and an excruciating need to piss, and figured it was probably a good time to make my exit. That is, if I could find my fucking clothes. The high school guidance counselor was out cold, her heavy breathing loud enough to officially register as snoring. I finally managed to find everything I remembered putting on that evening and quietly let myself out. I was due at work in four hours, and it was going to be a long day.

I breezed into the stationhouse sixteen minutes late after a short nap, and, as we used to say in the Army, a shit, shave and shower. What I needed most was coffee, but I was running so late I didn't have time to stop anywhere, and I was going to have to pay the price and take what there was at the stationhouse, which was not a particularly attractive alternative. Having an all-male police force with nobody skilled at performing domestic chores, or particularly interested in performing them, our coffee-making equipment was pretty atrocious. Adding to the problem was the fact that the stationhouse was manned twenty-four hours a day, seven days a week, which meant there was somebody there all night every night and whoever happened to be on duty on any given night always needed coffee to help get him through the shift, and of course he couldn't leave his post to go out and get some even if there were someplace around that was still open. That meant there was usually something akin to the sludge they drain out of your car's transmission sitting in the pot when the relief came on in the morning. Even somebody dumb enough to be a Cape Cod cop quickly figured out if you wanted a decent cup of coffee in the morning, you'd better stop somewhere on the way in and get it or risk someday having your insides sent to the Smithsonian or the Center for Disease Control.

I was in the process of washing out the previous night's remains and making a fresh pot, fresh being a relative term, when a call came in for the Chief, who hadn't come in yet. The call was from Balzano, who when told the Chief wasn't in, asked for me. He wanted to know if I could meet him and Cavanaugh to chat for a few minutes over coffee. They were at a place not far down the main street that I could walk to. I grabbed my hat and practically went skipping out the door.

It was the start of a typical July day on the Cape, and the main street was pretty busy even at that hour with a lot of people already in their beach clothes ready for another fun-filled day in the Cape Cod sun. Shops were beginning to open up, and I passed a heavyset blond woman with glasses perched down on her nose hanging out pink, lime green and iridescent orange hoodie sweatshirts that said Cape Cod across the front on a rack outside a store. On the other side of the street, I spotted one of the town's meter maids already out checking parking meters.

Balzano and Cavanaugh were at a bakery that made really good bread and pastry, and where you could also get a full breakfast or lunch if you wanted. The place was a storefront with the cutesy name, Plenty of Dough. It was one of those places where the smell of fresh bread hits you when you walk through the front door and makes you immediately start to salivate. The place was run by a group of young women I suspected were gay. Inside, there was a counter in the front with a big glass display case about twelve feet long loaded with all kinds of goodies, and some tables in the back where you could sit and eat if you wanted to. They also put a couple tables out on the sidewalk in good weather, which that morning were all occupied. Balzano and Cavanaugh were sitting at one of the tables inside in the back. There were empty plates and crumpled up paper napkins on the small table in front of them, and large paper cups of coffee that it looked like they were still working on. I gave them a friendly wave when I spotted them and Cavanaugh gave me a nod in return.

The bakery was a popular place, and, with the line at the counter stretching almost to the front door, it took me what seemed like forever to get up to the counter to order. I marvel at people who stand in a line like that looking at their phone or picking their nose or whatever, and it's only when they finally get to the head of the line and get waited on that they start to think for the first time about what they want and start looking to see what the choices are. And when it's two people together, then there's this long dialogue about who wants what and what looks good. And, of course, there's the chitchat with the counter help. All this made me about ready to scream when I finally got waited on. I ordered a large dark roast and an extremely delicious looking raspberry Danish about the size of a Frisbee, and brought them back to the table where Balzano and Cavanaugh were sitting. Cavanaugh moved the empty plates on the table around to make room for me to put my coffee and pastry down.

"You guys start early," I said, smiling as I sat down.

Neither of them returned my smile. "This isn't all that early for us," Balzano said flatly.

I took a bite of my scrumptious looking Danish and licked some bits of sticky frosting off my fingers. Then, I took a sip of coffee and could feel the sugar and the caffeine starting to flow into my system. "So, what's up?" I asked, putting my cup down. "How're things goin'?"

"Okay," Balzano replied. "Nothing major to speak of, we just wanted to pick your brain about something, see if you guys know anything about a certain individual here in town."

"Sure. Who's that?" I took another large bite of my Danish.

"You know a guy named Marty Blair?"

I tried not to show my surprise as I slowly swallowed my mouthful of Danish. "Yeah, I know him. The Chief knows him, too. Pretty much the whole town knows him."

"So tell us what you know about him."

I took another sip of coffee as I thought about what I was going to say. "Owns a couple restaurants here in town. I've heard he also owns a couple other restaurants on the Cape as well. Been around a while. Friendly. Like I said, knows a lot of people. Gives money to local charities, the hospital, Little League, that kind of thing. Always seemed like a nice guy. I've never been to his house or anything, just know him from around town." I looked at them trying to gauge where this was going.

Balzano said, "Ever hear anything about him dealing drugs?"

I took another bite of Danish and a sip of coffee. *This is getting interesting,* I thought to myself. "No, nothing like that, at least not as far as I know. Maybe the Chief knows something about it, but I don't."

"Well, our drug enforcement people think he's definitely in it up to his eyeballs," Balzano replied. "They've been working on it for quite a while now. Haven't been able to get anything on him yet, but they're pretty confident they're on the right track."

"What's he supposedly dealing?"

"Social stuff. Speed, ecstasy, pain killers, that kind of stuff. With all the partying on the Cape in the summer and lots of young people around with money, it's a pretty lucrative market."

"You think he sells the stuff around town here?"

"The drug guys think his market's a lot bigger than that, probably from the Canal to Hyannis, maybe even further."

"Wow. Where do they think he gets it from?"

"Probably Boston, or maybe New York. Somebody in the business who can't be bothered with a seasonal market and wholesales to him. Then, he peddles the stuff on his own free and clear."

"He have any competition?"

"Nah, not really. There're some other dealers around, but not enough to create any real competition. They mostly stay out of each other's way. Nobody wants problems."

"He do heroin or anything like that?"

"Not to our knowledge. Like I said, mainly pills. Less volume, easier to transport. People get hooked on the stuff, then they move to heroin. That's the market the big boys are interested in, it's a lot more profitable. So they sell the pills to guys like Marty, and then he does the seed work for their heroin business."

"Heroin's a big problem on the Cape."

Balzano nodded. "Thanks to guys like Marty."

"But all this about Marty Blair, it's just theoretical, isn't it? I mean, it sounds like you guys don't actually have anything on him."

"Like I said, our guys are working on it."

"Okay," I said, "so let's assume for a minute it's true. Is this somehow related to Valerie Gray, or is this something different?"

"Blair owns the Shanty Diner."

I stared at him. "I didn't know that," I said.

"Yeah, well, I'm not surprised," Balzano said. "Most people don't. You have to do a title search and know the ins and outs of all his corporations and trusts and stuff. The drug guys helped us figure it out."

"Okay, so he owns the diner, and she worked there part-time after school. Could be just a coincidence. You think he was mixed up with her? I'm told he's a big ladies man, and she apparently turned a lot of heads, but hooking up with a high school kid? He's probably in his forties, and, like I said, he knows a lot of people in town, and if it'd ever gotten out, his reputation would've been in the toilet. And her playing hide the kielbasa with a guy like him at the same time she's going out with a stud college baseball player who's half his age? I don't know, but it sounds a little dubious."

Balzano gave me one of his patronizing smiles. "Strange things can happen when a guy starts thinking with his other head. And he's got a lot of money to throw around, and that would explain where the money in her bank account came from a lot better than being a salesgirl for Bobby Frank."

"You think maybe Blair was paying her to fuck him? Considering what was in her account, though, that seems like a lot of nights on her back. Unless maybe she was doing something for him that was worth a lot."

"Maybe. Or maybe she was dealing drugs for him. Or both. She obviously didn't earn that much working part-time at the diner."

"You guys got any evidence of any of this? Other than she worked at the diner and he owned it? You sure he even knew who she was? He's got a lot of people working for him."

"Rongoni told us she thought her friend might've been seeing somebody else on the side," Cavanaugh said, "somebody her friend kept secret even from her."

"Yeah, I saw that in the file but it was pretty vague, at least in the report. I don't know exactly what she told you guys but my recollection is the report didn't have anything in it linking her to anybody specific. She may've been going out with a bunch of different guys for all we know. So that isn't going to get you very far, I wouldn't think."

"No, you're right," Balzano said. "It's all pretty much speculation at this point, but it would explain where the money came from better than anything we've got so far."

"Yeah, but it looks to me like you've still got a ways to go on this," I said. "Your drug guys have been after him for a while now and they haven't come up with anything solid on him yet. If it somehow turns out they're right, that means he's pretty clever and if that's the case, he's probably way too clever to bring some high school girl into his business just because she's got a pretty face and a nice pussy."

"Well," Balzano said, "let's suppose he falls for her and he brings her into his operation. After she sees what's going on, she threatens to expose him if he doesn't pay her off. He knows once blackmail starts it never ends, so he kills her."

"Okay," I said, "that's one theory. But like I said, it sounds like you don't have anything to back it up."

"There's another possibility," Cavanaugh said. "She's his little darling, and then all of a sudden she starts spending nights on the ballplayer's boat. Blair gets mad, she tells him to fuck off, and he hits her over the head."

I thought for a moment. "I'll tell you, I know the guy, maybe not well, but I know him and I can maybe see him fucking her a few times, but I'm not real crazy about the jealous lover bit. My impression is he's up to his neck in women. Let's say just for kicks he sees her working in the diner one day and decides he wants to get into her pants. He sweet talks her, maybe offers her money, which she needs for college, and eventually gets her onto her back. They have this thing goin' on for a while, and then she meets the ballplayer and she tells Blair she's moving on. He's gonna' whack her over the head? With his position in the community? Or does he just call up one of his other girlfriends to come over and help him ease the pain? Like I said, if he's as smart as you guys think he is, he couldn't be dumb enough to let his emotions get the better of him to the point where he kills a high school girl just because she ditched him. I suppose it's theoretically possible, but, like you just said, it seems like total speculation at this point."

Balzano nodded. "There's also another possibility, and that is she got involved in Blair's drug business and got whacked by some bad guy. We see that kind of shit all the time on the other side of the canal. Not a good business for a pretty young high school girl to be in."

"Well, again, I don't want to be a turd in the punchbowl here, but you haven't actually got him in the drug business yet, and then you've gotta' somehow get her there, too. And I don't think you want to screw this up and have his lawyers coming after you. But I shouldn't be telling you guys your business, you know this stuff a lot better than me."

Balzano nodded again. "Well, we came across this thing with Blair, and we wondered what you and the Chief might think about it. She's working at his place, he's got a lot of money and is selling drugs, she gets knocked off and leaves a bank account with more cash in it than most high school kids usually have and a lot of nice clothes while her family's supposedly broke. We don't think it's just a coincidence and wanted your reaction, see if you could think of anything we might be missing. So try it out on the Chief, and see what he thinks. We're gonna' keep working on it."

"I'm pretty sure the Chief'll say the same thing as me, but I'll run it by him."

"Where the hell did the money come from if it wasn't from Marty Blair?" Cavanaugh said. "That money's got to be linked to this somehow."

"Possibly," I replied, "but that's not really a lot of money. I mean, who knows, maybe she'd been saving since she was a kid."

"Yeah, and maybe the Tooth Fairy's coming in here for coffee any minute now," Balzano said, frowning.

"Maybe she was keeping it under her mattress for a long time and finally decided to put her nest egg in the bank. Didn't want to have to explain walking in with all that cash, so she did it piecemeal. Hey, I know that's probably not likely, but we both know that's the kind of shit you're gonna' hear from Marty's lawyers in the courtroom if you try to link him to the money. But, like I said, you guys know a lot more about this kind of stuff than I do."

"And we appreciate your opinion, don't think we don't," said Cavanaugh. "And you and the Chief know the guy, that's why we wanted to try it out on you. Every case needs somebody to pick holes in it. When there're no more holes, that's when you can close it. But talk to the Chief. Maybe this'll lead somewhere, you never know."

"We'll give it our best shot. So where does this leave us with Bobby Frank? He on the shelf for the moment?"

"No," Balzano replied, "definitely not, we haven't closed the door on anybody yet but for right now we want to keep exploring this Marty Blair angle."

"Well, good luck with it. Maybe it'll pan out, who knows."

There was a pause. Then, Balzano said, "So, Brian, tell us, where'd you get all those muscles?"

I gave him a slightly surprised look. "Body building," I said.

"How long you been doin' it?"

"Picked it up in the Army. Mostly out of boredom."

"You were in the Army?"

"Yeah, I was an M.P."

"Where'd you serve?"

"Iraq."

"A lot of guys in the State Police spent time over there. Not a nice place. We should thank you for your service."

"You joined the Army, that's what you got."

Balzano nodded. "On the body building thing, though, aren't you afraid of getting all bulked up and everything, and then having it turn to fat when you get older?"

I thought to myself, *I can't believe this fat little out-of-shape prick is actually saying this to me.* I gave him a phony smile. "I don't lift to add bulk," I said. "Just for tone. I'll probably never get any bigger than I am right now."

"You take supplements or anything?"

"Nah, just try to maintain a healthy diet."

Balzano smiled. "Like that Danish you just polished off?"

"I allow myself a treat every now and then," I said. "Trust me, I stay in pretty good shape."

"I don't doubt it," Balzano replied.

"So, have you guys had any more thoughts about the case?" Cavanaugh asked, changing the subject.

I thought for a moment. "We haven't talked about McGruder since you interviewed him. I guess he's got an alibi. That is, unless his buddies are covering up for him."

"That'd make it a conspiracy," Balzano said. "Pretty serious shit lying for a friend in a situation like that, you could go to prison for a long time. You'd have to be pretty stupid."

I shrugged. "I guess. What about Dowling?"

"What about him?"

"He apparently left the boat shortly after she did and is unaccounted for after that. And he's got a record. And he probably knew she had her friend's car. He might've figured out where she was going when she left the boat and gone after her. Wanted some pussy but she fought back, and she hit her head in the struggle. Or he whacked her."

Balzano nodded. "No sign of a struggle on her body, though, although we certainly haven't ruled Dowling out as a suspect. Frankly, we haven't ruled anybody out for that matter, but this has never looked like a sex crime."

"Maybe she was carrying drugs, and somebody knew it."

"Yeah, that's one of the reasons the Blair thing's so interesting. Maybe he didn't do it, but he has an idea who did."

"Well, whoever it was, the publicity's still ramped up," I said. "I guess Carmen Belafontaine did another story on it on TV the other night."

Cavanaugh frowned. "Yeah, she's milking it. Our media relations people tell us it's a big deal on social media now, too. We don't look at that stuff but they have to. Apparently, somebody posted some pictures of her on the internet, probably taken on a cell phone, and the thing went viral. Now, there're all kinds of nitwits out there chatting away with all sorts of theories, comparing it with other crimes and trying to show it was the same perpetrator, shitting all over us and claiming we're trying to cover up whoever did it because it's a celebrity or some big politician, all kinds of crazy shit like that. Our people have to read all that stuff just to make sure there isn't something there that might be useful, but it's just about all garbage. The cases has sure gotten a lot of attention, though."

"So it seems," I said.

"Too many people with too much time on their hands," Balzano replied.

"Yeah," Cavanaugh said, "but it's also got sizzle to it—beautiful girl, ugly crime, fancy part of the Cape. Not like just another gang member getting gunned down in lovely downtown New Bedford."

I nodded. "Well, I don't look at that stuff either. I'll try this thing about Marty Blair out on the Chief, and if he has anything to say we'll let you know."

"We appreciate it, Brian, and thanks for coming over," Cavanaugh said. "Let us know if there's anything you think we should follow up on."

"Will do, Guys."

"Well, we gotta' get rollin,'" Balzano said. "Lot's to do." They both stood up. I still had some coffee left that I knew I was going to need to get me through the day, so I stayed in my chair. "I'm gonna' stay and finish my coffee, if that's okay. You guys have a great day, and we'll talk soon," I said. They both nodded, and I watched them walk through the front of the bakery and out the door.

I sat there sipping the remains of my lukewarm coffee. *Fucking Marty Blair,* I thought to myself. *Mullally's gonna' love this.*

When I got back to the stationhouse, one of my colleagues called from across the room, "You got a phone message." He got up from his desk, and walked over and handed me a pink call slip. "Some teacher from the high school. Said it was important. Said she's got the information you wanted. The number's on the slip."

I looked at the slip. "When'd she call?"

"Right after you left."

"Thanks." I looked at the call slip again. "I'll call her right back." He shrugged and walked off.

This was not a call I was going to return in the stationhouse with everybody and his brother listening. I went to the john, came out and put my hat back on, and went outside and got into one of the cruisers. I sat there for a minute, and then dialed her number on my cell phone.

She picked up on the second ring. "Hello," she said. Not exactly cheery.

"Hi, it's me. Sleep well?"

"Too well, I guess. What happened to you?" Now she sounded pissed.

"Hey, I'm sorry if I snuck out but I had to be at work at eight, and you were sleeping so soundly I didn't want to wake you up."

"Yeah, well, you could've at least left a note or something. I felt like I got ditched."

"It was four o'clock in the morning and I didn't want to turn the lights on because I was afraid I'd wake you up. I had enough trouble finding my clothes in the dark. I figured I'd call you this morning, but I wound up getting called first thing for a meeting on that case, and I just got back. I'm really sorry, but I've got a lot going on and I'm not exactly operating on a lot of sleep. I sure as hell didn't mean to upset you, and I'm really sorry if I did." *Okay*, I thought to myself, *now shut up and let her vent.*

There was a brief silence. "Well, you can imagine how I felt," she said.

"I'm really sorry," I said again. "I didn't know this thing was gonna' come up this morning. What happened last night was really great. I hope you enjoyed it, too."

"Yeah, well, it was special for me, too. That's why I was upset, but I understand. You've got a lot going on. Let's just forget about it."

Inwardly, I breathed a huge sigh of relief. "Okay, am I going to see you again soon?"

"I thought I might cook dinner for you some night if you want."

"That sounds great. Maybe you could wear that same top again."

"The cook is off limits."

"What about after the cook goes off duty?"

"That will be a subject for future discussion."

"Is it going to be a long discussion?"

"That depends."

"Let me call you later to set something up once I get my work schedule."

"Okay, but don't try playing it cool again. Call me, or the police are going to be getting a lot of calls asking for your whereabouts."

"Got it. Now enjoy your day, and think about last night."

"Believe me, I am. Bye."

"Bye," I said and ended the call. *Jesus,* I thought to myself, *you knew this was probably going to get complicated.*

Mullally showed up around 11:00. "Need to talk to you, Chief," I said as he walked past me heading toward his office. He kept walking without responding, but motioned over his shoulder for me to follow him. Once we were in his office, I closed the door behind me.

"So, what's up?" he asked as he sat down heavily in his chair.

"The state cops called this morning," I said. "When they found out you weren't here, they asked for me. Wanted me to meet them for coffee down the street. Seems they're exploring a rather interesting new theory and wanted to know what we thought of it."

"What's the theory?"

"That Marty Blair's mixed up in this."

"Mixed up in what?"

"Val Gray."

Mullally frowned. "You're shitting me."

"I wish," I said. "It's even more complicated than that. It seems the State Police drug guys have been after Marty for quite a while. They think he's running a drug cartel on the Cape, but they haven't been able to come up with enough on him yet to make it stick."

"Marty Blair's in the drug business? Jesus Christ."

"Who knew, right? Well, Balzano and Cavanaugh talked with the drug guys and between them they figured out Marty owns the Shanty Diner, where Ms. Gray worked part-time. So now they're guessing maybe Marty was the source of the money in her account, and she was doing more for him than waiting on customers."

"Like what?"

"Well, that's a problem. They're trying to find a link between the two of them. The drug guys think Marty's in it up to his eyeballs, and the money makes them think she was working for him somehow in his drug business."

"A high school kid? Jesus, I can see her maybe selling a little stuff to her friends at school for Bobby Frank but the big time drug business? She was what, eighteen years old for Christ's sake?"

"Nineteen. But yeah, that was my first reaction, too. So Marty's supposedly running this sophisticated drug business that the state cops can't figure out for the life of them with a high school kid as a partner? But the money does at least make you stop and think."

"How do they think the two of them got into business together? Was she doing such a good job at the diner that he decided to give her a promotion?"

"They think maybe he was fucking her, and she got into the business that way."

"What way? First of all, even if Marty is stupid enough to fuck a high school girl, which I doubt, he's so in love with her he tells her he's in the drug business? That is, assuming he actually is in the drug business, which the state cops apparently can't prove. And then he decides to invite her into the business so they can be lovey-dovey partners in crime together like Bonnie and Clyde? Jesus, the whole thing sounds like a load of shit to me."

"Or maybe he tells her about his little side business, and some night when she's got his dick in her hand she asks him for a job and it's at a critical moment, and he can't say no."

Mullally shook his head. "I'm telling you, Marty can't be that stupid. And if he was so in love with her, why the fuck would he kill her?"

"One of their theories is she was blackmailing him."

"Oh, Jesus Christ, what next? They got any evidence?"

"No," I replied, "of course not. It's all just a theory. They don't have any evidence of any of this, not even the drug stuff. They just wanted our reaction."

"What'd you tell them?"

"I was basically non-committal. I just pointed out that they were going to need more than a theory."

"What'd they say to that?"

"They wanted me to try it out on you."

"Well, okay, now you've tried it out on me, and I'm not buying it. At least not until they come up with a hell of a lot more."

I nodded. "Love can sometimes make people do crazy things, and I guess she was a real piece of ass. And then there's the money. But frankly, I think the state cops have got a hard-on for Marty, and they're trying to get something on him any way they can. Maybe they think this is a new angle that may put pressure on him on the drug thing. But you do kinda' have to wonder where she could've gotten the money from if it wasn't from Marty."

"The money could've come from a lot of different places. Maybe she borrowed it for college. Remember she asked Phillips if she could borrow some money from him? Maybe she found somebody else to loan it to her. Or maybe working for Bobby Frank. Who the fuck knows." Mullally shook his head. "Here we've got a drug problem, and it turns out maybe the main source of our problem has been right here under our noses the whole time. That is, if the state cops are right."

"I somehow doubt they're just making it all up."

"Well, if they nail Marty on the drug thing, we're not going to look very good."

"They've supposedly been after him for a long time. If they haven't been able to figure it out after all this time, how could we've done it?"

"Hindsight's twenty-twenty. We're right here in the same town with him." Mullally was silent for a moment. Finally, he said, "You think there's anything we oughta' do?"

"What about having a little talk with Marty off the record? Try to get a feel for whether the drug thing is real and whether there really was anything going on between him and Ms. Gray?"

He paused. "That's a little tricky."

"I know, I know. But it's likely he already knows they're after him on the drug thing and if that could turn out to be a problem, it'd be good to know. And if the thing about him and Ms. Gray's got something to it, it'd be nice to know that, too. On the other hand, if this whole thing's just somebody's imagination working overtime, that'd be nice to know as well."

"We can't be interfering with a State Police investigation. I'd like to keep my pension."

"If this thing explodes, who knows where the finger pointing might lead. This department's had a pretty cozy relationship with Marty over the years, and people probably wouldn't like it if this blew up and they got wind of what's been goin' on with him. Like we've been protecting him or something. If our asses are hanging out there in the wind, it'd be better to know about it sooner rather than later. Just a few simple questions, that's all. See what we think then."

"I shouldn't be involved in this. You talk to him. That way, we can at least say it was part of our background investigation."

Yeah, I thought to myself, *and I'll be the one who gets hung out to dry if it blows up*. At the same time, though, I very much wanted to hear what Marty had to say. "Okay," I said, "I'll talk with him and let you know what he says."

"Just be careful, for Christ's sake. It's one thing for somebody to claim we've been protecting him, but let's not open ourselves up to a charge of interfering with a State Police murder investigation. Or a State Police drug investigation. Let the state cops go after him if they want. If he's mixed up in this, there's nothing we can do about it."

"I hear you, Chief" I said, and walked out.

12

July 27, 2012 I'd always thought Marty Blair was a pretty smooth guy. He was handsome with curly black hair and always looked tan and in good shape with a great smile that made me think he'd probably had his teeth capped. He was single and rumor had it he'd fucked half the women on the Cape, including the married ones. He had money but did a good job of concealing how much. He drove a new car every year but nothing flashy, and he mostly wore blue jeans. He supposedly had a nice house overlooking the ocean, but I understood relatively few people ever got to see it except for maybe some of his girlfriends. Whatever entertaining he did was usually at one of his restaurants.

Marty was everybody's friend and he seemed to know half the town personally. And he was extremely generous. Whenever there was a needy cause, Marty was there. Some fireman hurt in a fire? Marty would arrive with a carful of groceries for the family. The town needs money for Christmas lights for the main street? Marty'd take care of it. The senior class at the high school is short of money for a class trip? Marty'd make up the difference. Little League needs a new outfield fence? No problem. And he was particularly generous to our little department. He gave out turkeys to everybody at Thanksgiving, and every year he threw a Holiday party for us and our spouses and girlfriends in a private room in one of his restaurants with everybody going home with a nice bottle of booze. And he took us all out on his boat every summer to fish and drink ourselves silly. One time, he brought along an extremely well-endowed young lady to serve drinks and snacks who looked like she was about to fall out of her bikini top at any minute. Needless to say, nobody paid a lot of attention to fishing on that trip.

Marty was also the department's personal banker. Short of cash for some reason or want to take the wife on a nice vacation? Go see Marty, he'd fix you up with an interest free loan you could pay back whenever. I'd personally never borrowed any money from him, but I'd often wondered how many of those loans ever actually got paid back. Yeah, Marty was the department's special friend, and approaching him about this little problem was going to be a delicate conversation.

After I'd talked with Mullally , I called Marty's assistant, Suzie Blanchette, to see if he was around. Suzie had been with Marty for years, and if you wanted to talk to Marty, you had to go through Suzie. I sometimes wondered whether Marty's girlfriends all had to go through Suzie, too. Suzie was a petite little thing, probably in her sixties, with dyed hair and the biggest pair of glasses I'd ever seen, which made her look like some kind of giant insect. When I called, Suzie told me the boss was in his office and I should come on over.

Marty had his office on the second floor of one of his restaurants that was situated on the harbor about a hundred yards up from where McGruder's boat was tied up. The name of the restaurant was the Harbor Club, and it was about the most expensive restaurant in town with a panoramic view of the harbor. You got to Marty's office by going up an outside staircase in the back of the building. Suzie was sitting at her big desk in the outer office when I walked in, and she gave me the same big smile she always gave everybody. "Hello, Brian. It's nice to see you," she purred. She nodded toward the red light on her phone console. "The boss is on the phone right now. Can I get you a cup of coffee or some water?"

I took my hat off. "No thanks, Suz, I'm fine. How're you?"

"Oh, I'm just my usual self, Brian, thank you for asking. How're you doing?"

"Can't complain."

"He may be on for a few minutes. Why don't you sit down," she said, nodding toward the leather couch against the wall on the far side of the room. "I'll let him know you're here as soon as he gets off."

I went over to the couch, sat down, and put my hat down beside me. There were copies of the New York Times, Wall Street Journal and the local paper on the coffee table in front of the couch. I pulled the copy of the Times over and glanced at the front page. Suzie went back to doing what she'd been doing.

About ten minutes passed in silence. Then, having seen the light on her console had gone out, Suzie announced, "He's off the phone."

She got up, knocked on the door of Marty's office, and opened it a crack. "Brian's here," she said through the opening.

"I'm on my way," I heard Marty say. A few seconds later the door swung open and out he came. He was wearing his usual blue jeans, an expensive-looking polo shirt, boat shoes and no socks. His hair looked damp like he'd just come from the gym. "Hey, Brian, how's it going," he said in his usual exaggerated way as he came over to the couch with a big smile and his hand stuck out.

I stood up and we shook hands. "Hi, Marty," I said. "Thanks for having me over on such short notice."

"You caught me at a perfect time. Come on in," he said gesturing toward the door to his office. I picked up my hat and went in. "Suzie, dear, take my calls for a few minutes while I talk with Brian," he said as he followed me in and closed the door behind him.

I sat down in an expensive-looking leather chair in front of his sleek modern desk that had what looked like a state-of-the-art computer on it. He went around the desk and sat down, and put his feet up on the desk. Behind him was a big picture window that provided a panoramic view of the harbor. There was a rich oriental rug on the floor. The walls were covered with plaques and framed awards from the Boy Scouts, the Little League, the local hospital, you name it, and a lot of pictures of Marty shaking hands with a bunch of people, most of whom I didn't recognize, with the usual big smile on his face. *The most popular guy in town,* I thought to myself.

"Nice view," I said, looking past him out the large window.

He glanced back at the window and then turned back to me again. "Yeah, it's nice, even in the winter when the boats are gone. When I bought this place, I guess it was about eight years ago, I had my eye on this space for my office and it's worked out really well. So," he asked with a wry smile, "you come over to take in the view?"

"No, I'm sort of here on business, but not really."

"Oh?" he said, the smile fading slightly. "Well, this should be good. What's up?"

"I have to be somewhat careful in what I say for reasons that will become obvious," I said. "I'd like this to be a conversation that never took place, but it is taking place so I have to assume it may surface someday, and I don't want either of us to take a hit if it does."

The look on his face was serious now. He took his feet down and faced me squarely across the desk, his hands folded in front of him. "Brian, you want to talk with me about something confidential, it's completely confidential. Whatever it is stays within these four walls, I promise you."

"Well, let's get started and see how it goes," I said. "I'm trying to protect us both. I think you'll figure out in a hurry what I'm talking about."

He nodded. "Okay, go ahead, shoot. If I've got a problem, I'll stop you."

"Fine. Okay, so you know the girl whose body was found in the Sound and who they think was murdered?"

"Sure, Valerie Gray. Awful tragedy. She was a lovely girl. I hope you catch whoever did it real soon."

"Yeah, well, it's really the state cops that're investigating it, and me and Mullally are just doing odd jobs for them, but they keep us informed about what's going on. It's apparently turned up that Valerie Gray worked at one of your restaurants."

He looked surprised. "Yeah, the diner. I don't own it personally, but one of my businesses owns it. She worked there part-time after school. That a problem?"

"She do anything else for you besides work at the diner?"

He frowned. "What the fuck's that supposed to mean?"

"Well, the State Police are the ones who figured out you own the diner."

"Yeah, good for them."

"Sounds like you knew her."

"Yeah, I knew her. I know most of my employees."

"The question is, how well did you know this drop dead gorgeous high school girl who worked at the diner part-time?"

"Jesus, Brian, this is getting a little insulting."

"Whoa, Marty, take it easy, I'm on your side. I'm trying to take this slowly. You'll see why in a minute. So how well did you know her?"

He turned and looked out the window behind him for a minute, and then turned back to me. "Okay, I was in the diner one day not long after she got hired, and I spotted her. I mean she was pretty hard to miss, let me tell you, she was a real piece of ass. I asked, who the hell's that? Part-time high school student, I'm told. Jesus, I thought, high school? You gotta' be kiddin' me. So I go over and introduce myself. Blond hair, blue eyes, great tits. I'm Val, she says. We chat for a couple minutes, just small talk. Then, I go back and tell the manager to put her out front, she'll attract every horny truck driver and mailman in town. You go to the diner, Brian, you must've seen her, didn't you?"

I hesitated. "I might've."

"Well, you probably know what I'm talkin' about, then. She was really something."

"Yeah, well, now you're going to see why this is a little tricky," I said. "I'm about to tell you something I'm not supposed to, so can I be sure you're never going to say you heard this from me? I could get into some really deep shit over this."

"I told you, anything you say here is strictly confidential. Whatever it is, I didn't hear it from you. Okay?"

"Okay, well, what you ought to know is the state cops are trying to connect the dots between you and her."

He stared at me for a moment. "You're shitting me. I mean, you are shitting me, aren't you?"

"No, Marty, I'm not shitting you. And it seems they're also focused on a little side business you supposedly run."

"Jesus, that shit again? I swear, those fucking guys never give up."

"Apparently not. Okay, look, if you have some other business interests besides restaurants, I don't want to know about it, okay? That's your business. We're not involved in anything that's going on with that." He nodded slowly. "But without talking about those kinds of things, let me ask you did Ms. Gray ever do anything for you other than pour coffee behind the counter at the diner?"

"What do you mean by anything?"

"I mean anything at all. You name it."

He looked out the window again for a long time and then turned back to me. "Yeah, she did some other stuff for me."

"Like what?"

"That's not something I can really get into."

"Why not?"

"It's just not something I can get into, Brian, that's all."

"I don't get why not."

"Because you're a fucking cop, for Christ's sake. That's why not. Jesus."

I paused and took a deep breath. "Okay, now I get it. But please understand I'm also your friend. And I came all the way over here to tell you something I could get into some really big trouble for like I said, okay?"

He stared at me for a minute. "Yeah, I can see that."

"So, okay, like I said, as far as Mullally and me are concerned, this is a murder investigation. Anything else is somebody else's problem. We're just trying to figure out what she might've been doing that could've gotten her killed, and we don't really give a shit how she may've gotten there. We're looking for leads any way we can find them and whatever she was doing for you might lead us somewhere, and that's all we're interested in. We were hoping you might be able to help us out with that. As a friend. And the sooner we solve this thing, the sooner the state cops are hopefully gonna' get off your back. They're swarming around now because a pretty high school girl got murdered, and it's on TV and everybody's bustin' their balls."

He nodded slowly. "Okay, I see where you're goin'."

"So, can you help us out?"

"Let me think about it."

I stared at him. "This is a murder case, Marty. Other kinds of illegal activities, that's one thing, but murder's something else. Mullally and me don't think you did it, but the best way to prove that is to figure out who did. So by helping us, you'll be helping yourself. You didn't hear it from me that the state cops are trying to connect the dots between you and her, and, likewise, if you tell me something that could help solve this thing, I didn't hear it from you. Okay?"

He thought for a long time. I sat there in silence waiting for him. Finally, he said, "Okay, I see what you mean about the murder thing. It's a whole different ballgame. Let's give it a try. I'm not sure I can help you, but I'll tell you what I know. But I'm talking to a cop now, and I need to be absolutely sure what I'm going to tell you isn't going anywhere beyond this room."

"Nobody's going to know anything. I'm not wearing a wire or anything, or taking notes. You want to search me for a wire or a tape recorder you can. As far as I'm concerned, once this conversation is over, you say nothing and I say nothing. Nobody's gonna' know where any information you give me came from, you have my word."

"Okay, I don't need to search you, Brian, I trust you. Like I said, she did some other things for me."

"Okay. Why don't you could tell me generally what types of things without getting into specifics."

He furrowed his brow. "She ran some errands for me. Delivered some stuff, that kind of thing."

I paused. "Okay, I assume she was like your Fed Ex person, delivering stuff as part of your business?"

He nodded. "Yeah, she was like Fed Ex."

"And I assume you paid her?"

"Yeah, sure, I paid her something."

"How many times did she make deliveries for you, approximately?"

"A few. Maybe a dozen."

"And how much did you pay her?"

"Why do you need to know that?"

I shook my head. "Jesus, Marty, this is confidential, remember?" He stared at me and didn't say anything. "Look," I finally said, "I'm already in enough trouble, so I might as well tell you they've found out she had a bank account with a good sized chunk of change in it. And they're looking to find out where the money came from, and they think it may've come from you."

"Well, if it's a good sized chunk of change, it didn't come from me."

"Great. So convince me. How much did you pay her?"

He paused again. Finally, he said, "Three hundred bucks a delivery. Hey, for the number of deliveries she wound up making, that doesn't add up to a whole lot if you're talking about the kind of money I think you're talking about. Let me tell you how it happened. After that time I met her at the diner, maybe a week later, she suddenly shows up here unannounced. You should've seen her, she was dressed to kill. Sat there in the same chair you're sitting in now. High heels, low cut top, short skirt with her legs crossed in a sexy way, big smile like she and I are old friends. We talk. She says she needs money for college, tells me she lives with her mother and they can't afford college unless she can find something that pays a lot more than working at the diner. She asks if there's something else she can do for me to earn some money. Hey, a lotta' guys in my position might've said, honey, you wanna' make some money, why don't you come over here and crawl under the desk and sample some of my DNA. But I'm thinking, no, this is just a high school kid, for Christ's sake, although you'd never know it to look at her sitting there. She really knew how to get under a guy's skin, let me tell you. Then, I thought to myself, hey, this lady seems to know how to handle herself and nobody'd ever figure she was somebody's Fed Ex, so I asked her if she'd like to make a delivery for me sometime and earn a few bucks, you know, try her out. Well, you mighta' thought I'd told her she'd won the lottery or something. I really thought she was going to come around the desk and kiss me. So anyway, she does the delivery, and bingo, everything goes smoothly. So now I'm thinkin' I'm a fucking genius. This beautiful, young thing, a fucking high school student for Christ's sake, who'd ever think she was somebody's Fed Ex? And after that, everything worked great like she was a pro. She helped me out, and I helped her pay for college, although unfortunately she never got that far."

"You pay her in cash?"

"Yeah, cash."

"These deliveries, where'd she take 'em?"

"Some places around the Cape."

"As far as Hyannis?"

"Maybe."

"When was the last time?"

"Maybe middle of June. After that, for some reason she quit. I have no idea why. Maybe she figured she'd made enough, or maybe she found somebody else to get the money from, I don't know."

"Okay, so you paid her for running these errands for you. Now, I want you to assume hypothetically that, as you've already guessed, her bank account had substantially more in it than what you paid her to work the counter at the diner and be your Fed Ex person. And you've told me she never crawled under your

98

desk. So, is there any place else you can think of, hypothetically, where that money could've come from?"

He looked at me blankly. "No, other than she got it from somebody else and not me."

I paused again. "What about the people she made these deliveries to. Could she've gotten money from any of them?"

He shook his head. "No, not unless she made deliveries or did something for one of them, too."

"Or she crawled under the desk for one of them?"

"I don't know what your hypothetical amount of money is, but I have a feeling it's more than a high school girl would probably get for crawling under somebody's desk once or twice. And I don't see her as being the type who likely would've become a regular at that kind of thing."

"Well, the question is then, where the fuck did the money come from?" I paused for a minute to think and something dawned on me. "Let me ask you this, would it've been possible for her to have taken something out of the packages she was delivering for you without anybody noticing?"

He thought for a moment. "You mean skimming?"

"That's your word, not mine. Let's just say, hypothetically, she wanted to do something like that. Could she have?"

"Yeah, theoretically it's possible. It happens from time to time. A little bit here and a little bit there might not get noticed. But she would've had to've been pretty careful."

"Okay, let's follow that along. Let's say somebody was doing this and got caught? Would that have put that person in danger?"

He shook his head. "No, not that kind of danger, not getting killed. Maybe somebody would've gotten mad and wanted to teach her a lesson or something so she wouldn't do it again. But murder? Nah, the one thing the person who was short would be looking for would be either to get back what was taken or get back the money they were out. If you kill the person who robbed you, you'll never get anything back. Anyway, one way or the other if somebody'd discovered a problem, they definitely would've come to me about it right away, figuring they'd gotten shortchanged."

"If she was skimming, to use your word again, do you think she could've found a market for what she'd taken?"

"Around here in the summer? Are you shitting me? Of course." He paused. "So, how do I fit into all this? Even if they thought she was doing Fed Ex for me, they don't think I could've killed her, do they? Why the fuck would I do that?"

"Well, they've got a couple theories, neither of them all that great. One is she knew about your side business and she was blackmailing you, and you had to get rid of her. The other is you two were lovers and you got jealous when you found out she was fucking one of the guys on the Middies, so you killed her in a crime of passion."

"She was fucking one of the Middies, huh? Well, lucky him. Look, she was a real piece of ass, no question about it, but she was in high school, for Christ's sake. I get all the sex I need, maybe more than I need. And I've got women who do a lot more than any high school girl would ever know about, let me tell you. You wouldn't believe some of the stuff women do these days, Brian. I mean, I don't want to insult you, I'm sure you probably know."

I bit my tongue. "I'm afraid I lead a pretty sheltered life."

"Whatever. Anyway, blackmail? Jesus, a high school kid? Her word against mine? My lawyers would tear her to pieces. This stuff's garbage, Brian, total fucking garbage."

"I thought so too when I heard it, Marty. Maybe they think if they throw this out there, something else'll fall out."

"Yeah, I see what you mean. Well, nothing's going to fall out, I can promise you that. You can go back and tell the fucking state cops they can kiss my sweet ass. This is stupid and it's never gonna' go anywhere. You can tell 'em that, too."

"Marty, I'm not going to tell 'em shit, remember? They're never going to hear about this conversation from either one of us, right? I came over here because we thought you ought to know, that's all, and we also thought maybe you could help us out."

He nodded slowly. "Okay, sorry, Brian, I'm just pissed off about this whole fucking thing. The fucking state cops've been driving me nuts for a long time now, and now you tell me this shit. You can understand why I'm pissed. I'm not mad at you, though, please don't misunderstand me."

"Look, Marty, I know, this is a pain in the ass for all of us. But there's one more thing you should probably think about. If anybody questions you about any of this, there's one question that's sure to come up and that is, where were you the night she disappeared."

He looked at me blankly. "That'd be easy if I knew when the fuck that was. What night was that?"

"July 8th."

He stared out the window for a moment, and then turned back to me. "I don't know. I'd have to go back and reconstruct my schedule. Hopefully, I was with some broad and she's believable."

I nodded. "Well, figure it out. It may turn out to be important."

"Okay. What else?"

"You know about anybody she might've been going out with?"

"Like a boyfriend or something? Jesus, how the fuck would I know that? You said she was fucking one of the Middies. Well, that's news to me."

"You never saw her with anybody? She never mentioned any male friends?"

"No."

"Ever heard of a guy named Bobby Frank?"

He shook his head. "No, who's he?"

"Old boyfriend. Small time dealer here in town. If she was in business for herself, she may've been using him as a distribution outlet. I take it his name doesn't ring any bells."

"Nope. Like I said, if she was in business for herself, I didn't know anything about it. Maybe she met somebody along the way and went to work for them, maybe that's why she quit working for me. Then, she got in over her head and paid the price. It's not a very nice business. But how the hell would I know? One thing's for sure, though, if I'd known she had her hand in the cookie jar when she was working for me, trust me, I would've fired her on the spot. That kind of shit can cause a lot of problems I don't need. But I wouldn't have killed her, for Christ's sake, that would've been totally fucking crazy. You believe me, don't you, Brian?"

"Yeah, I believe you, Marty. This whole thing's just a lot of crap."

"Well, good, I'm glad you think so, too. What else?"

"I can't think of anything else right now. I think we're done."

"In that case, then, can I ask a favor?"

"Depends on what it is, Marty."

"I know, I know, I'm just asking. If you can't, you can't, I understand."

"If I can't what?"

"Keep me informed about what's going on. I don't mean like every day. I just mean, you know, like if you think there might be a problem coming my way, give me a heads up. Nothing major, like maybe if you see something coming, you just say to me, hey, Marty, remember what we talked about that time, well there's a problem, something like that, it doesn't have to be any more than that, I'll get the message."

"I'll try to do what I can, Marty, but I can't promise anything so you better watch your back."

"Trust me, I will, you can be sure of that. Hey, Brian, I owe you. I know coming over here took some big ones with the state cops swarming around and everything. I appreciate the heads up, I really do, and I want to make sure you know how much I appreciate it. How about starting with dinner downstairs on me. You must have some lovely lady stashed somewhere you'd like to score some points with. Just pick a night and call the folks downstairs, they'll take care of it. Like I said, everything on me."

"Jesus, that's really nice of you, Marty, thanks. I'm definitely gonna' take you up on that."

"Look, it's my pleasure, Brian, my pleasure. And maybe you can think of something else I can do for you sometime. You just let me know."

"Thanks, Marty," I said. "I definitely will."

I sat in the cruiser in the Harbor Club parking lot and dialed her number. "Hi, it's me," I said when she picked up.

"Who's me?" she said. Very funny.

"I must have the wrong number," I said.

"Oh, is this the horny cop who's looking for a free meal?"

"Yeah, and the cook for dessert. Glad you finally recognized my voice."

"Well, I was just playing it cool."

"Touché. How about Tuesday night?"

"Sure, why not. It'll give me plenty of time to figure out dinner and pick up some groceries."

"Well, there's been a slight change in plans."

"Uh, oh, I'm not sure I'm going to like this."

"You will. Instead of you cooking dinner, how about we go to the Harbor Club?"

"The Harbor Club? Somebody die and leave you a lot of money?"

"I cannot tell a lie. It's a freebie."

"A freebie at the Harbor Club? Wow, you weren't kidding about the perks of being a cop. I'm lucky if I get an apple that isn't rotten."

"It's a little unusual. I did somebody a favor."

"Who's that?"

"Sorry, I can't say."

"I hope it was a he and not a she."

"Trust me, it was a he."

"We're going to be able to get in there on such short notice in July?"

"It's all taken care of."

"Well, I graciously accept. Now I'm thinking I better go shopping for something to wear."

"I kind'a liked the outfit you wore the last time."

"Yes, well, I've never been to the Harbor Club before, but I understand it's a classy place and I think I'm going to have to find something a little more conservative. And something that will promote better eye contact with my dinner companion."

"Better wear a tent, then."

"I'm going to assume that was intended as a compliment."

"You want me to come right out and say it?"

"Say what?"

"That you've got nice boobs, and I enjoy looking at them."

"Well, I prefer to call them breasts but thank you, that's very nice. And they enjoy you doing more than just looking at them."

"You busy? Maybe I could stop over for a little while."

"I'm on my way to school. And I suspect you're on duty."

"Yeah, which means I'm supposed to be available to respond to emergencies."

"Sounds like you're the one who's having an emergency. See if you can make it to Tuesday night."

"And then what?"

"I'll let you use your imagination."

"I have a pretty wild imagination."

"I hope so," she said.

We were sitting in Mullally's office. "Okay, I talked to Marty," I said.

"That was fast."

"He was around so I popped on over."

"And?"

"He was actually pretty candid with me after I coaxed him a little. He told me besides her wiping the counter at the diner, he was using Ms. Gray to make deliveries for him. We didn't get into what it was she was delivering, but he admitted he was paying her three hundred bucks a pop to be his delivery girl. Says she came to him asking whether he had anything else for her to do besides working at the diner because she needed money for college."

Mullally frowned. "Three hundred bucks to deliver something? Jesus, I hope that never comes out. But even at three hundred a pop, that's a lot of deliveries to come up with the little nest egg she had."

"Yeah, and he says he only used her about a dozen times. He claims the bulk of the money must've come from somewhere else."

"Was he fucking her?"

"He denies it. Says he gets all the sex he needs and doesn't need to hit on high school girls who lack the experience of the women he's accustomed to."

"Jesus, you believe him?"

"He was pretty convincing, but then Marty's always a charmer."

"You try the blackmail theory out on him?"

"Yeah. He scoffed at it, says it's pure bullshit. Says if she'd ever tried to blackmail him, his lawyers would've made mincemeat out of her. He's probably right, although if she'd come forward it would've at least raised more suspicions about him, which he certainly doesn't need, and his reputation would've no doubt taken a major hit. Who knows, maybe he was paying her to make deliveries and fuck him at the same time. The main thing is, there doesn't seem to've been a good reason for him to kill her. At least not according to him."

"By any chance, did you ask him where he was the night she disappeared?"

"He claimed not to know what night it was. Said he'd have to go back and reconstruct his schedule."

Mullally shrugged. "So, whatta' you think?"

"Well, like I said, Marty's pretty convincing. But it looks like she was fooling around in a not so nice business, at least making some deliveries, and who knows what kind of creeps she may've run into along the way. She would've been a tempting target in a business that attracts a lot of bad actors and where she was probably in way over her pretty head."

"Well, one thing's for sure, and that is this department had probably better start distancing itself from Marty starting right now. No more freebies, no more socializing, nothing. The guy's radioactive at this point."

I nodded. "I guess that pretty much goes without saying."

"Nobody around here's going to be real happy about it, but there's nothing we can do. Fucking guy's a snake for sidling up to us like he's been doing and handing out all those favors to everybody like we're all dumb as dog shit. This whole thing isn't anything we want to go into any further. We already know more than we should. Let the state cops figure it out, if they can. If we tell them anything about this, we're going to have a lot of explaining to do ourselves, including talking to him when we know he's being investigated. Let's shut this thing down right now. Marty's on his own. He hired her, that was his decision. If the state cops can link her to him, or they can get him on the drug thing, that's his problem. We gave him a heads-up, that's all we can do. Whatever happened between him and her, or between her and anybody he does business with, there's nothing we can do about it."

"He asked me if I could let him know if we ever thought there was any trouble coming his way."

"What'd you tell him?"

"I told him I'd do what I can but no promises."

"You think if Marty got into trouble he'd try to drag us into it? I've borrowed money from him a few times, probably everybody in the department has."

"He might, although I don't know where that'd get him. Might even make things worse for himself instead of better."

"What about your conversation with him? Obstruction of justice?"

"He said he'd keep it confidential."

"Even if he's charged with murder?"

I thought for a moment. "Where would that get him? I'd just say I was investigating the case like we talked about. The state cops might be pissed, but what're they going to do? I'd deny he told me anything about her making deliveries for him or any of that stuff. It's my word against his, and I'm a cop. And I'd say if he'd told me anything like that, I'd have gone to the state cops about it right away. So, I think we're probably okay."

Mullally nodded. "Right. So, let's just go about our business and play dumb. If any of this surfaces, we can just say you were just doing what we thought they wanted us to do and you never heard anything about her working for him other than at the diner. And pray this whole thing blows over."

"I'm with you, Chief," I said.

13

July 27, 2012 The town's Rec Center was an old, two-story brick elementary school the town no longer had a use for as a school, so they'd made it over into a recreation center that was used for yoga classes, scout meetings and activities like that. The town also ran a day camp there every summer for kids six to twelve, which was really just day care for kids out of school for the summer whose parents didn't want them hanging around the house doing nothing. The counselors took the kids to the beach and on nature hikes and stuff like that, and on rainy days they played games or watched movies in the Rec Center. It also allowed the town to provide a few summer jobs for high school students as part of the program. The camp's activity schedule was posted online so the parents and the kids would know what was happening on any given day. I checked the schedule and picked a time late in the afternoon when I knew they'd be back at the Rec Center to drop by to talk with Gina Rongoni.

When I pulled into the Rec Center parking lot, the kids and the counselors were all outside gathered around the front steps. The smaller kids were sitting in a group on the steps with one of the counselors, and the older kids were hanging around in bunches. Several boys were kicking a soccer ball around with another one of the counselors, and there were backpacks strewn all over the place. I looked at my watch and figured it was just about pick-up time. Before I got out of the cruiser, I took my sunglasses off and hooked them on the pocket of my shirt to try to look a little more friendly. I spotted Gina Rongoni standing with a group of older girls. As strikingly mature as Val Gray had looked, Gina Rongoni looked like she was barely out of middle school, never mind having just graduated from high school. She was short and a little overweight with a dark complexion and thick black hair that seemed resistant to a comb or brush. She had relatively attractive facial features except for an unfortunate nose that was a little too large. She was wearing athletic shorts and a white t-shirt that said "New

Salisbury Seniors Rock" in red letters across the front, and her hair was piled up on her head and fastened with a scrunchie. As I made my way toward the group, they all stopped talking and turned and stared at me. At that moment, it suddenly dawned on me that with all the kids hanging around, I needed to dream up some excuse for being there and wanting to talk with her. The last thing I needed was for every kid in the stupid camp to go home that night and tell their parents a cop had showed up at camp today asking about some murder.

"Hi," I said to Rongoni as I walked up, forcing a smile. "Are you in charge?"

She was staring at me like she thought I was about to arrest her. Cops can have that effect on people sometimes. "I'm one of the ones in charge," she said nervously. "There are actually three of us. Greg over there with those guys," she said, pointing to the boys kicking the soccer ball around, "and Sarah on the steps with the little kids, we're all, like, sort of in charge." She continued to stare at me like she was terrified.

"Great," I said, still smiling stupidly, hoping to get her to relax a little. "Why don't I just talk with you. I wanted to check on how pick-up and drop-off are going and whether there are any safety issues you think we need to deal with." Hearing this, the kids around us all started to move away and talk with each other again, undoubtedly figuring this was going to be about the most boring conversation on the planet. "Maybe we should go over there and talk," I said, gesturing toward an open area away from everybody else. She seemed to hesitate at first and looked at me apprehensively, and then finally said, "Okay," and we separated ourselves from the others.

"So," I said, trying to sound like we were colleagues as we moved away from the group, "how is pick-up and drop-off going? Any traffic problems or safety issues we need to be concerned about?"

She shook her head slowly, still looking extremely nervous. "No, I don't think so, I think everything's going okay. It gets a little, like, crowded sometimes when there're a lot of cars, but the parents all seem to be pretty careful. People mostly wait their turn, and we're watching the kids pretty closely so that, like, nobody gets in front of a car or anything."

I nodded. "Good, that's good to hear. Any ways you think we could make it go more smoothly?"

She thought for a moment, at the same time scanning around like she was looking for someone. "No, I don't think so," she finally said. "A lot of the kids have gone here before and, like, everybody pretty much knows how it works, including the parents."

"You don't think we need an officer here, then?"

"No, I don't think so. This is my third year here as a counselor, and, like, we've never had one before, and there've never been any problems as far as I know."

Boy, is she nervous, I thought to myself. "Well, if you ever need our help, just call the police station. We'll have somebody come right over."

She nodded. "Okay, thanks, we will."

"Looks like things are going well," I said as we stood there for a minute watching the kids milling around. Then, I said, "There's something else I'd like to talk to you about if you don't mind."

She looked at me nervously, and then slowly nodded. "Okay."

"We're helping the State Police investigate Valerie Gray's death. I know they've already talked with you, but I wanted to do a little follow-up."

She nodded slightly again. "Okay," she said in a soft voice.

"The two of you were going to go to UMass together in the fall, is that right?"

"Uh-huh."

"You were going to room together?"

"Yes."

"I understand the money was an issue for her?"

"Yeah, it was."

"Do you know how she was doing coming up with the money?"

"No, that wasn't any of my business."

"Had she been talking to people?"

"I have no idea."

"Do you know whether she was considering any other options besides UMass?"

She hesitated slightly. "That was the only place she applied last winter, as far as I know. We both applied at the same time."

I thought for a moment. "You mentioned to the other officers that during this past spring she borrowed your car a number of times to go out at night. Is that right?"

"Yes," she said softly.

"I want to focus on that a little more. I'm wondering about the time frame. Let's use graduation as a reference point. Do you recall her doing that, say, after graduation?"

She looked away at the kids clustered around the stairs, obviously thinking. Finally, she turned back to me and said, "I don't know. Possibly."

"But you had that sense before graduation?"

She nodded her head. "Yeah, for a while before."

"Do you think she might've been seeing somebody?"

"I don't know, maybe. It was, like, because of a couple of things she said. And there were nights when she didn't come home until late. And I could tell she had a change of clothes with her like she was going out. One time, I asked her if she was going somewhere after work, and she put her finger up to her lips and said, 'It's a secret. I'll tell you someday.'"

"But I take it she never did?"

"No, but I'm sure she was going to."

"It wasn't to see the guy on the Middies, McGruder?"

"No, this was before him. Maybe the first time was, like, in March, sometime around in there. "

"But you have no idea who she might've been seeing? No clues or anything?" She shook her head. "No."

"You don't think it was her old boyfriend, I take it?"

"Which old boyfriend?"

"The guy with the motorcycle, Bobby Frank."

"Oh, God, no, I'd be really shocked if it was him. They had, like, a pretty big fight when they broke up. That was a while ago, around the end of the winter. And if she was back with him, I don't know why she would've wanted it to be a secret. Maybe she might've been, like, embarrassed or something, I don't know. But she said some pretty nasty stuff about him when they broke up, and I really doubt it was him. And she wouldn't have needed my car, he could've picked her up."

"What about somebody from school?"

"That'd be, like, a real surprise, too. I don't think she ever went out with anybody in school the whole time we were there."

"Any of the male teachers take a particular interest in her you're aware of?"

"You mean in like a sexual way? No, not that I know of. She always got better grades from the male teachers than from the female teachers, though. It was, like, pretty funny."

"I understand she talked with Mr. Phillips a lot. What was their relationship like?"

"He was her favorite teacher, she liked him a lot. I think she went to him for, like, advice about college and stuff like that."

"Do you think there was anything going on between them?"

"You mean like sexual? With Mr. Phillips? Wow, if there was, I sure didn't know about it. A lot of the girls thought he was, like, to die for, but I never got the impression Val felt that way. Her having a relationship with a guy his age would've been kind of a surprise, but you never really knew with Val so I suppose anything's possible. But, like I said, if there was something going on between her and Mr. Phillips, I never knew about it."

"And she never said anything about where she'd gone any of those times she came home late?"

"No."

"Did you ever stay up and listen for her to come home?"

"No, there was no reason for me to do that. The car was always in the driveway the next morning. It went on for a while, and then she hooked up with McGruder."

"And it stopped?"

"Yeah, she was pretty wrapped up with him."

"She was serious about him?"

"That's what it seemed like."

"What'd you think of him?"

"I thought he was a conceited jerk."

"Ever go on his boat?"

She shook her head. "Nope, I was never invited."

"But I take it Val went there a lot?"

"Yes."

"Once she started seeing McGruder, she must've borrowed your car quite a bit."

"Yeah, not every day, but maybe, like, three or four times a week. She always put gas in it. She was my friend and I didn't mind her using it when I wasn't. It wasn't doing anybody any good just, like, sitting in the driveway, and there was no way she could've ever afforded a car."

"After she started seeing McGruder, you knew where she was going when she borrowed your car?"

"Uh-huh."

"But not before that?"

"No."

"Before she started up with McGruder, did she go on any long drives you can recall?"

"I don't know what you mean by long drives. Like to Boston or someplace? I don't think so, although I never actually looked at the mileage or anything. Just the gas gauge, and like I said she always made sure to put gas in it. I don't ever remember thinking, Jeez, she used, like, a lot of gas or anything like that."

"She ever talk about running errands for anybody or making any kind of deliveries?"

She looked puzzled. "Deliveries?"

"I don't know, delivering packages or anything like that?"

"Packages? Like what?"

"Doesn't ring any bells?"

"No, not really."

"Did she do drugs?"

"You mean socially?"

"Yes."

"Sure."

"How do you know?"

"I know."

"What kinds of stuff?"

"Social stuff. She wasn't an addict or anything. It was just social. Like, sometimes when she went out."

"You didn't tell the other officers about that."

"They asked me if I ever saw her using drugs. The answer to that is no, I never actually saw her. But I knew she used them sometimes, like, when she went out. And I didn't think it was that important really. It's not like she did it a lot. A lot of people use drugs socially. I don't think it's any big deal."

"Do you do drugs?"

"I have once or twice. Practically everybody has at some point. Like I said, it's not a big deal."

"When did she start?"

"I think with Bobby Frank. I think that's why she stayed with him as long as she did. He seemed to be able to get stuff whenever he wanted."

"You know he's been arrested a couple times for dealing?'

"Yeah, pretty much everybody knows that."

"She do drugs with McGruder?"

"I assume so. I'd be really surprised if she didn't although I was never there so I couldn't, like, actually swear to it."

I thought for a moment. "Do you know whether she ever dealt drugs?"

"No."

"Would it surprise you if someone told you she did?"

"It'd be a surprise to me, but I wouldn't be shocked. She needed money, her mother's on welfare. But if she did, I never knew anything about it."

"I think you told the State Police the last time you saw her was when she borrowed your car the night she disappeared?"

She hesitated slightly. "Uh-huh."

"What time was that, approximately?"

"I don't know. Maybe eight o'clock, something like that. She was off work that night. She said she was going down to the harbor. I assumed it was to McGruder's boat."

"Did she say when she'd be home?"

"No. I assumed that night sometime."

"You told the State Police you didn't see her again after that?"

"That's right."

I paused for a moment. "You go out that night yourself?"

She hesitated again. "No."

"She had your car, right?"

"Right."

"You live a couple houses up from her?"

"Yes."

"You have a boat?"

"My family does, yes." She looked back nervously toward the others congregated in front of the steps. "A Whaler. My father uses it to fish. We have a dock."

"You use the boat much?"

She paused briefly again. "No, not as much as I did when I was a kid."

"You fish?"

"No."

"Where do you go, then?"

"I might take it out every once in a while. Maybe when it's calm and the weather's nice. I don't go very far."

"Over to the harbor?"

She shook her head. "God, no, not that far."

"You just go out and motor around for a while and then go home?"

She nodded. "Like I said, I used to use it more when I was a kid."

Just then, a car pulled into the parking lot and swung around in front of the Rec Center. It looked like the first parent arriving for pick-up. "Sorry," she said, "if we're done, I gotta' go. Pick-up's starting."

I nodded. "Sure, go ahead. Any traffic problems, just let us know, okay?"

"I will," she said over her shoulder as she hurried back toward the Rec Center.

14

July 30, 2012 Sitting in the stationhouse's common area sipping a cup of coffee and doing some mindless paperwork, I was surprised to see Balzano and Cavanaugh come through the door unannounced. They asked for the Chief and although I was sitting in plain sight right in front of them, they ignored my presence. Mullally quickly came out, they said something to him I couldn't hear, and he immediately took them into his office and closed the door. *Shit,* I thought to myself, *this isn't good.* I sat there trying to act like I was doing something but I couldn't keep my eye off the door to Mullally 's office. Everybody knew I was supposed to be working on the case, and I felt pretty conspicuous sitting there by myself trying not to look nervous while the two state cops were closeted with Mullally .

After about twenty minutes had gone by, which had seemed like forever, Mullally 's door finally opened and he came out, a grim look on his face. He came directly over to me and said in a low voice, "We need you in there," gesturing toward his office. Then, he turned abruptly without giving me a chance to say anything and headed back into his office. I grabbed a chair and followed him in. When I got inside, he said, "Shut the door." After I'd done so, I looked for some space to wedge my chair in beside Balzano and Cavanaugh, who both had deadpan expressions on their faces as they watched me squeeze my chair in and sit down. I looked around at the three of them, hoping they couldn't see I was shaking. From all appearances, it looked like the shit was about to hit the ventilating system.

Mullally spoke first, an angry tone in his voice. "Brian, did you know this young woman, Valerie Gray?"

I stared back at him, and then looked at the two state cops, who were watching me with undivided attention. "Not really," I said, looking back at Mullally .

"What's that supposed to mean?" Mullally asked sharply.

"You mean, did I know who she was?"

"Okay, let's start with that. Did you know who she was?"

I paused. "Yeah, she worked at the diner."

"And you saw her there?"

"Yeah, a few times," I said.

"Did you talk with her?"

"Yeah, when she waited on me."

Balzano and Cavanaugh continued to sit there deadpanned, watching me. "Did you talk with her about more than what you wanted in your coffee?" Mullally asked in a sarcastic tone.

"We'd chitchat a little. Over the counter stuff. The weather, how busy they were, that kind of stuff."

"How often did you see her there?"

I paused again. "I don't know, a few times."

"Over what period of time?"

"It was this past spring. I'd never seen her there before that."

Mullally looked at Balzano and Cavanaugh. Balzano spoke up. "We've interviewed a number of people at the diner, Brian. It seems Valerie Gray was a very popular waitress. Her end of the counter was always pretty crowded with guys. The people at the diner remembered a couple of those guys in particular because they came in so often and seemed to like to chat with her, and you were one of them."

"I don't think I went in there that often. Maybe they remembered me because of the uniform."

"Did you know her by name?"

"Just as Val," I said. "Her name tag said Val on it. I didn't know her last name."

Mullally said, "So when did you figure out it was the same girl who was murdered? You must've known it was her when the body was identified."

"I know this is going to sound crazy," I said, "but at first I really didn't recognize it was the same girl until I read the report that said she'd worked at the diner. At that point, I thought the fact she served me coffee at the diner a few times seemed more like a coincidence than anything else and I didn't see how it was relevant to anything. So I knew who she was, so big deal, anybody around here could've known who she was, it's a small town. A bunch of people who go to the diner knew who she was. So what? Okay, I guess in hindsight I probably should've said something, but I couldn't have told you anything about her except she worked at the diner, and that's it. And everybody obviously knew that already."

There was a silence. Then, Mullally spoke. "You ever see her outside the diner?"

"No. Never. I saw her in the diner and that's it. She was in high school, for Christ's sake. Hey, she was damned attractive with a great body and was really something to look at moving around behind the counter in this skin-tight waitress uniform she wore. You want to know the truth, I think she really liked all the attention and tried to act sexy to get guys who went in there all worked up. Okay, I'm human and she was really something in the looks department, and that's why I stopped there sometimes, probably like a lot of other guys. Maybe I did go there fairly regularly for a while, now that I think about it some more. Hey, she was one sexy babe, and she looked a lot older than somebody who was in high school, that's for sure. But hit on her? Are you kidding me? Maybe if she'd been a little older I might've tried something, although I doubt it would've gotten me anywhere. She was way out of my league looks-wise. But she was sure nice to look at."

"So you never saw her outside the diner, and you never talked with her about anything except making small talk? Is that it?"

"That's it. Period."

There was another silence. Then, Balzano said, "Okay, Brian, is there anything else you want to tell us?"

"No, that's it."

"Then could you step outside for a minute then and let us talk with the Chief?"

"Sure." I got up and went back out into the common area, shutting the door behind me and leaving the chair inside. I sat down at my desk and waited, knowing everybody else in the room was probably wondering what the fuck was going on.

About five minutes passed, maybe the longest five minutes of my life, and then Mullally stuck his head out the door and motioned for me to come back in. When I was back inside and the door was closed again, Mullally said, "Okay, Brian, we're gonna' give you a pass on this one and chalk it up to a combination of inexperience and just plain stupidity. Other than this, you've done a pretty good job of staying on top of the case and helping out, and it'd be stupid to try to bring somebody else into it at this stage. But you should've told us about this. For Christ's sake, no more mistakes like this one, okay? You've wasted a lot of these gentlemen's time on this, and that's the last thing we need right now. Understand?"

I looked at them. "Yeah, Chief, I've got it," I said, relief washing over me like a huge wave.

15

April 6, 2012 The problem was, I was lying. Big time. I'd known Val a lot better than I'd let on, and one of the main purposes of my little investigation had been to try to find out if anybody could link me up with her, at least outside the diner. So far, it didn't appear anybody could, but the last thing I wanted was to wind up as a suspect in the case myself. Like I told Mullally and the state cops, I met Val at the diner. It was back in the spring. Before that, I'd rarely gone to the diner, and when I did it had always been in the morning before work. But that afternoon I'd been cruising around in a fog, fighting to stay awake. Summer was still a couple months away, the town was dead, and I decided I'd stop at the diner for a cup of coffee and see if that would help get me through to the end of my shift.

The diner was an institution in town. The menus said it had been in operation continuously since 1927. Situated on the main street in the middle of town, the place had a real fifties look to it with the front covered with a polished metal finish to make it look like a railroad car and an old-style sign on the roof that spelled out the name of the place in pink neon lighting. Inside, the front section was probably the original layout with an L-shaped counter, some booths along the windows facing the street, and the kitchen in the back. Over the years, the place had been expanded out the back a couple times so it was now the size of a regular restaurant, although the preferred spots were still either at the counter or in one of the booths in the front.

The cuisine was old fashioned diner food, with breakfast by far the most popular meal: eggs, pancakes, French toast, bacon, sausages, the works, and in enormous portions. You could also get muffins, toast, Danish and fantastic donuts. It was enough to make a cardiologist freak out. Lunch and dinner were either a sandwich or one of their blue plate specials like fried chicken, meat loaf, or ham. And the prices were extremely reasonable, especially for the amount of food you got. On any given Saturday or Sunday morning, even in the off season, there was always a huge line outside waiting to get in and pig out on one of their gargantuan breakfasts, which, after you'd staggered out, would pretty much anesthetize you for the rest of the day.

That afternoon, I went in and sat down at the counter, and immediately noticed a tall, shapely blond waitress behind the counter with her back to me, her long blond hair piled up on her head and fastened with a big clasp. The light yellow waitress outfit she was wearing had a tight skirt that accentuated her gorgeous ass and was cut well above her knees, showing off a fantastic pair of legs. I sat there ogling all this waiting for her to turn around. When she finally did, I was blown away by her gorgeous face, her sparkling blue eyes, and her sumptuous breasts, which, together with her tight skirt, made her uniform look like it was about two sizes too small for her. All I could think of was a Sports Illustrated swimsuit model with her incredibly youthful, sexy look.

Seeing me sitting there, she smiled, sauntered over, and stood in front of me with one hand on her hip. The expression on my face probably made me look like I'd just been struck by lightning. Her nametag said "Val" on it. "What can I get for you, Officer?" she purred in a sweet voice.

I smiled back. "Coffee, please," I said, barely able to get the words out.

"Cream and sugar?"

"No, thanks. Just black."

"We have some homemade apple pie this afternoon. Would you like a piece to go with your coffee?"

Lady, if you only knew how much I'd like a piece, I thought to myself. "Sounds tempting," I said, "but I'd better pass. Just the coffee, thanks."

I watched her intently as she went to get the coffee and bring it back, her hips swaying as she moved. "Here you are," she said, setting the cup in front of me. "I don't think I've ever seen you in here before."

"No, I don't think you have. I'm Brian, by the way. I don't usually come in here in the afternoon, but today I needed something to keep me going. Is Val short for Valerie?"

She grinned and raised an eyebrow. "Hey, you're pretty sharp. You sure you're not Sherlock Holmes?" I chuckled. "Well, enjoy your coffee, Sherlock," she said, and strolled off down the counter to check on another customer, her hips moving seductively in that tight skirt. *Wow,* I thought to myself, *what's her story?*

And that was the beginning. Suddenly, I had an unquenchable thirst for coffee in the afternoon. I quickly figured out which afternoons she worked and was careful to arrange my schedule so I'd be sure to be able to stop by the diner on those days. I even figured out when business was the slowest so I could grab as much time with her as I could. She always greeted me with a big smile and was extremely solicitous, asking me how my day was going, and what I was doing as if my job was fascinating and not dull as dog shit. The first few times we talked about the weather, how busy the diner had been that afternoon, and that kind of small talk, but pretty soon things got more personal. She asked me a lot of questions about myself and I told her about my humble upbringing and about Iraq, although I left out the part about getting blown up. She told me she'd never met anybody who'd fought in a war before and said I must be a brave guy. It was quite a jolt when I asked her at one point what she did with the rest of her time when she wasn't at the diner, and she told me she was in high school. For the most part, though, she dodged questions about herself. She was charming and funny, and flirtatious without being overly so, and she always wore that same waitress outfit that looked like she'd been poured into it. I couldn't get enough of her.

It wasn't long before I began to fantasize about her and how she'd look with her clothes off, and what it would be like to be in bed with her. I was having horny thoughts about her practically nonstop. Even in my fantasies during my horniest nights in Iraq, I never dreamed I'd ever actually meet somebody like her. I wanted to ask her out in the worst way, but there were some obvious problems with that. First and foremost, she was in high school, and I was much older than she was and a town cop, and there would've been a shit storm if I'd ever been seen anywhere with her. And where would I go with her anyway? She wouldn't have been served a drink anywhere, although she looked a lot older than she was and she might've had a fake I.D. But I was a cop, for Christ's sake, and how would it have looked if she'd been caught with a fake I.D. and I was with her? So, what was I going to do, ask her out for ice cream? Or over to my place? Yeah, sure. But even if I could've come up with someplace to take her where we wouldn't have been seen and would've been legit, I doubt I would've had the balls to ask her out anyway because I was convinced she would've said no for a gazillion obvious reasons, including she probably had a lot more attractive options than me, and if she'd blown me off as I expected, that probably would've put an end to the little fantasy world I was living in.

April 23, 2012 This went on for a while until finally one day she solved my problem for me—she asked me out. It was a few weeks after I'd met her for the first time. We were talking over the counter and out of the blue she suddenly asked me if I was seeing anybody, to which she'd probably already figured out the answer given all the time I'd been spending hanging around the diner chatting with her. When I told her no, she said she was a little surprised I'd never asked her out and maybe I didn't like her. *Didn't I like her? Jesus, I was practically having wet dreams about her.* At that point, I didn't wanted to start going through all the reasons why I hadn't asked her out, which I thought were pretty obvious, so I just told her I'd thought she probably would've said no, which was the truth. She smiled and leaned over the counter, and folded her arms under her breasts. An extra button on her uniform had somehow come unbuttoned providing me with an unobstructed view of some pretty unbelievable cleavage. Well, she said, you'll never find out unless you ask. I glanced down at her breasts for a brief second. She made no move to cover them up. Then, I looked back up at her and I said, okay, would you like to do something together sometime? Sure, she said, that'd be nice. Then, she proceeded to tell me there wasn't any place in town that was any fun, but she knew a place she thought I'd like in Hyannis, and would I like to take her there sometime? Sounds great, I said, barely able to get the words out.

April 27, 2012 Hyannis was about a forty minute drive from New Salisbury. We arranged that I'd pick her up after work that Friday night. They closed the counter down around eight o'clock, and I was waiting for her in the parking lot out back in my car. She came out about twenty minutes after the counter had closed wearing flat shoes, a skin-tight pair of silver designer jeans that looked like they'd been painted on and cost a lot, and a pink hoodie sweatshirt. It was the first time I'd ever seen her with her hair down, and it made her look even more dazzling. She had a large purse about the size of a small beach bag slung over her shoulder that looked like it was stuffed to the gills.

She slid into the car and grinned, and squeezed my arm. It was the first time we'd ever made physical contact and it sent what felt like an electric shock right through me. She was wearing a scent that was intoxicating, and I guessed was expensive. "I need to put my makeup on," she said. "Can we go somewhere and park for a couple minutes?"

"Sure," I said. "Some reason you wanted to do that in the car?"

"I didn't want to make a big deal in front of everybody over the fact I was going out. I like my privacy."

I nodded. "Got it," I said. "I think there's a shopping mall on the way to Hyannis with a big parking lot. That okay?"

"Perfect," she said.

I pulled out and headed for Hyannis. "What's in the bag?" I asked her. "Looks like you cleaned out the safe."

"Oh, a bunch of stuff. My waitress uniform, a pair of shoes, my makeup, some jewelry and a few other odds and ends."

"You gonna' lug all that stuff around with you all night?"

"I'm going to take the shoes out and put them on when I do my makeup. Then it won't be so stuffed."

"You might want to leave the bag in the car."

"Thanks, it'll be okay."

"You going be able to find this place? I've got GPS on my phone if we need it. You know the address?"

"I've got GPS, too, but we won't need it. I've been there before and I'm pretty sure I can get us there. Downtown Hyannis isn't all that big."

"Great," I said. *I wonder where the hell we're going,* I thought to myself. *I guess I'll just let it be a surprise.*

The shopping mall was about half way to Hyannis. We made small talk on the way. It felt strange being in the car alone with her where there'd always been the counter between us and a lot of people around. I looked over at her a few times as we talked not able to believe this was really happening. I was really nervous and scared that if I screwed up somehow that'd be the end.

When we got to the shopping mall, I swung around to a corner of the parking lot away from the stores where there weren't many cars, and parked under one of the overhead lights that illuminated the lot. "This okay?" I asked her. "You see alright?"

"It's fine if you could turn the light on," she said.

"No problem," I said, shutting the car off and turning on the overhead light.

Then, I sat back, leaning against the door, and watched her. She pulled the hoodie over her head and took it off. Underneath she was wearing a low-cut, form-fitting sleeveless silver top that looked stunning on her and incredibly sexy. She dug around in her bag and pulled out a pair of matching silver stilettos and slipped them on, stuffing her flats back into the bag. She pulled a couple long neck chains out of a compartment in the bag and put them on. Then, she pulled a heavy, silver chain link bracelet out of the same compartment and fastened it on her wrist.

"Nice bracelet," I commented.

She glanced down at it. "Thanks. It was a gift. From me."

"Special occasion?"

"Sort of," she replied. I wondered to myself what that was supposed to mean, but I let it go.

She pulled down the visor on her side and spent the next couple minutes putting on her makeup in the little mirror on the back of the visor. When she was done, she took one last look in the mirror and said, "There, that should do it." She started putting the makeup away in her bag. "Let's go."

"You look great," I said, starting the car up. *The understatement of the year*, I thought to myself.

"Thanks," she said. She looked down at the hoodie in her lap. "Maybe I'll leave this in the car. I don't think it'll fit in my bag. I'll toss it in the back seat, if that's okay."

"Fine," I said. I thought to myself, *am I in a dream or what?*

Hyannis is the largest urban enclave on Cape Cod, although it's technically just a village in the City of Barnstable. Its large natural harbor makes it the biggest recreational boating spot and the second biggest commercial fishing port on the Cape. The town's attractions include a major shopping mall and the headquarters for Cape Cod Potato Chips, and it's where you get the ferry to Nantucket. It even has an airport for small planes. And it also has what passes for night life on the Cape.

She didn't have any trouble finding the place, which was a club named Cure on a side street off the main drag in town. It was in a two story building that stood alone with alleys running along both sides and looked like it had once been a furniture or hardware store that had been converted into a club. The front was painted black with the big windows painted over in purple and lit from behind with the name Cure printed in large black tattoo script over the purple paint in one of the windows. It was about 9:30 in the evening and there was already a line of about twenty people out front waiting to get in, the women all dolled up for a big night out in Hyannis. We had to park in a lot a couple blocks down the street and walk back. As we got out of the car, I thought to myself, *should I take the Glock with me?* As usual, it was locked in the glove box. I didn't want to make a scene pulling it out in front of her, but I couldn't see trying to explain to somebody later on why I'd gone out somewhere at night in a strange environment without it.

"I gotta' get something out of the glove box," I said, going around to her side of the car. I reached in and unlocked the glove box. She stood there, her bag over her shoulder watching me as I pulled the Glock out and strapped it on under my leather jacket. "Sorry," I said, "this is what it's like to go out with a cop."

"Hey, that's okay," she said. "You've gotta' do your job."

I looked at her standing there in her sexy sleeveless top in the cool night air. "You gonna' be warm enough?" I asked her, wondering whether I should offer her my jacket, but of course then I'd have nothing to cover up the Glock with.

"We don't have far to go," she said, probably thinking the same thing I was. "I'll be okay."

When we got back to the club, the line out front seemed to have gotten even longer. "Looks like it's gonna' be a wait," I said, eyeing the crowd.

"We don't have to stand out here," she said. "Come on this way."

We walked past the line and around the corner into the alley on the far side of the building. It was dark with the only light coming from the streetlights out in front. At the far end of the building was a short set of wooden steps with a handrail leading up to a heavy metal door with a sign on it that said "Employees Only." She went up the steps and banged on the door a couple times with her fist. I stood below watching her. We waited about thirty seconds but nothing happened.

"You want me to try?" I asked her.

She shook her head, and banged a couple more times. Finally, the door opened and a young woman in a short black skirt, a skin tight black top, stilettos and black mesh stockings was standing there. She was overly made up, especially her eyes, with dark lipstick and big hair that was jet black, and I couldn't help thinking maybe we were going to a Halloween party. She eyed us without saying anything, her arms folded in front of her. Loud music was coming from inside behind her.

Val said, "Can you tell Rhino Val's here?"

The woman looked her up and down and nodded, and then turned and closed the door. We stood there for about a minute and then the door opened again, and standing there this time was a guy who literally filled the doorway. Every part of him seemed huge, his arms, his body, his legs. He was wearing black jeans, a black t-shirt and a pair of huge black sneakers. His huge head was shaved bald, and he had an enormous hooked nose with an extremely large earring in his left ear, and tattoos running up both forearms and under his t-shirt, reappearing at his neck. I assumed this was Rhino.

He gave Val a big smile. "Hey, Little Babe," he said, "glad you could make it." Then, he looked past her down at me standing at the foot of the stairs and his smile faded slightly. "I see you brought somebody with you."

"Yeah, this is my friend, Brian," she said, turning slightly towards me. "Brian, this is Rhino."

Rhino stared at me for a moment. "Hey, Brian," he said flatly, "pleased to meet you."

I nodded. "Same here," I said.

"Well, come on in," he said, stepping back to let us in. When I got inside the door, he stopped me. "You got a license for that thing?" he asked.

Very observant, I thought to myself. "'Course," I told him.

"Well, keep it out of sight, okay? You won't need it in here. Normally, I wouldn't let you in with it."

"No worries," I said.

He looked me up and down again. "You lift?"

"Yeah."

"How long you been doin' it?"

"A few years," I told him. "It's a hobby."

He nodded, and then turned and gestured for us to follow him.

He led us through a large darkened space that looked like a utility room with metal shelves on the walls filled with supplies and maintenance stuff, and then down a darkened corridor with a door at the far end, the music getting louder all the time. He opened the door and we were in the club. It was a large, darkened space extending up two stories with fancy high tech lighting that continuously changed the color of the room. On one side of the place, a large glass booth extended out over the room at the second floor level where a black DJ with dreadlocks wearing a black t-shirt, black pants and a huge pair of white-framed sun glasses was spinning the music with the help of an attractive female assistant. People were packed in with a lot of folks jammed together dancing and everybody else either standing around or perched at high tables around the outside of the room. Waitresses dressed like the sweet young thing who'd met us at the back door were wading through the crowd carrying trays of drinks. The music was loud enough to make the walls and the floor vibrate.

We stood there for a minute taking in the scene. I'd never been in a place like this before. Rhino flagged down a guy who was clearing tables, said something in his ear over the music, and pointed to Val and me. The guy nodded and left. He was back a couple minutes later with two other guys, the three of them carrying a high table and two chairs. They put the table down in an open spot against the wall, and the first guy waved to us and pointed to the table.

Rhino leaned over to us and said, "There you go. Have a nice time." Then, he said to Val, "Come on up to the office for a few minutes when you get a chance."

Val smiled and nodded. Rhino turned and walked away, and we went over to our table and got ourselves up onto the high seats. "VIP treatment," I said, leaning close to her over the noise of the music. She nodded, scanning around the room. "Nobody carded you," I said.

She shook her head. "They won't."

A waitress materialized out of nowhere and put a drink napkin in front of each of us. "What would you like?" she asked.

I looked at Val. She looked at the waitress. "A Cosmo. Grey Goose," she said.

The waitress nodded and looked at me. "Vodka martini straight up. Grey Goose as well," I said.

"You want some food?" Val asked me. "It's all comped so have whatever you like."

I shook my head. "No, thanks, the drink's fine. You?"

"No, I'm fine." She looked at the waitress. "Just the drinks, thanks." The waitress nodded and disappeared.

We looked around at the crowd. "You seem to have a lot of clout in this place," I said.

She looked over at me and smiled. "Rhino's very sweet to me. Sweet in a nice way."

"You two related? You don't look much alike."

She chuckled. "No. Just friends. Very platonic."

The waitress was back with our drinks in no time. They were enormous. I figured there was probably about four ounces of vodka in mine. The waitress carefully set the two huge martini glasses down in front of us and asked, "Anything else?"

"No, thanks," Val said, "I think we're all set." The waitress nodded and disappeared again.

I picked up my martini and looked at it. "Wow," I said. "Not exactly what I expected in a place like this."

"Like I said, Rhino takes good care of me," she said. We clinked glasses and sipped our drinks, and then she put hers down. "Speaking of which, I've got to go talk with him for a few minutes. Can I trust you to guard my drink?"

"Absolutely. It's completely safe in my hands."

She grinned. "Back in a few," she said, and slid down and started making her way around the crowd, her bag over her shoulder. I sat there sipping my drink and eyeing the females on the dance floor, a number of whom were pretty scantily dressed, and wondered what the fuck was going to happen next. *Okay, I thought to myself, she looks a lot older than she is, and she's stunning, and she's obviously been here before, so maybe the club likes to have her here to spice up the décor. Maybe she's not the only babe in the room who's getting comped. Who the fuck knows how they run these places. If there's anything more to this whole thing than that, though, I don't want to know about it.*

She came back about twenty minutes later. I'd finished my martini and had ordered a second. She put her bag under the table and climbed back up on her chair. She looked at her drink still sitting there and then at me. "I see my drink's still here," she said. "Nice job guarding it. Sorry that took so long. I wouldn't have been surprised if you'd drunk it on me."

"I wouldn't want to be seen drinking one of those things," I said. "Too big a risk to my masculinity. So I ordered a second martini instead. You're lucky I'm not under the table. These things are lethal."

She grinned. "Enjoy yourself," she said, picking up her glass and taking a sip. She swallowed and made a face, and put the glass down.

"Should we get you a fresh one?" I asked.

She shook her head. "No. The vodka's still good and that's what counts."

We stayed for another half an hour. I nursed my second martini, hoping I'd be able to walk when it came time to go. It was too loud to carry on any kind of an extended conversation, so most of the time we just sat there and watched what was going on around us. At one point, perhaps emboldened by the second martini, I asked her if she wanted to dance, figuring that's what we'd come for, but she shook her head and said she didn't like to dance.

Finally, after we'd both finished our drinks, she leaned over to me and asked, "You want to go?"

I was a little surprised after we'd come all that way to get there, but we were just sitting there and it'd gotten a little boring. Of course, I was scared shitless at that point that I'd been a total loser as a date, and she was looking to escape as quickly as possible.

"Whatever you'd like to do," I said. "Two of those martinis are enough for me."

She nodded. "Let's go," she said.

"Do you need to say good-by to anybody?" I asked.

"No, we're all set."

"Should I leave the waitress a tip?"

"No, she's fine. All taken care of."

This time, we went out the front entrance. The line outside was even longer than when we'd gone in. Everybody in line perked up when we walked out, no doubt figuring there was now room for somebody else inside. It was chillier now, and as we walked back to the car I was tempted to put my arm around her just to try to keep her a little warm, but I didn't, figuring a move like that might be misinterpreted and the evening already looked like it was headed in the wrong direction. We got into the car, and I started it up and turned the heater on full blast.

"It should be warm in here in a minute," I said.

To my surprise, she snuggled over against me and said, "That sounds good."

We sat there like that in silence for a few minutes as the heat started to pour out of the vents. Finally, I said, "You want me to take you back and drop you off?"

She sat up and looked at me. "Was it that bad?" she asked.

"Oh, Christ, no," I said. "It was fun. And you're very lovely."

She snuggled back down against me. "Yeah, right, it was fun, kinda' like a root canal. I'm really sorry. I hope I can make it up to you."

I tentatively put my arm around her. "No, really, it wasn't bad. The place was pretty cool, although I'm glad we didn't have to wait in line to get in. And those drinks were incredible."

She looked up at me and smiled, and said in a husky voice, "Shut up and kiss me." I looked down at her, startled. "Is there something you're waiting for?" she asked.

"No," was all I managed to get out before she was all over me, her lips pressed hard on mine, her tongue probing, trying to get into my mouth. It was if a dam had broken inside me. Before I knew it, she was down on the seat and I was on top of her, my mouth not wanting to let go of hers. My hands groped at her breasts and tried to get under her top. Suddenly, I felt her hands on my shoulders as she forced me back up, our mouths finally separating. We were both breathing heavily.

"Not here," she said softly.

"Where?" I asked.

"There's someplace I want you to take me. Someplace nice."

"Tell me where."

"I'll show you. Drive."

I sat back behind the wheel and she sat up. She smoothed her top with her hands, and then ran them lightly through her hair, brushing it back. "It's not far," she said.

We drove down toward Hyannis Port and the ocean. When we got to the ocean, we took a right turn and followed the road for about three miles with the ocean on our left. It was dark and there weren't many cars on the road. The sky was clear, and there was a half moon over the ocean and plenty of stars. Finally, we reached a spot where there was a turnoff to the right with a sign that said The Beach Rose Inn.

"That's it," she said, pointing to the sign.

We turned in and followed the road up a hill about a hundred yards to the Inn, and pulled into the parking lot in front. It was a beautiful old mansion, three stories high looking straight out at the ocean. The whole place was shingled in classic Cape style with the trim painted white. There was a lawn in front with a white fence around it, and a lighted walkway leading up to a large porch that wrapped around the house with a bunch of white rocking chairs on it. The lights were on over the entryway and the porch and inside on the first floor, but the rest of the house was dark. There were only a couple other cars in the parking lot.

"Wow," I said, looking up at it. "How'd you know about this place? Or maybe I shouldn't ask."

"I found it online," she said. "I've never been here before. Trust me, I couldn't afford it."

"You think they have room?"

"Doesn't look like that many cars. It's the off-season. During the summer, you've got to book this place months in advance. Let's check it out and see if they've got anything."

She reached over into the back seat and grabbed her pink hoodie, and pulled it on. We got out and went up the walkway to the porch. There was a fancy plaque beside the front door certifying that the place was a member of some fancy chateau organization in France. When we opened the door, I could hear a faint chime go off somewhere inside. The door opened into a wide hallway with a beautiful crystal chandelier overhead. An elegant stairway on the right led upstairs and immediately off the hallway to the left was a small study with a gas fireplace, a desk with a computer, and a couple leather chairs. Everything was beautifully appointed with original art work and expensive-looking oriental carpets on the floor. In my mind, I started calculating the outstanding balance on my credit card.

As we stood there by the doorway to the study, a short, pudgy guy in dark green corduroy pants, a dress shirt and a black cardigan sweater came around the corner from the other end of the hallway toward us. He looked to be in his fifties with a bushy beard flecked with gray and half-glasses hanging on a chord around his neck. He welcomed us with a friendly smile and asked how he could be of assistance. I told him we didn't have a reservation but wondered if he had anything for one night, to which, after sizing us up for a moment, he responded that he believed he did. *Probably don't get a lot of walk-in one night stands*, I thought to myself.

He led us into the study and invited us to sit down while he checked the computer. He called up a screen and took a quick look, and told us the main house was full but he could give us one of the cottages out behind the main house. I told him that would be great. The cottages were apparently named after flowers, and the one he gave us was named "Lavender." It had a king-size bed, a mini-bar, a Jacuzzi tub and a gas fireplace. Breakfast was included, and was served in the main house between 7:00 and 10:00 am. He slid my credit card through a hand-held machine that spit out a charge slip for me to sign. $495 for one night. I took a deep breath. At least the machine didn't reject my card. He gave us a key on a chord that had a large wooden disk with a lavender flower painted on it and told us check-out time was at noon, and to check out all we had to do was leave the key in the room, and if we had any additional charges they'd put them on the credit card. He explained we should bring our car around to the rear of the house where we would see three cottages and ours was the one on the far right. He wished us a pleasant stay, and told us if we needed anything to just call the office.

We drove around to the back and found our one-room cottage, which was right out of one of those decorator magazines. The color scheme was, not surprisingly, a misty lavender and grey with long drapes, deep plush carpeting and accent lighting. The centerpiece was a king size four-poster bed made out of what looked like birch with a sheer grey canopy over it. There was also a little sitting area with an expensively upholstered loveseat and a glass-topped coffee table with a beautiful vase of fresh flowers on it adjacent to the silver-grey gas fireplace. The bathroom was all grey marble with elegant fixtures. I wondered to myself what this place went for in high season.

"Wow," I said, "pretty nice." After the last ten minutes, I'd almost forgotten what we were there for.

She hadn't. She came over to me and put her fingers up to my lips. I kissed them as I felt her slide something into my mouth. It felt like a small pill. She smiled and said, "Just swallow it, you'll like it, and crank up the fireplace. I'm going to use the bathroom for a minute." She disappeared into the bathroom with her bag and closed the door.

I stood there for a moment with the pill slowly dissolving in my mouth. It didn't taste very good. There were two bottles of water on a small table at one end of the loveseat. I opened one of them and took a swig, washing what was left of the pill down my throat. I took another slug and put the bottle down, and started to tackle the fireplace. It wasn't all that hard even for a cop; there were instructions on a small sign on the wall beside it, and all I had to do was hit a switch and it started right up. *Now what*, I thought to myself. She was still in the bathroom. I took off my jacket and the Glock and put them on the loveseat with the Glock under the jacket. I turned the light off so that the only source of light in the room was the fireplace, sat down on the bed and took my shoes off, and then leaned back, propping myself up with a couple of big decorator pillows. At that point, I started to feel a strange sensation coming over me like I was floating, and I was beginning to feel a little flushed.

The door to the bathroom finally opened. She'd flipped off the bathroom light and was standing there in the light of the fireplace wearing a low-cut turquoise bra and a matching pair of bikini panties. I couldn't believe how sensual she looked in the firelight.

She came over to the bed and stood there about two feet away from me. "Are you going to take your clothes off?" she asked in a soft voice.

I stood up and we were practically against each other. I began to take my shirt off. She started to unbuckle my pants. The next thing I knew, we were standing there naked, her hands messaging my chest and my biceps while my hands roamed over her hips and her breasts. Her skin felt almost electric to the touch. I put my face in her hair and felt the incredible softness of it. Her scent was mesmerizing. I realized whatever she'd given me had magnified all of these sensations, and as we stood there for a long time just rubbing our hands over each other I figured she must be experiencing the same thing I was. The fireplace had warmed the room up and it was beginning to feel like we were in a sauna. The room seemed to be spinning a little. She slowly turned me so that the bed was just behind me and gently forced me backward onto it. Then, she climbed on top of me, her golden hair hanging down over me in the firelight. I closed my eyes. It was like I was in a dream.

In my semi-conscious state, I felt somebody shaking me. A voice was telling me, "Hey, I'm sorry but we've got to get going." I had no idea where I was for a moment, and then I remembered. Then, I realized I was naked, lying on my stomach on the bed with a cover partly over me. The lights were on but I didn't want to open my eyes. I had what felt like the worst hangover I'd ever experienced.

"You okay?" she asked. I nodded slightly. All of a sudden, I was incredibly thirsty. "Sometimes that stuff can make you feel like shit afterward," she said. "Especially if you're not used to it. Sorry, but I've got to go home."

I turned my face toward her. She was already dressed and sitting on the loveseat with her bag packed. I pulled my wrist up and looked at my watch. It was 2:47 am. "Shit," I said.

"You going to be okay? I can drive if you want."

"No, I'll be okay. Just give me a minute." I took a deep breath.

"Sure, take your time." She continued to sit there on the loveseat, watching me.

A lot was suddenly going through my mind. I wondered what it was she'd given me; whatever it was had given me a major buzz, and the vodka had probably magnified it. I didn't want to go, but I didn't feel like sex right then, and anyway she was all dressed and we were obviously leaving whether I wanted to or not. My mind was pretty much a blank. I wondered whether she'd enjoyed it. She was certainly all business now. Maybe it hadn't been all that great for her. Maybe I'd never have another chance to go to bed with her again. I was naked and I was going to have to get up and find my clothes and get dressed, and I felt strangely modest where she was already dressed and sitting there watching me. And I needed to piss really badly.

Okay, I thought to myself, *you don't have any choice.* I rolled over and tossed the cover off, and sat up on the side of the bed. My head was spinning from just that little exertion, but I knew I had to keep moving. I stood up and started looking around for my clothes. The fireplace had been turned off.

It took me a couple minutes to get dressed. "I'm going to use the bathroom," I told her. "Is there any water in the fridge?"

"I'll look," she said.

I went into the bathroom, flipped on the light and shut the door. I took a long piss, flushed the toilet and then stood over the sink looking at myself in the mirror. Fortunately, the damage to my brain didn't show much on the outside. I splashed some cold water on my face and wiped it with a towel. I ran my fingers through my hair and then went back out, flipping the bathroom light off. She was standing in front of the mini-bar holding a bottle of water out to me. I took it, unscrewed the cap, and drank about half of it. I took a deep breath, and then finished the rest.

"What'd you give me?" I asked her.

"Ecstasy," she said. "Ever had it before?"

"No, I haven't done much with drugs."

"Well, that's not exactly a surprise, seeing as how you're a cop. You like it? You acted like you did."

"I enjoyed myself, that's for sure. You?"

"Yeah, but we've got to get going now."

"After you," I said, gesturing toward the door.

We rode back in silence. I glanced at her a couple times out of the corner of my eye and she was sitting there staring straight at the road ahead of us, her mind seemingly elsewhere. She told me to drop her behind the diner where she'd left her car. There was only one car in the lot when we got there, and I pulled up beside it.

She leaned over and squeezed my arm. "Thanks," she said, "that was nice."

"Thank *you*," I said. "We do that again?"

"Sure. We'll talk." She leaned over and kissed my cheek. Then, she got out, and went over to her car and got in. I sat there and waited for her to leave before

I pulled out. As she headed out, she gave me a wave as she crossed in my headlights. I continued to sit there after she'd gone, lost in thought. *Was I imagining all this?* Nothing about it seemed real.

16

April 30, 2012 And that was the beginning. I didn't see her again until the following Monday at the diner. She was all smiles as usual, but it was almost as if nothing had happened. Early on in our conversation when I softly broached our little adventure together, she made it clear in a low voice that this was not something to discuss in public, nodding toward the other customers at the counter, and of course she was right. But I couldn't help undressing her again in my mind. I badly wanted to touch her agin, but she seemed to sense that and kept her distance, even staying back away from the counter so I wouldn't be tempted to reach over it. So, we made small talk for a few minutes while she maintained the space between us. Finally, totally frustrated, I asked her in a whisper if we could talk someplace. She thought for a minute and then asked me in a normal voice if I'd go outside with her and take a quick look at her car and see if it would pass inspection, or whether there was a chance she might get pulled over. I, of course, said sure. She explained it was actually a friend's car, but she didn't want to get stopped if there was something wrong with it.

She called out to one of her co-workers that we were going outside for a second to look at her car, and I followed her out. We went out the back door and over to where the car was parked, and I asked her what the problem was. She said there wasn't any, but we should look at the car as if there were while we were talking. I made a big deal out of squatting down beside the car and looking under it at the exhaust. Then, I stood up and asked her when I was going to see her again. She told me she was fine going out with me, but she didn't want it to get too serious, and she also didn't think it was a great idea for us to be seen hanging around together in public, which I certainly couldn't argue with. She told me she was free a week from Friday night, and if I wanted to go out then that'd be fine, maybe back to Hyannis.

Not get too serious, I thought to myself. *Jesus, I was borderline insane about her and she would've had to have been brain dead not to have known it.* But I told myself, *shut the fuck up, this is no time to say anything about your feelings, that's obviously the last thing she wants to hear right now. Just tell her whatever will make her happy.* So I told her, fine, a week from Friday. And I told her I was going to stop showing up at the diner every day because I was probably hanging around there too much, and from now on I'd limit it to maybe once a week, which she thought was a good idea. It pained me to do that but sitting there in the fucking diner making small talk with her while I had a hard-on under the counter was almost worse than not seeing her at all. Then, we went back inside, and I paid for my coffee and left.

May 11, 2012 Waiting to go out with her again was excruciating. After our first encounter, my fantasies were now much more real, but at the same time our little conversation outside the diner had thrown me for a loop and I had no idea what to expect from this woman next. One thing was clear and that was she was in complete control as she had been from the beginning. All I wanted was to be with her again, and it didn't much matter how that came about.

We'd arranged that I'd pick her up after work again, and as I sat in my car behind the diner that night waiting for her I was pretty nervous. She came out wearing the same designer jeans and pink hoodie and carrying her over-stuffed bag, but this time she didn't need a makeup stop. We were going to Hyannis again, but this time to someplace different. It turned out to be a sports bar situated on a back street. No sexy top or stilettos this time, she kept the hoodie on. No line out front, this place was obviously a whole different scene. It was a big place with about fifteen TV's spread around the room showing every kind of sporting event being televised that night, and obviously catered to construction worker and fisherman types. The few women in the place were big-haired, overweight and pretty unattractive, and it looked like the guys and the gals all used the same tattoo parlor. Not surprisingly, Val got a lot of attention as we followed our host, a burly guy with a beard and a shaved head who probably doubled as a bouncer, between the tables to an empty booth across the room. There were a lot of rude stares and exaggerated body language, and a few off-color remarks directed at her that were loud enough for us to hear. She ignored it all, although it seemed to be a little unnerving to her. After we'd sat down, I told her I hadn't known she was a sports fan, and she said she really wasn't. *Then, why the fuck did we come here,* I thought to myself. *Was she trying to show herself off or something?*

We ordered drinks. I ordered a beer and she had a Cosmo. Nobody asked her for an I.D. While we waited for our drinks, I scanned the TV's around the room, vainly looking for something worth watching. She was still getting rude stares. The drinks arrived and I paid for them. We'd taken a couple sips when she announced she needed to use the ladies room. Once again, she got all kinds of stares and some more rude remarks as she made her way back across the crowded room, her bag over her shoulder, leaving me there alone feeling pretty uncomfortable with some of the stares now being directed at me. I subconsciously felt for the Glock strapped under my jacket. It didn't look like it'd take a whole lot to set off some of the morons who were giving me dirty looks and who probably thought beating the shit out of somebody was part of their regular Friday night entertainment. I doubted anybody'd try to start anything inside the place, but outside afterward might be a whole other story. I wasn't afraid of taking on any of these yoyos, but I didn't want Val in harm's way if things got out of hand. I could feel the tension building inside me. It was like the tension I felt in Iraq when things started to look like they might get hairy. I took a few slow breaths to try to relax myself. *Stay calm*, I told myself, *just stay calm. Nobody's going to try anything, they're just having a few beers at the end of the work week and feeling it a little. And you've got the Glock and a badge if anybody's stupid enough to try anything, so just relax. She picked this place, so try to act like you're enjoying yourself and focus on her.*

She was gone for a while. When she finally came back, I had pretty much calmed down. She sat back down opposite me and asked if I'd ordered a second round. Her drink was still sitting there practically untouched. When I told her I hadn't, she asked if I wanted to go. I nodded at her drink and asked her if she wanted to finish it. She shook her head, so I said, fine, let's go. We got up together and made our way out. I wanted to ask her how she'd gotten so plugged into the club and bar scene in Hyannis, but I let it go. There was nobody waiting for us outside. When we got back to the car, I asked her if she wanted to go someplace else for a drink but she told me she didn't know any place where she wouldn't get carded, particularly on a Friday night, and when I then asked her if she wanted to go back to Cure, she said she didn't want to wear out her welcome there. She suggested if I wanted to, we could stop at a liquor store and I could pick up a pint of vodka, and we could go somewhere and drink it in the car. So that's what we did. We found a public parking lot down by the harbor and sat there in the dark passing the bottle back and forth like we were in high school, only I wasn't in high school but a police officer feeding hard liquor to a minor who was also an attractive female and who, one could easily surmise upon observing us, I was trying to get drunk. So we sat there slugging down vodka while I furtively scanned around, praying the local cops wouldn't show up.

After about half an hour of this and the pint more than half gone, she told me she needed to go home pretty soon. Needless to say, that wasn't exactly what I'd been hoping to hear after the last time, although I wasn't going to be able to afford many more trips to The Beach Rose Inn, and I'd been planning to talk to her about maybe trying to find someplace a little cheaper. But even after our conversation outside the diner, I hadn't been expecting a big zero. I sat there staring out the window blurry-eyed from the vodka trying to figure out what to say next. It was silent in the car for a minute. Then, almost as if she'd read my mind, she slowly slid her hand over onto my crotch and began to softly rub me. I was startled for a moment, but I wasn't about to tell her to stop. I leaned my head back and spread my legs, and sat there like I was paralyzed holding the stupid bottle of vodka in my hand while she gently massaged the hardness in my pants. Then, she unbuckled my belt and pulled my zipper down, and slid her hand inside my briefs and grasped me. I closed my eyes and breathed deeply. Slowly at first, and then more rapidly, she moved her hand up and down. It was obvious she'd done this before. I couldn't believe how soft her hand felt and the pleasure that was consuming me. It began to build, and then suddenly I felt it coming. I groaned, and then it came, over and over like it was never going to stop, and then finally it did. I felt the wetness all over me; my briefs were soaked, and I imagined it was on my pants as well.

She pulled some tissues out of her bag and began cleaning me up as best she could. Finally, when she'd done the best she could and disposed of the soaked tissues in her bag, I slowly sat back up and started to zip myself up. Everything was still pretty wet. She sat there watching me. "Wow," I finally said.

"Thanks for bringing me," she replied. I took a swig of vodka and offered her the bottle. She shook her head. I put the top back on the bottle and dropped it on the floor. "We'd better go now," she said. We drove back to the diner in silence. When we got to her car, I got a kiss on the cheek and a little squeeze, and then she was gone, leaving me sitting there in the dark in my damp underwear.

And that was the last sex I had with her, if you want to call it that. We had two more dates, both of them pretty perfunctory. I picked her up, we'd go someplace in the Hyannis area she'd chosen, have a drink or two, and then I'd bring her back and drop her off. The places we went both times were real dives. One of them was a gay bar, for Christ's sake. Fucking place gave me the creeps as soon as we walked in, and we were out of there in a hurry. She never got carded at any of the places we went, and I figured that's why she picked them. I thought maybe somebody was giving her intel on places where enforcement of the drinking age was lax, and she certainly looked a lot older than she was. She was nice toward me and chatty enough, but it was like the other stuff had never happened. I thought maybe she sensed I was getting too serious, or maybe she was just having her period or something, I didn't know. I was scared shitless to say anything or ask any questions, but just tried to act non-serious while inside I was going crazy. I thought a million times about how I could broach the subject of our earlier encounters and try to find out what was going on in her mind, but I could never get up the courage. I probably sensed the answer was going to be something I didn't want to hear. So I just went along, telling myself over and over that she wouldn't be going out with me if she didn't like me, and maybe she was just trying to gauge whether our relationship had any long term potential beyond the sex part. I knew sometime in early June the high school held its graduation, but she never said anything about it and neither did I.

June 21, 2012 Finally, one day in the latter half of June, I dropped by the diner in the afternoon, and she was really cold toward me and didn't seem to want to talk. I finally asked her if there was something wrong, and she told me in a soft voice she'd started seeing somebody and it was serious, and it'd be best if I stopped coming by. It was like a bomb had gone off. I just sat there shell-shocked, unable to say anything. It wasn't like things had been going great between us, but I was crazy about her and as long as she'd kept going out with me I'd figured things still might improve. I finally put some money down on the counter for my coffee, got up, and staggered outside. I sat in the cruiser in the parking lot for a while trying to collect my thoughts. I couldn't believe the most beautiful, sexy creature I'd ever known, and who I was madly in love with, had just told me to fuck off. It was like somebody had pushed me off a cliff and I was falling through space.

June 23, 2012 It didn't take me long to find out who she was seeing; I just followed her a couple nights after she got off work. I knew what time she got off, so the first night I parked behind the diner away from the back door in a darkened area where there were some other cars and waited for her. I was off duty so I had my own car; a cruiser would've been way too obvious. I slouched way down in the seat so I could just barely see over the dashboard, hoping she wouldn't spot me. That first night, she came out in her waitress outfit and got picked up by the girlfriend who apparently loaned her the car when she needed it. I followed them at a safe distance as they drove to the town's Dairy Queen together, and then to the girlfriend's house. I parked up the street some distance away from the house and waited. After a while, she came out and walked a couple houses down the street to a small house I assumed was hers. I hung around until I was pretty sure she wasn't going out again, and then left.

Two nights later, when I knew she was working again, I waited for her in the same place. This time, she came out dressed like she was going out and had her friend's car. I followed her down to the harbor where she parked in the parking lot across from the large boat docking area and went aboard a big cabin cruiser with a Confederate flag painted on the bow that was tied up there. The boat was all lit up and it looked like there was a party going on on board with people out on deck and music playing, and a lot of laughter. I waited until she was on board the boat before I pulled into the lot, where there were a lot of other cars, and I parked as far away from her car as I could. As the evening went on, more people arrived and nobody seemed to be leaving.

Finally, a little before midnight, after I'd been sitting there for a couple hours, everybody inside the boat's main cabin started coming out on deck. I leaned my head over to the open window to try to hear what was going on. Eventually, Val emerged with a guy who had one arm around her waist with his hand resting on her ass and a beer in his other hand. He raised the beer over his head and said in a voice that probably carried all the way across the harbor, "Aw' right, you fuckers, I hope y'all had a good time 'cause the party's over. Everybody off. Some of us've gotta' ballgame tomorrow."

There was laughter and a lot of jokes, but eventually people started to disembark, many of them heading toward cars in the lot where I was sitting. Val and the guy watched them go, and then turned and went back inside. I stayed there for a while longer to see if she'd come out again. Finally, somebody turned the lights on the boat off, and I figured I'd seen all I needed to see. The next morning I called the harbormaster to find out who owned the boat. Then, I went online and Googled the owner, and found out I'd been ditched for a stud baseball player whose daddy was a rich lawyer.

July 31, 2012 Now, it was six weeks later, Val was dead, and I was part of the team investigating her murder, but I couldn't get McGruder out of my head. It didn't make a lot of sense to try to pretend I wanted to question him about the case where he'd already given a statement to the State Police and had a big-time lawyer and everything, but I still wanted to meet the fucking guy face-to-face. I figured if I showed up in uniform, he'd just call his lawyer, and there'd be a shit storm and I was in enough trouble with Mullally and the state cops already. Anyway, this was personal. So late one morning on a day I was off duty, I put on a t-shirt, shorts and a pair of flip-flops, and drove over to the harbor. I parked in the parking lot near his boat and strolled over to the dock. It was a beautiful sunny day with a lot of people out and about.

I stood there on the dock looking at the boat like I was inspecting it. I walked back to the stern and looked it over, and then walked back around to the bow. I reached my hand up and felt the smooth teak work like I was admiring it, hoping all these dramatics would draw somebody's attention on board. If all else failed, my fallback plan was to knock on the hull to see if I could stir up some activity, but I didn't have to go that far. As I stood there massaging the teak work, McGruder's head appeared over the rail looking down at me from the deck. He was wearing a red visor, a gray t-shirt that said "Middies" on it, and a pair of black shorts that said "Gamecocks" in red letters along the bottom on one side.

"Y'all lookin' for somebody?" he asked in a homey Southern drawl.

I looked up at him and smiled, trying to act like we were old, long-lost buddies. "Just admiring it," I said. "Beautiful boat. South Carolina, huh?"

"Yep."

"Up here for the summer?"

"That's raht."

"Nice. You take it out to the islands?"

"Nah, stays here. Too much for me to handle by myself. It's mah' daddy's boat. He'd shoot me."

I nodded and continued to examine the teak work. "Too bad. The islands're nice this time of year."

"Yeah, so ah've heard. We may take in a little island tour on the way back to Charleston. Raht now, though, we're not goin' anywhere."

"Mind if I come aboard? I'd just like to see what the deck looks like, if that's okay?"

He shrugged. "Sure. Come on up."

I climbed aboard and stuck out my hand. "I'm Brian by the way."

"Sean," he said as we shook hands. He was taller than he looked on the baseball field, and standing there in shorts and a t-shirt, more powerfully built. And close up, he was even more of a pretty boy than I'd thought with high cheekbones, dark eyes and almost feminine eyelashes. It struck me how beautiful any kids he might've had with Val would've been, and with his athletic bloodlines thrown in. "This's Ras," he said, gesturing toward a large black figure in a tank top and bathing shorts stretched out on a lounge chair like he was dozing. Close up, his teammate was an imposing specimen with bulging muscles in his arms, chest and legs.

"Hey, Ras," I said like we were all good buddies. Dowling raised his hand a few inches in greeting and then dropped it without opening his eyes.

I looked around. It was a beautiful boat, although it could obviously use a little cleaning up. The deck was soiled from foot traffic and there were a couple of bulging trash bags in one corner, one of them on its side with a pizza box, some used napkins, and a few empty beer cans spilling out of it onto the deck.

"How many feet?" I asked him, looking around.

"Sixty-two."

"Wow. No wonder you need help."

"Yeah, it's a lotta' boat."

"You get a captain to take it back and forth to South Carolina?"

"Yep."

"Must be a big gas tank."

"Yeah, but ya' can go a long way on one tank. Almost all the way to Charleston from here."

I nodded. "So, what brings you up here so far from home?"

"Ras and me're playin' for the Middies this summer. That's why we're up here."

"No shit."

"Yeah, no shit. You go to any games?"

"Nah, not a baseball fan."

"You look like you might've played football."

I shook my head. "No. Just do some body building. It's a hobby."

He nodded. "You from around here?"

"Yeah, I'm a Cape Cod boy."

"Ah'd offer you a beer, but it's a little early."

"Yeah, too early for me, thanks. I bet a fair amount of beer gets drunk on this thing, though."

He smiled. "Amen, Brother. We almost always got a party goin' on."

"You don't mind being surrounded by Yankees?"

He chuckled. "Hell, we're the ones've got them surrounded."

"Sounds like you're havin' a good summer."

"Can't complain. We got some really nice Yankee ladies takin' good care of us. Ain't they nice, Ras?" The reclining figure nodded without opening his eyes.

"Glad to hear you're not lonely."

"Wouldn't mind a night off once in a while, to tell ya' the truth. The girls around here're downright voracious."

"You fall in love yet?"

"About twenty times so far this summer, but who's countin'."

I stood there grinning and thinking what a fucking asshole this guy was. He was an even bigger jerk than I'd thought he'd be. Standing there, I wondered whether I could've taken him in a fight. Before this, I'd figured I probably could, but up close he was a lot stronger than I'd thought and no doubt more athletic than me, and with his buddy there, I wouldn't have stood a chance. Of course, I was just playing mind games with myself. This wasn't middle school, and the thought that I'd actually get into an altercation with a murder suspect while I was off duty was obviously beyond stupid and would've certainly cost me my job if not worse after his lawyers had gotten through with me. There didn't seem much point in continuing this charade.

"Well, thanks for the tour," I said.

"Glad you enjoyed it. Come back any time."

"I may take you up on that."

"It'd be our pleasure, Brian."

"Good luck with the rest of the season," I said, as I descended back onto the dock.

"We'll give it our best shot," he said as I turned away.

I strolled up the dock and didn't look back.

At night, the Ocean Club looked pretty fancy when you drove up with the front of the place bathed in soft lighting. A short flight of broad steps led up to a landing where ceramic urns filled with beautiful native plantings framed double glass doors with the restaurant's name etched across them in fancy script. A valet appeared immediately to take our car. My favorite high school guidance counselor and I walked up the stairs and through the glass doors into a large foyer where there was a huge fish tank filled with exotic species built into one wall. The décor was classic South Beach with muted pinks, aquas and mauves. Our hostess was a striking brunette in a strapless lavender dress that showed off her fabulous tan. The deep carpeting felt luxurious under our feet as we followed her across the busy dining room to our window table overlooking the harbor. The lighting in the room was subdued, and there was a small floating candle on each table along with an orchid in a lovely clear vase. The wait staff was all tuxedoed.

An ice bucket with a bottle of expensive-looking champagne in it was sitting beside our table when we arrived. The reserved sign on our table was removed, our tastefully upholstered armchairs were pulled out for us, and, once we were seated, our napkins were gracefully opened for us and placed in our laps. Our gorgeous hostess gave us leather-bound menus and a wine list, told us to enjoy the evening, and departed with a lovely smile. A waiter instantly appeared and asked if we'd like our champagne opened. We both nodded simultaneously, and he immediately went about the business of uncorking the champagne with a practiced flourish. We sipped our first glass of champagne while enjoying the view as it gradually grew dark outside and the lights on the boats in the harbor began to come on. I'd never been in a place like this before.

"Well, congratulations," she said. "I don't know what you did to deserve this, and I probably don't want to know, but it's awfully nice."

"I'll drink to that," I said, as we touched glasses again and sipped some more champagne. I was wearing my only sports coat and an open-neck shirt.

There was a silence for a moment. Then, she said, "You seem a little distracted tonight. Is everything okay?"

"Yeah, I'm okay."

"It's not my outfit, is it?" she said, glancing down at herself. She was wearing a dress that wasn't particularly sexy and made her good sized ass stick out.

"No, you look lovely. I think I said that already."

"Well, you did, but I wasn't quite sure. I know it's not a lot of cleavage like you seemed to like the last time."

"You look lovely. There, I said it again."

"Thank you. As they say, three's a charm. I won't mention it again."

We sipped some more champagne and gazed out the window. Finally, she asked, "How's the case going?"

"Slow," I said, and drained my glass. I reached for the bottle. "More?" I asked, holding the bottle up.

She nodded. "Sure, why not. I wonder how many people go out of this place feet first."

"You probably wouldn't be the first. Or the last," I said as I poured some more champagne into her glass.

"Well, I'm going to try to stay in an upright position this evening given it's my first time here. I don't want to get a reputation." I smiled. Her eyebrows shot up. "Is that a smile? I knew there was one in there someplace."

"Sorry, but I've got a few things on my mind right now. I'll try to lighten up, I don't want to spoil this."

"You're not, believe me," she said, and took another sip from her freshened glass. "So, you don't want to talk about the case?"

"I can talk about it if you want, but I can't really say much about what's going on right now."

She nodded. "Of course. But understand that for a small town high school teacher who leads a pretty dull life, the whole thing's pretty interesting. And the media's really playing it up."

"Yeah, that's another problem. You'd think it was the crime of the century."

"Well, it is pretty fascinating."

"Somebody said there are whackos on the internet who're claiming the murderer was some celebrity we're trying to cover up for. Like there're a lot of celebrities around here."

"I hadn't heard that one. Anything new on McGruder you can tell me? That part's really intriguing. I'm a little surprised the media hasn't picked up on him yet."

I shrugged. "Yeah, it's a little surprising. Not much new as far as it goes. Other than he's a fucking asshole." I sipped some more champagne.

"Well, I've had the impression you don't particularly care for him, but what made him a fucking asshole, to borrow your expression?"

"I met him."

"Oh, wow. Did you get his autograph? Sorry, sorry, just kidding. So, was this part of the investigation?"

"Sort of."

"Sort of?"

"Let's just say I met him on his boat today."

"And he was a fucking asshole to you?"

143

"No, he was fake best buddies like all those Southern assholes usually are. I knew a bunch of 'em in the Army, and they're all the same. Bunch of phony jerks."

"I assume he's still a suspect?"

"Technically, I guess he is, but he and one of his teammates swear they were on the boat together asleep the night she disappeared."

"You believe them?"

I shrugged. "I don't know. His daddy's got him all lawyered up, and there's a real shortage of evidence. And then there's also Dowling."

"What's his problem?"

"He was on the boat that night too but left early supposedly to go home. But nobody can actually vouch for where he went after he left the boat. And there's this little problem of an arrest record. Seems Dowling's somewhat prone to violent behavior."

"Like that time on the ball field?"

"Yeah, and like rape, although the victim decided in the end not to testify."

"My God."

"Yeah, another college student. He and some of his friends. No conviction, though, so you can't use it on him on the witness stand. Also, assault on a police officer, reduced to a misdemeanor."

"Wow, McGruder's got some great friends. Maybe they killed her together and are covering up for each other. Or maybe it was Dowling."

I shrugged again and took another sip of champagne. "Lots of possibilities, but like I said, no evidence."

"Speaking of possibilities, what about Hunter Phillips? Did you ever follow up on him?"

I frowned. "Yeah, I had a chat with him. He admitted they had a pretty close relationship, which is interesting considering her attitude toward everybody else at the school. And, like you told me, he seems like quite the ladies' man and he's got a lot of money, which seems to've been a particular interest of hers."

"Do you think she actually slept with him?"

"At the moment, there's no evidence to link the two of them sexually, but who knows."

"Sounds like a tough case."

I nodded. "Yeah, like I said, it's slow goin'. Maybe we oughta' talk about something else."

"Yes, we should talk about something more uplifting. Maybe try to make something uplifting happen under your side of the table."

I smiled. "I don't think you can reach that far from where you're sitting."

"No, Silly, I didn't mean actual touching. Not in a classy place like this, for God's sake. No, I meant maybe we should talk about things that are, shall we say, mutually pleasurable. And I can see this line of conversation has already brought another smile to your face."

"Weren't you saying something a minute ago about trying to stay in an upright position tonight?"

She grinned. "In the restaurant, you dope."

"Ah, you had me worried there for a minute."

At that moment, our waiter reappeared. After our glasses had once again been refilled, she ordered swordfish and I ordered a steak. Our thoughtful waiter, having emptied the bottle of champagne into our glasses, showed up a few minutes later with another bottle so by the time dessert was over I was feeling pretty looped, which was no surprise given we were then more than halfway through the second bottle. As I contemplated pouring myself a little more, not wanting such an expensive bottle to go to waste, I glanced across the table at my companion, who'd been quiet for a couple minutes. I suddenly realized her face had turned a deep red and her eyes looked pretty glazed, and she had a strange look on her face.

"You okay?" I asked, hoping it didn't sound slurred.

There was a slight pause as if she was considering my question. Then, she said in a half-whisper, "I'm really shitfaced." She swayed a little, and for a moment I thought she was going to fall forward and smash her face on the table.

Oh, shit, I thought to myself, *I'm just barely going to be able to get out of here on my own. What the hell am I gonna' do with her?* I looked around for our waiter and flagged him down. We were all set, no check, all taken care of including the tip. I asked him if somebody could bring our car around and handed him the ticket, again hoping my speech wasn't too slurred. No problem, he said, and off he went. *Now, to get her up and moving in the direction of the door,* I thought. I slowly stood up and put my hand on the table to steady myself, and then slid around holding onto the table until I was standing behind her chair. I leaned down and whispered in her ear that I was going to help her up. She nodded. I reached down and grabbed her under her elbows, and lifted her up. She was like dead weight, but once she was up and I'd let go of her she remained standing, braced against the table. *So far, so good,* I thought to myself. I quickly moved around to her side and whispered to her to grab my arm, which she did with both hands like she was grabbing onto a life preserver, her nails digging into my bicep. I took a half step forward toward the door and she did the same, still clinging to my arm and leaning against me. Utilizing this half-step technique we

145

managed to make it across the dining room, through the foyer and out the front door with only a few stares.

My car was at the foot of the steps, the passenger door held open by a smiling young man in a white shirt, black slacks and a black bowtie. He saw us and, quickly sizing up the situation, bounded up the steps to help me get her down and into the car like she was somebody's ninety-nine year old grandmother. We got her in, he closed the door and I went around to the driver's side with one hand on the car to keep my balance. I got in, started it up, remembered to close the door and turn the lights on, and slowly pulled out. *The restaurant staff will be yucking it up about this one for a week,* I thought to myself.

Fortunately, her house was only a couple miles away through mostly residential streets so I didn't look like a complete idiot driving at about fifteen miles an hour. All I could think about was not getting stopped by one of my colleagues. She didn't say anything during the drive but just stared straight ahead. *Don't throw up until we get there,* I thought to myself. She wasn't exactly looking like a candidate for sex, and I wasn't sure of my own capabilities at that point either. I managed to park in front of her house without running into the curb. It was about thirty feet from the street to her front door. It was dark and nobody was around, and I figured I could probably carry her if I had to. I managed to get her out of the car and upright, and we started up the walk together much like we'd made it across the dining room. The last obstacle was the two stone steps up to the front door, which at that point looked like a climbing wall. I put one foot up onto the first step and I felt her start to follow, and then suddenly she lost her balance. I tried to hold her up but with my diminished reflexes and her clutching onto my arm with both hands, I couldn't get my other arm around her and before I knew it she was pulling me down with her.

We crashed in a heap at the bottom of the steps with me on top of her. She let out an awful scream and immediately followed with a couple more. *Oh, shit,* I thought to myself in my semi-intoxicated state, *this isn't good.* I got to my knees. She was lying sideways across the walkway at the bottom of the steps writhing in pain. I looked down and saw that one of her ankles was badly twisted at an unnatural angle, obviously broken. I knew she needed to stay put and not try to move while I got some help. I tried to calm her down but she was still writhing and screaming in pain, no doubt waking up the entire neighborhood. While I firmly held her down, with one hand I managed to get my cell phone out and hit the speed dial for the stationhouse. I told whoever answered to send an ambulance ASAP.

When the ambulance finally arrived, I saw in addition to the fractured ankle she'd been cut pretty badly and there was blood all over her new dress. She was obviously in a lot of pain, and it was a relief when we finally got to the emergency room and they whisked her away, no doubt to shoot her up with painkillers. I needed to sober up and stay awake, but the only coffee I could find was out of a machine in the cafeteria. The rest of the place was closed. The coffee tasted like shit, but I needed it. I spent the next three hours on a hard plastic chair in a hallway near the emergency room fighting to stay awake. Finally, around 4:00 am a cute blond nurse in blue scrubs with a stethoscope around her neck found me and told me they'd had to operate on her and put a couple pins in her ankle, and she was still in surgery, and I should go home and try to get some rest. The expectation was that she was going to be in the hospital for at least a couple days.

I called the local taxi company to get a cab to take me back to her house to pick up my car. I went home and took a hot shower to try to get the last of the booze out of my system. Then, I called the stationhouse and told them I was taking a sick day, and went to bed. Besides feeling like shit and having had no sleep, I knew my exploits of the night before would be all over the stationhouse, and I didn't feel up to the razzing I knew I was going to get. My one and only visit to the Harbor Club, along with a chance to get laid, had turned into a monumental disaster and I didn't feel like making it even worse.

18

August 1, 2012 I slept until a little past noon, got up, took another shower, ate something, and went back to the hospital. They told me she was sleeping and I could wait or come back later. I decided to wait, which was probably a mistake. I wound up sitting in a waiting area where there was a TV tuned in to some stupid daytime television show with the volume turned up in case anybody who sat down there was hard of hearing. There were a few magazines scattered around, most of them over a month old, and that was about it. Finally, after about two hours they came and told me I could go in and see her.

People in hospital beds after surgery usually don't look their best, and she was no exception. She was lying there in a hospital johnny, her hair sticking out in all directions, and dark patches under both her eyes like somebody'd punched her lights out. Her left leg, which looked like it was in a cast or a large brace under the bedcover, was elevated in a position that looked uncomfortable as hell, and there was an I.V. line running into her left forearm. She looked like she'd aged about fifteen years. On the far side of her bed, a curtain was drawn with another patient on the other side of the curtain I couldn't see. Not exactly the place for a private conversation.

When I walked in, she looked like she wanted to hide, undoubtedly knowing she looked like hell. The first words out of her mouth were she was sorry, which she must've said about fifteen times. I asked her how she was feeling and she told me she felt like shit. She said she wasn't in a lot of pain, but that was because she was still all doped up, and they'd told her she was probably going to feel pretty uncomfortable once the drugs started to wear off. I asked her if she needed anything, and she thanked me and told me she was okay for the moment and that her mother was flying in from Rochester, New York because she was going to need somebody to take care of her once she was discharged. I asked her what the doctors had said about recovery time and she told me it was a bad break, and she wouldn't be able to put weight on the ankle for probably six weeks, and then she'd still have to have a boot for at least another month after that before she could start physical therapy. That's if everything went okay. She said she was worried about her job with school starting soon, particularly her position as the school's guidance counselor, and at that point she started to tear up.

I did the best I could to try to buck her up, but it didn't seem to do much good. She kept saying she was sorry and didn't want this to screw up our relationship. Of course, I told her the usual bullshit you tell somebody in the hospital who's been through a rough time, that everything's going to be okay, that she was going to be fine, and so on, but I tried to stay away from the relationship part. I stuck it out for about forty more minutes, and then finally I told her I was going to let her get some rest. A pained look came across her face like she was suddenly fearful I was dumping her. I took her hand and kissed the back of it and told her again to get some rest, and then I left, still wondering in my mind how I was going to deal with all this.

August 2, 2012 I was checking the cars in a parking lot by one of the town's playgrounds for parking stickers. The lot was about two hundred yards up the street from one of the town's beaches. To park at one of the beaches, you needed either a visitor's sticker, which cost forty bucks for the season, or a resident sticker, which the town gave out for free to everybody who owned property in town and paid real estate taxes. There were attendants at all the beach parking lots who wouldn't let you in without one kind of a sticker or the other, but of course there were always people who were only in town for a few days, or maybe a week, and who wanted to avoid shelling out forty bucks for a visitor's sticker. This obviously required them to try to find alternative parking for the beach, and this playground lot was a spot they frequently tried. In season, to park in this lot you also needed one kind of sticker or the other, which was clear from signs posted in the lot, but there was no attendant on the premises, which encouraged stickerless beachgoers to try to park there and run for luck. One of our important responsibilities when we were out patrolling in the summer was to check this lot for violators, to whom we handed out, not coincidentally, forty dollar tickets.

I was sitting in a cruiser writing out a couple of those when my cell phone vibrated. I was surprised to hear Marty Blair's voice on the other end of the line where I couldn't remember him ever having called me before.

"Hey, Brian, it's Marty," he said in his usual chummy way. "Thought I'd just check in and see how everything went Tuesday night. Hope you had a good time and everything."

"Hi, Marty," I said, probably without much enthusiasm. "Yeah, it was great. Thanks again."

"Everybody treat you okay?"

"Like royalty. Everything was great, the food, everything. Perfect evening." I wondered whether he'd gotten a report from the staff on our less than graceful exit.

"Well, we try to make it a special dining experience," he said. "I was thinking maybe you'd like to go back again sometime. On me, of course. Or maybe you've come up with something else I could do for you as a thank you."

I took a deep breath. Mullally had said we needed to distance ourselves from this guy, and that was obviously true for a lot of reasons. It had also crossed my mind that hopefully my accepting a free dinner at the Ocean Club right at that particular point in time hadn't been a huge mistake. And here he was, trying to drag me in deeper. "Hey, Marty," I said, "I really appreciate the night out and everything, and it's not like we're not friends and all, but with the state cops buzzing around I think it'd probably be better for both of us if we kept our distance for right now. You'll probably hear the same thing from Mullally if you talk to him. I'm sure you can understand."

There was a slight pause. "Jeez, Brian, I'm sorry to hear that. Is there something more I oughta' know about? Something else come up since we talked?"

"No, nothing I know about, Marty, but I only hear about what goes on in the part of the case we're working on. Like I told you, we're not plugged into whatever else they may be looking at."

"Gotcha'. Okay, well, I'll stay out of your hair, then. I don't want to make this any more complicated than it already is. Eventually you're going to catch whoever killed her and this other thing is all going to go away, and then things'll be back to normal."

"That's right, Marty, everybody's just gotta' be patient."

"Hey, I'm with you, Brian. Okay, well, thanks for that and I'm glad you had a good time at the Club. And maybe you'll cut me some slack next time you catch me driving too fast."

I feigned a chuckle. "Don't press your luck."

He laughed. "Fucking cops. Never give anybody a break. You be well, my friend."

"You, too, Marty," I said and ended the call. *Fucking sleaze,* I thought to myself. And getting tagged with being mixed up with Marty Blair was not something I needed right at that particular moment.

19

August 3, 2012 I figured my role in the case gave me a credible excuse to go to the memorial service for Val and observe. As it turned out, holding it in the high school auditorium was an unfortunate choice given not that many people showed up and the big empty auditorium made the lack of attendance even more obvious. About a dozen kids from school and two teachers came, one of whom was Hunter Phillips. Nobody else showed up, including her mother. The sparse crowd didn't even fill up the first two rows of the center section of the auditorium. Everybody was neatly dressed and a couple of the guys wore ties. One thing that was striking was how young the kids all looked in comparison to Val even though they'd all been in the same class together. On the stage beside the podium was a small table with an eight by ten of Val's graduation photograph in a nice frame along with a vase of flowers. I stood in the back by the door like I was there in some official capacity.

The first person who spoke was a guy who'd graduated with Val. He spoke for a couple minutes and talked about what a great classmate she'd been and that kind of stuff. It was all pretty impersonal, and he could've been talking about just about anybody in the class. Then, Gina Rongoni got up and spoke. She was wearing a dress and low-heeled shoes, and it looked like she'd gotten her hair done. Right from the start you could see this was very emotional for her, and she got even more emotional as she went along. She talked about what a wonderful friend Val had been, and how hard she'd worked to support herself and her mother. She talked about Val's plans for college, and how fate had cruelly intervened and had taken her away just when a lot of wonderful opportunities were about to open up for her, and how Val had been destined for stardom in whatever path in life she'd chosen to take. She had a couple tissues rolled up in her hand and she used them to dab her eyes as she went along. She talked for about ten minutes, and then suddenly stopped, as if the whole thing was too much for her, and sat down. There was a silence for about a minute after she'd finished. Then, Hunter Phillips got up and, in what I thought was overly dramatic fashion, read a poem he said was one of Val's favorites. It started out talking about life and happiness, but ended up talking about death and dying, which made the whole thing even more depressing. After Phillips sat down, there was another long pause. Then, probably sensing nobody else was going to get up and say anything, Rongoni got up and started going around thanking everybody for coming, signaling it was over. The whole thing took less than half an hour.

Knowing the crowd would be filing past me to get out of the auditorium, I left before anybody started out and went out and got into the cruiser, which I'd parked some distance away from the front door. There was some brief milling around outside as people filed out and I even heard some laughter, and then everybody dispersed. I watched Phillips make his way to the parking lot and get into a snazzy black Audi convertible and drive off. Hopefully, his seeing me there, if he had, wasn't going to precipitate another call to Mullally from his lawyer. I continued to sit there in the cruiser for a while. Finally, Rongoni came out carrying the vase of flowers and the framed photograph. I wondered what had taken her so long. She glanced nervously over at the cruiser, and then walked quickly to the parking lot, got into her car, and drove away like she was in a hurry.

I sat there for a while after she was gone. It was another beautiful summer day, the kind that usually puts you in a good mood and not the kind of day people often spend pondering somebody's death. I sat there feeling numb. The sadness of the whole situation had really hit me, perhaps from seeing her picture and the flowers and all that, but nobody knew what had gone on between Val and me and I needed to keep it that way. Finally, I got up the strength to start the car and slowly pull away. Time to put the game face back on.

That afternoon, Mullally called me into his office and had me take a seat. "One of the selectmen, Todd Millbrook, just called asking what's going on in the Valerie Gray case," he said. "The selectmen're getting concerned there doesn't seem to be a lot of progress, and the media and that television woman are busting everybody's balls with the whole town holding their breath there won't be a lot of cancellations in August. I told him I'd give him an update. Any idea what the fuck's going on with the state cops?"

I shook my head. "No, nothing new as far as I know. You want to know the truth, I don't think they're putting a whole lot into this."

He frowned. "We haven't seen much of them lately, that's for sure."

"I think they're probably busy over on the other side of the bay with their New Bedford street gangs and don't want to be bothered with this stupid case. It's probably too long a drive for them over the Canal."

"Don't they pay attention to the media? They're getting slammed all over the place, and that includes us as well."

"I guess they don't care."

"You think they're still hung up on Marty Blair?"

I shrugged. "Who the fuck knows. You know everything I do. Nothing's come into the file lately or I would've told you about it."

"Well, we've got to have something to tell the selectmen or we're going to look awfully stupid. You've been poking around. Anything new I ought to know about on your end?"

"Frankly, I've pretty much run out of ideas. Seems the victim kept to herself a lot and didn't have many friends. We've known all along about two of the guys she went out with but that's about it. I'm sure the state cops've run into the same thing. If they're anywhere close to an arrest, they haven't told me about it."

"Jesus, it's been almost a month now and so far nothing. Remember they said if you don't come up with a suspect in the first couple weeks, it may never get solved? That wouldn't sit well around here. Attractive young girl who's just graduated from high school gets murdered and dumped in the Sound, and nobody can figure out who did it? People would have a right to be pissed."

"It's pretty much out of our hands, isn't it?"

"Try telling that to the people around here. We're the police, for Christ's sake."

"Know anybody at the State Police you could call? Somebody higher up?"

Mullally shook his head. "No, and I doubt that would do any good anyway. Except to piss those two off."

"I guess we'll just have to wait it out, then."

"It really sucks that whoever did this is still out there walking around, and it may be somebody close by."

"I don't know. There's always been the possibility it could've been a stranger, some pervert who wandered through and spotted her. A lot of people go through here in the summer. And then there's the drug thing and all the not so nice people in that business. Still a lot of possibilities."

"Well, it'd be pretty hard to track down some pervert now if that's who did it. And our friends seem to be hung up on the drug angle, even though they haven't been able to come up with shit. And they're the ones who said at the outset there's a good chance it's somebody she knew from around here. Maybe those are the people we ought to concentrate on while they're screwing around and try and come up with something. Do some more snooping around and maybe come up with a suspect we can try to build a case against, see if we can somehow force the issue. Didn't the baseball player say when he was questioned he thought she may've gotten a call or a text from somebody? That would have to've been somebody she knew. We need to find out if she did get a call and who it was."

"Well, he admitted he was just guessing. And her phone wound up in the Sound with her and they couldn't salvage anything out of it, so where are you going with that? And you'd think the state cops would've been down that road already anyway."

Mullally frowned again. "You're right, you're right. I'm just trying to think of anything else we could follow up on. Let's go over the list possible candidates we know of."

"Well, obviously there's McGruder, and Dowling. And there's Bobby Frank, although McGruder and Frank've got alibis."

He snorted. "Yeah, and their alibis both suck."

"I'm just sayin', they've got alibis. But any way you look at it, if the state cops are going to do anything with either McGruder or Dowling, they'd better do it soon because the two of them are going to be heading back down south before long and that isn't going to make trying to put a case together against either of them any easier."

"I can't understand why the state cops haven't done more with them. One interview and that's it. And Dowling doesn't have even a half-assed alibi. And the guy's got a record of violent behavior, for Christ's sake."

"Yeah, but none of it's admissible."

"That doesn't mean he wasn't capable."

"He says he went home and went to bed."

"But he can't prove it."

"Yeah, and nobody can prove he didn't."

"What about Frank?"

"What about him?"

"She was still in touch with him, wasn't she? And it looks like they were both in the drug business. I'm wondering, do you think Frank's linked to Marty Blair somehow?"

"I tried that out on Marty. He claims he's never heard of him."

"Marty's not at the top of my list of credible witnesses these days."

"I hear you, but isn't that the part of the case the state cops are supposedly working on? The drug thing? And the part we want to stay out of?"

"Yeah, you're right. "

"You have anybody else in mind?"

"Who else is there? What about the teacher, what's his name?"

"Hunter Phillips? You told me to stay away from him."

"Yeah, yeah, I know, but he's got money, doesn't he? The state cops think this is all somehow tied to the money she had stashed away. They don't know about Phillips, though, do they?"

"No, not as far as I know."

"I'm just exploring all the angles. Maybe he became obsessed by her, paid her a lot of money to fuck him, or loaned it to her, and then, not wanting to risk being exposed, killed her. Or maybe she was blackmailing him. He'd be as good a target for blackmail as Marty. Maybe better."

I shrugged. "Yeah, except the only thing that could've happened to him is he could've lost his teaching job, which he doesn't really need. So I'm having trouble with the idea she was blackmailing him."

"Maybe she ditched him for McGruder and he got pissed. Maybe he was the mystery man she went to see at night with her friend's car before McGruder came along. And she was wheedling money out of him in exchange."

"Maybe. But like with Dowling, how're you gonna' prove it?"

"Have we figured out whether there's anybody else she may've gone out with? She was an attractive girl, not the type who would've been sitting at home very much, I wouldn't think."

"I don't know how we're supposed to do that. I've asked everybody I've talked to whether they know who else she may've been seeing and nobody knows anything, not even her best friend. The state cops've done the same thing and gotten nowhere either as far as I can tell. Maybe this is going to be one of those cases that never gets solved."

"I don't even want to think about that. But right now, we've at least got to do something, or make it look like we're doing something. Telling the selectmen we're sitting on our hands waiting for the state cops while at the same time we don't know what the fuck they're doing isn't exactly going to inspire confidence in this department."

"Why do I have this feeling you're looking for me to get this thing off the dime?"

Mullally frowned. "Look, nobody expects you to solve the fucking thing. But you wanted to be a cop, and you wanted to help on this case. Okay, now it's time to find out how smart you are. Just try to get it moving in some direction where maybe we can build something, or at least have something to report. Instead of just sitting here playing with ourselves waiting for those two dumb fucks to come up with something. Maybe there's somebody else out there we can take a look at, somebody we haven't considered yet who's right under our noses. You came up with Phillips and that was good police work. I want you to think about it some more and see what else you can come up with, maybe find another new angle."

I left the stationhouse to go for a drive and as I was walking across the parking lot to get into a cruiser, my cell phone vibrated. I pulled it out and looked at the number. Then, I let it go to voicemail. I got into the cruiser and sat there for a minute, and then played the voicemail recording back.

"Hi, it's me. I know you're probably busy, but I just wanted to catch up and give you an update. I'm home, and my mother's here, and I'm sitting in a chair in the living room with my leg all propped up with pillows and thinking about you. I really miss you a lot, and I'm really sorry this all happened, but it really shouldn't affect anything. I assume you haven't called or come by because you wanted to give me some time to rest, but I'm feeling a lot better now, and if you wanted to come over I could get rid of my mother for a while, maybe put that top on you like. We can't do very much, but I bet I could still put a smile on your face. So call me when you get a chance. I'll be here. Miss you a lot. Bye."

I sat there for a moment staring at the phone. I actually thought about calling her back, but then stopped myself. *What the fuck was I going to say, for Christ's sake? That I was sorry, but I was just in it to get laid?* I sat there for another minute staring out the window, and then I pressed DELETE.

I drove down by the ocean and swung the cruiser into the parking lot at a beach they called the Bluffs. The parking lot was situated at the top of a high bluff looking out over the Sound and the Vineyard, and a wooden staircase of about sixty steps zigzagged down to the beach below. It was a nice beach, although it could get a little crowded when the tide came all the way in, and it was a real pain in the ass if you had to haul a lot of stuff back up the stairs at the end of the day, not to mention a couple screaming urchins who wanted to be carried up. And there were no toilet facilities down on the beach. There were a couple port-a-johns in the parking lot, but it was a long hike up if you needed to pee so most people just went into the water when they needed to relieve themselves, which at least made the water warm to swim in.

The weather had turned dark rather suddenly, and it wasn't a particularly nice afternoon for the beach. It had rained a little, and the sky was heavily overcast, and there were only a few cars in the parking lot. I pulled into a space that looked out over the Sound at the Vineyard in the distance. Out on water there was a sailboat race going on, about fifteen or twenty 420's from one of the local yacht clubs skimming along across the gray water like little moths. The wind had come up, and a few raindrops were hitting the windshield. *Not the greatest day to be out there in one of those things,* I thought to myself. *A lot of people who race those things are pretty nuts, though; they even race them in the wintertime, for Christ's sake.* I sat there watching the little boats as they maneuvered in a pack around one of the big round orange balls that marked the race course and changed direction, pondering what to do next.

As I sat there, a woman came up the stairs from the beach in a bathing suit holding a little boy in her arms who looked too big to have to be carried, a large canvas bag loaded with beach stuff hanging from one of her arms. The woman had the little boy wrapped up in a beach towel with his scrawny legs covered with sand hanging out below. He was wailing at the top of his lungs, and the woman was obviously trying to quiet him as she made her way to one of the few cars still left in the parking lot. *Probably stayed on the beach too long and got cold,* I thought to myself. I saw the woman glance in my direction as she made her way quickly to her car, probably worried I was going to get out and arrest her for child abuse. She got the back door of the car open and managed to tuck the little guy, still bawling, into a car seat with the towel still wrapped around him; and then she closed the door, opened the front door, tossed the canvas bag into the front seat, and got in and started the car up. I thought about my little brother when he was that age and how my mother had comforted him when he was upset like that. And now he was almost sixteen. I wondered what he was like. Hopefully, not like me. My friend the high school guidance counselor had told me I should try to connect with him again, but this was definitely not the time. I continued to watch as the woman pulled out and drove away, wondering whether I'd ever have kids myself someday.

Sitting there, I thought for a moment about the nightmares and how I hadn't had one in while, although I knew I wasn't over them. There seemed to be no pattern to when they occurred, nor any correlation between what I was thinking or doing in the hours before I went to bed and the awful images that suddenly materialized later in my sleep. I just wished they'd go away and leave me in peace.

I looked back out at the Sound again. A month had gone by, but the commotion hadn't died down at all and people were obviously starting to get antsy. The silence from the state cops was frankly making me a little concerned, and while my little secret seemed safe for the moment, there was no telling how long it would stay that way. What was amazing to me was the most logical person for Val to have gone to meet up with alone that night had seemed fairly obvious from the start, but for some reason nobody had been able to piece it together. Up to this point, I'd stayed out of it for obvious reasons, but now it looked like it was going to have to be up to me to figure out that part of it.

20

August 6, 2012 The following Monday morning, I parked my cruiser just off the road by the entrance to the town's DPW garage and storage area. If you were coming down the road, you couldn't see the cruiser where I'd parked it until you were almost on top of it. The spot was about half a mile from Gina Rongoni's house on the road she'd have to take to get to her job at the Rec Center. I'd been sitting there for about twenty minutes watching the cars as they went by when I spotted her car coming down the road. She looked like she might be going a little over the speed limit, but not enough for me to stop her where I didn't have radar on her. I saw her glance over at the cruiser as she went by, and by the time she was past her brake lights were on, the reflex reaction most people have when they spot a police car on the side of the road. I pulled out and put the blue lights on. She was watching in her rearview mirror, and when I put the lights on she immediately put her blinker on and pulled over to the side of the road in a clear area. I pulled in behind her and left the lights on. I took my time getting out of the car and walking up to the driver's side door of her vehicle. Her window was down and she looked extremely nervous.

"Hello," I said calmly, "would you please get out of the car and come with me."

She nodded, pulled the keys out of the ignition and got out. She was practically shaking. "Do you want my registration or anything?" she stammered.

"No, not right now," I said. "Let's just talk for a couple minutes."

She nodded again and followed me back to the passenger side of the cruiser. I opened the door and gestured for her to get in. She slid into the passenger seat and I shut the door behind her. Then, I walked back around to the driver's side and got in, figuring at that point she was about as vulnerable as she was ever going to be.

"I want to talk to you about the night Valerie Gray disappeared," I said. I could see she was really tense. She'd turned away and was staring straight ahead at the windshield. There was a brief silence. Then, I said, "I don't think you've told us everything that happened that night." She didn't say anything but just continued to sit there staring straight ahead.

"I shouldn't have to tell you," I said, "but this is pretty serious business. Lying to the State Police can get you into serious trouble. Lying in a murder investigation can get you into a lot more trouble. As in serious jail time. Do you understand?"

She nodded almost imperceptibly, but kept staring straight ahead. I detected a tremor run through her body. I remembered how nervous she'd been the first time I'd talked with her and figured she must be the nervous type. Then, it suddenly dawned on me maybe I was pushing things a little too far and she might become hysterical, and that obviously would've been counterproductive. *Let's keep going and pray she doesn't break down,* I thought to myself.

I tried to soften my tone a little. "Look," I said, "we're trying to solve a murder here. The victim was your best friend. We need your help if there's anything more you can tell us. Nobody's accusing you of anything. The main thing now is finding out what happened that night. You come forward now, maybe everybody forgets what you said before. You're young, and young people make mistakes. But if you keep holding back information, there are definitely going to be serious consequences."

She nodded slightly. There were tears in her eyes. "What makes you think I haven't told you everything?"

"I can't reveal our sources of information," I said. "I can only tell you we now have solid information that after she borrowed your car that night, you saw her again later before she disappeared."

She kept staring straight ahead, not looking at me. "How do you know that?"

"We have a witness who's come forward and told us you met your friend on the Yacht Club dock that night sometime after midnight. You went there in your boat."

She turned and stared at me blankly, seemingly unable to speak.

Telling a suspect you've got a witness to something when you actually don't is an old ploy cops use to try to get a suspect to talk. Sometimes it works, and sometimes it doesn't. And it can backfire on you. But this time I had an actual witness. That witness was me.

21

July 8, 2012 It was one of those really hot nights you can get in July on the Cape with a lot of humidity and hardly any breeze. I always figure there are probably going to be about five or six nights like that every summer and you just have to suck it up and get through them if you don't have air-conditioning, which of course I didn't have in my little cottage. With no breeze, the place was like an oven and the little fan I'd rigged up on the dresser didn't really do much except blow the hot, sticky air around the bedroom. I was lying on top of the sheets in a pair of briefs and a t-shirt with the sweat dripping off me soaking the sheets and the pillow. The more I tossed and turned trying to get to sleep, the more uncomfortable it became. The other problem was I couldn't stop thinking about Val. I'd barely seen her the past few weeks, just a couple stops at the diner for coffee when I'd gotten up the courage. She clearly hadn't wanted to talk with me, and I was getting the pretty clear message she wanted me to just disappear. I'd also been keeping track of her nighttime activities enough to know she was still hot and heavy with the ballplayer, and I knew my chances of ever getting back with her had pretty much faded into the sunset. I was going back and forth feeling depressed one minute and really pissed the next, which wasn't helping me try to get to sleep. And I couldn't get that image out of my mind of her on top of me naked in the firelight.

I finally looked at my watch. It was almost midnight, and I wasn't going to get to sleep anytime soon. I got up and stood in front of the fan in the dark, trying to cool my body off a little. I knew that one way to cool off on a hot night when you don't have air-conditioning is to just get in the car and go for a drive, so I threw on a pair of shorts, a t-shirt and some sneakers, and grabbed the Glock. I went to the refrigerator and put some ice in a glass, filled it with water from the kitchen tap, and slugged down the whole glass, which made me start to sweat all over again. Then, I went out to the car thinking I'd go down to the harbor, where it was probably cooler, and see if anything was happening on McGruder's boat.

I pulled into the parking lot on the other side of the park from where the boat was tied up. There were only a couple other cars in the lot, and I immediately recognized one of them as the car Val borrowed from her friend when she went out at night. Before I shut off the engine, I lowered all the windows to try to catch whatever breeze might be coming in off the Sound. The harbor was quiet with nobody around, and the moon and the stars were completely hidden in the dense humidity. There were no lights on the dock or in the park, and down at the end of the harbor the Yacht Club was also completely dark, the only light around coming from a boatyard on the other side of the harbor that stayed lit up all night. There was a faint glimmer of light in the cabin of McGruder's boat, but the drapes were closed and otherwise all the lights on the boat were out and there was no sign of any life on board.

I sat there for a while watching the boat and getting bored. I closed my eyes to see if I could nap, something I'd learned to do in Iraq, where you never got enough sleep. There were even times over there when I was so sleep deprived I actually fell asleep on a concrete floor or in the back of a moving truck. Sitting in the car trying to catch whatever breeze there was, I may've dozed off briefly but at some point I was awake again. Everything was still quiet and it wasn't a hell of a lot cooler than it had been at my place, and there didn't seem to be any activity on the boat, so I finally decided I'd go back and give my place another try. I was just about to start the car when somebody came out on the deck of McGruder's boat. It was hard to see who it was but I could tell it was a woman, and from her blond hair I knew it was Val. It looked like she had her phone out and was texting somebody. Then, she went back inside briefly, and then came back out again, climbed down onto the dock and headed down toward the Yacht Club. *This is pretty strange*, I thought to myself. On impulse, I decided I'd get out and follow her from a distance and see where she was going, figuring she wouldn't be able to spot me in the dark if I stayed far enough back and was careful.

I got out of the car and closed the door as gently as I could so it wouldn't make any noise. I could just barely see her now moving along fairly quickly down toward the Yacht Club. The thought occurred to me that maybe I ought to take the Glock with me, but at that point I was afraid I might lose her if I took the time to get it out of the glove box, so I left the Glock in the car and took off jogging diagonally across the park down toward the Yacht Club, moving as quietly as I could in the darkness while I tried to keep her in sight.

Just before she got to the Yacht Club, she veered off onto a path that ran through a grove of pine trees out to the Club's outer dock that extended out into the Sound. As she disappeared through the trees, I increased my pace to try to get closer behind her. When I got to the trees, I stopped and peered through them out toward the dock. She was heading down the path toward the wooden walkway that connected the dock to land. The friend she'd borrowed the car from was out on the dock standing next to a small boat with an outboard tied up to one of the large metal cleats on the edge of the dock. *Boy, this is really weird*, I thought to myself. *I wonder what they're up to.*

I moved cautiously along the path through the pine trees keeping low. On the other side of the trees, the Yacht Club had planted a low hedge of evergreens on both sides of the path leading down to the wooden walkway. Where the path met the walkway, there was a three foot high concrete wall that ran along the shore in both directions to prevent surf erosion. I figured if I stayed low and used the hedge on the side of the path as cover, I could get down to the wall and get behind it without them seeing me. Crouched where the wall met the hedge, I figured I'd be hidden from both the dock and anybody on the path, and where it was a calm night I could probably hear what was going on. I crouched down the way I'd been trained in the Army, and, knowing I had the element of surprise and they probably wouldn't be looking in my direction, I moved quickly down to the wall without any sign they'd seen me. The wall turned out to be not as high as I'd thought, and I had to get down on my hands and knees behind it and keep my head down low to stay out of sight, and it was pretty uncomfortable kneeling there in the gravel behind the wall and the hedge.

As I knelt there, I heard Val say in an agitated voice, "God, Gina, is there some reason you had to come all the way over here in the middle of the night in a freakin' boat, for God's sake? Couldn't this have waited until tomorrow?"

"It's, like, I really need to talk with you, Val, and you've got my car. What'd you want me to do, walk all the way from my house?"

"But couldn't this have waited until tomorrow? It's after midnight, and you shouldn't be out in that boat alone at this time of night. This is totally insane."

"It's not that big a deal, Val. The ocean's calm and I didn't have any trouble getting here. Give me a little credit, for God's sake, I'm not stupid, you know."

"Yeah, well, what if we get a thunderstorm, or the wind picks up? It's a long way to your house from here. You've got to be crazy coming all the way over here alone at night in that thing. Tie the boat up here and I'll drive you home, and we can come back and get the boat tomorrow."

"You don't need to worry about me, Val, I'll be fine. I just need to talk with you."

"Gina, what in God's name is so freakin' important that we need to talk about it out here in the middle of the night on this stupid dock? Seriously, are you okay?"

"I'm fine, Val, really I am, but I need to talk with you. We used to talk all the time, but, like, we haven't talked in weeks."

"It's summer, Gina. It's not like when we're in school together every day. You've got your job and I've got mine, and we're not together as much. If you'd wanted to talk, all you had to do was say so, for God's sake."

"You used to come over a lot at night, especially in the summer, and we used to talk all the time. Now, you're out every night."

"Gina, I've got a social life. We're out of high school now and we need to explore new things. You need to get out of the house, too, and get your own social life. We can't just hang out together all the time. If I'm using your car too much, just tell me and I'll figure something else out. I don't want to keep you from going out if that's what you want to do."

"I don't care about the car, Val, I just care about you. I understand your wanting to, like, go out and have fun and stuff like that, but I don't think your sleeping with Mr. Big Deal Baseball Player on his boat every night is frankly such a terrific idea."

"So, that's it. This is about Sean. You don't think I should be seeing Sean."

"No, frankly, I don't. I don't think he's your type, and I don't think your fucking him nonstop every night is really such a great idea. It makes you look like a slut, if you want to know the truth."

"Well, that's really nice of you to say, Gina, thanks a lot. I don't know what I did to deserve it, but thanks very much."

"Look, Val, I'm sorry, I didn't mean it the way it sounded. It's just that, like, I'm your friend and I'm worried about you."

"You've never even met Sean."

"No, but I don't need to meet him to know he's a conceited asshole who just wants to get his rocks off, and when the summer's over he'll disappear."

"Is this what you came all the way down here in the middle of the night to tell me?"

"No, I came down here because there're a lot of things we need to talk about, and I've had the feeling you've been avoiding me."

"I haven't been avoiding you, that's stupid."

"Well, what about school? You and I are supposed to start college in a month. Are you going to be able to go?"

"That's something we need to talk about, but I don't think this is either the time or the place. But we'll talk about it soon, I promise."

"Is it the money?"

"It's a long story. We'll talk about it, but not tonight."

"Why can't we talk about it now? What's going on, Val? You're still avoiding me."

"Like I said, it's a long story and I'm not in the mood to talk about it at this hour out here on this stupid dock. I'm tired and I want to go to bed, and you're probably tired, too."

"What, did he wear you out?"

"Come on, Gina, let's not be snarky."

"Okay, okay, that wasn't very nice, I'm sorry. But if there's something about school, I think I have a right to know about it. You're talking about my life, too, you know. And we're supposed to be friends, remember?"

"Yes, you're my friend and you'll always be my friend, although you're not exactly acting like it tonight."

"Look, I said I was sorry. I'm just upset, that's all, and now you've got me even more upset. I need you to tell me what's going on, Val. I think you owe me that."

There was a pause. Then, Val said, "I may not be going to UMass in the Fall, Gina. It's not final yet, but I think I may be going somewhere else."

"Where, for God's sake?"

"The University of South Carolina."

"I can't believe you're telling me this, Val. You're going to go there to be with him?"

"No, not just to be with him, although that's obviously part of it. But it sounds like a really cool place with lots of parties and sports and stuff, and it would get me away from here. Sean's old man is a big alum and gives a lot of money to the school, and Sean's pretty sure he can get me in even this late. His dad's talked to the admissions people and we're waiting to hear. It'd be a full ride scholarship and everything, and if it comes through I really can't turn it down because of the money. I'm sorry, Gina, I know you had your heart set on rooming together, but we can still stay connected and see each other on vacations and stuff."

"Val, do you know what this means? I chose UMass because that was the only place you thought you'd be able to go. We've both got a deposit down, and I've already been shopping for stuff for our room. And what if he dumps you? You'll be stuck down there with all those Southerners. South Carolina's not like Massachusetts, Val. The people down there are a lot different from the people around here."

"He's not going to dump me, Gina, trust me, I know how to handle him. He's really just a big baby. And his family's got lots of money and he's going to be in the major leagues, and I'm going with him. We're going to be on the big stage, Gina, that's what Sean and his friends call it, and I'm not going to be stuck in this freakin' town and be poor for the rest of my life."

"Val, don't you know about all those big sports stars? They all have children by a bunch of different women, and they beat up their wives and girlfriends. They're all, like, just a bunch of arrogant jerks that abuse women."

"You're just lumping them all together, Gina. They're a lot of good ones out there, too, that have great relationships. And I can handle Sean, trust me."

"And here I thought all this time he was using you when it turns out you're the one who's using him. It's like the two of you were made for each other, for God's sake."

"Gina, I know you're upset and you're saying things you don't really mean. I'm sorry, I really am. I wanted to wait for the right time to tell you but now you know. Just please know I still want to be friends."

"Friends?" Her voice was rising. "You're supposed to be my friend and you're doing this to me?"

"Gina, please keep your voice down, the sound carries. Look, it's not the end of the world. You're going to meet a lot of new people at UMass and you're going to have fun, I know you are. And we'll stay in touch. And if things don't work out in South Carolina, I can always transfer, or maybe you could transfer to South Carolina if you want."

"Val, you don't understand."

"I do understand, Gina, but it's not the end of the world, it's really not."

"No, you don't understand, Val." There was a slight pause. "I love you."

"Of course you do, and I love you, too, and we're never going to stop loving each other."

"No, Val, I mean, I really love you. Like I want to be together with you."

There was a pause. "Gina, I know you're upset and everything, and I'm sorry this has all happened. I didn't want to tell you this way, I really didn't. But you'll be fine. You're a strong woman, and this isn't the end of the world."

"No, Val, you're not getting it. I love you, as in I'm seriously in love with you. Not just as friends."

There was another pause. "Gina, I'm not sure what you're telling me. You almost make it sound like you're coming out of the closet on me. I know you don't mean it that way, but that's almost what it sounds like."

She was sobbing now. "Yes, Val, I'm coming out of the fucking closet on you. I can't help it, I love you. I've loved you for I don't know how long. This isn't the way I wanted to be, but it's the way I am. I'm sorry. I don't know what else to say except I'm sorry. I hate myself right now."

"God, Gina, I'm not sure I know what to say." There was another pause. "Look, there's no need to be sorry, I respect you for telling me, I really do. I know it wasn't easy. But please understand it's not exactly easy for me, either. I'm just not sure I can love you the same way you love me. I hope you can understand that. But we'll work it out somehow, I know we will. We just need to think about it. But I really think this is enough for one night. I think we both ought to go home now and talk about it some more tomorrow. Let's go out together tomorrow night and talk. We'll make it a special night out together, just the two of us. Here, untie the boat and I'll get in with you, and we'll go back to your house together. We'll get the car in the morning."

"You're going to ditch me, aren't you?"

"No, I'm not going to ditch you, you're my friend."

"Yes, you are, you're my only friend in the world and I love you, and you're going to ditch me, and I don't know what I'm going to do, Val."

"Gina, for God's sake, get a grip. I said we'll talk tomorrow and we will. I'm not going to ditch you. Now, please untie the boat and let's go."

"I don't want you to go with me."

"Gina, I was scared about you being in the boat alone before, but now I'm definitely not letting you go alone."

"Okay, Val, you want me to go, I'll go. You can go back to your love nest."

"Gina, shut up, I'm going with you. I'm not going to leave my friend alone, not when I'm worried about her."

"Val, believe me, I'm not going to do anything stupid. And what about Sean, isn't he expecting you back?"

"Oh, Christ, don't worry about him. They're watching a stupid baseball game, and it's probably over by now and they've gone to sleep. I was intending to go home soon anyway. Come on, let's go."

"Don't be stupid, Val. You're afraid something's going to go wrong out there, well what if something actually did go wrong and there's, like, a storm or something? You don't know anything about boats. What are you going to do out there that's going to help? Look, I'll take the boat. I know how to handle it. Trust me, I'll be alright."

"No, Gina, you're not going all that way alone. Come on, untie it and let's get going. I'm not letting you go without me."

I heard somebody get into the boat and start the motor. Then, I couldn't hear anything over the noise. A couple minutes went by while I crouched there on my hands and knees with the boat's motor running wondering what the fuck was going on. At one point, I could hear their voices like they were yelling at each other, but I couldn't make out what they were saying over the noise. Finally, after what seemed like an eternity, I heard the motor rev up as the boat started to move away, and then the noise gradually subsided as the boat moved off into the distance leaving me alone there in the darkness. I stayed there for a while not moving, wanting to be sure they were gone. It was completely still, and I was alone. *Well,* I thought to myself, *now she's definitely going to be out of your life for good, so time to get over it and somehow move on.* All of a sudden, I felt completely drained and almost didn't have the strength to get up. My life had hit bottom. I needed to go home and get some sleep, and somehow try to sort things out in the morning.

22

August 6, 2012 So, I'd known all along Rongoni had been lying about the last time she'd seen Val, but of course I hadn't been able to say anything about it because then I would've had to explain what the fuck I was doing out there on the dock that night, for which there was obviously no good answer. The state cops' report on their interview with Rongoni hadn't indicated she'd seemed particularly nervous when they'd talked with her, but I couldn't imagine she hadn't been given the way she'd acted with me the day I'd talked with her at the Rec Center and then again there in the car, and I would've thought experienced cops would've seen that kind of demeanor in a witness, particularly somebody Rongoni's age, as a red flag. It had certainly struck me at the time. I'd also thought the state cops would've surely figured out that if Val had in fact gone to meet up with somebody that night, Rongoni would have been the obvious candidate where it had to have been somebody she knew and would've felt safe with, and there weren't a whole lot of other possibilities. And if they knew Rongoni had a boat, which wasn't all that hard to discover, I figured they could've easily connected the dots by themselves, but it had finally reached the point where I had to do something myself where she sure as hell wasn't going to up and confess. So, I'd taken a shot to see if I could get it out of her myself, and it had worked.

As we sat there in the cruiser, she was shaking as she admitted she'd met up with Val that night on the Yacht Club dock. Once she'd gotten started, it had seemed to all just flow out. She told me she'd been sitting at home worried about her friend and the way she was throwing herself at McGruder, which Rongoni had thought was a huge mistake. And she'd wanted to talk with Val about college, but she'd had the sense Val had been avoiding her for some reason. It was a hot night, and she was cooped up alone in the house. Her parents were out in Longmeadow in the western part of the state where her grandfather lived.

169

He'd been taken to the hospital that afternoon, and her parents had rushed out there when they'd gotten the call, and she hadn't known when they'd be back or when she might hear from them. She'd thought maybe if she went out in the boat it would be cooler, and it would help take her mind off things, but it didn't and she kept getting more and more worked up as she rode out to the Sound. Finally, she decided she needed to confront Val and get it all out in the open. Knowing Val was on McGruder's boat and it was a calm night, she made a quick decision to head down the coast to the harbor, sticking close to the shore in case the weather changed. When she got to the harbor, she tied her boat up at the Yacht Club's outer dock and texted Val. According to Rongoni, Val was none too pleased to have her show up in the middle of the night like that. Rongoni went over their conversation on the dock, but left out the part about her telling Val she was gay, which wasn't exactly surprising. I had to press her to get that part out of her, and the fact that she'd been jealous of Val's relationship with McGruder, but all that was obviously important. Then, according to Rongoni, after they'd argued for a while, she'd left Val alone on the dock and gone home.

There was a silence. Then, I asked her, "Why didn't you tell the State Police all this?"

She looked at me nervously. "I was still in shock about her being murdered when they questioned me, and I, like, probably wasn't thinking straight. I wanted to stay out of it, and that conversation on the dock that night wasn't anybody's business and had nothing to do with her getting killed, it was personal between her and me. I wasn't trying to hide anything, I just didn't think it was, like, that big a deal. And I never thought anybody would find out about it. I thought we were alone out there that night. And she was fine when I left her there."

"The State Police are probably going to want to talk to you again," I said. She nodded. "Other than the State Police, you shouldn't talk with anybody else about this, understand?"

"I'll have to talk to my parents."

I nodded. "Okay. But nobody else. You can go now. Drive carefully."

She got out of the car without saying anything, walked back to her car, and got in and started it up. She put her blinker on, pulled out and drove off, glancing in her rearview mirror briefly as she pulled away.

I continued to sit there by the side of the road rolling things over in my mind. Okay, as I'd known all along, this was somebody who had: a motive—love, anger, jealousy; the opportunity—having lured the victim into meeting up with her alone late at night in a secluded place; and the means to dispose of her body—a boat. And who I'd now gotten to admit she'd lied about the last time she'd seen the victim. And who said she'd left the victim alone on the dock after their conversation, but the victim was never seen alive again afterward. It was amazing how the state cops had missed all this and I had to be the one who'd supposedly figured it all out.

I went back to the stationhouse and tried it out on Mullally. He listened to me in silence. When I was done, he sat there for a minute staring off into space. Finally, he turned to me with a grim expression on his face and said, "What a fucking mess."

"What's a mess?"

"The whole thing's a mess. Don't get me wrong, it all makes sense. But two girls who're close friends and just graduated from high school, going off to college together without a care in the world, and then all of a sudden one of them kills the other? I'm sorry, I know I'm getting old, but I'm almost not believing this."

"I know, it's hard to get your arms around."

"Why the fuck would she kill her best friend?"

"Crime of passion. She was in love with her friend, who was ditching her and taking off with somebody she despised. In a rage, she just lost it and killed her. Same as if they'd been boyfriend and girlfriend and she told the guy she was ditching him. Happens with some people, they just go berserk. Especially with kids. Adolescence, hormones, you read about plenty of cases like this."

He shook his head. "I guess so. Doesn't make the town look very good, though. I was hoping it'd been a stranger."

I shrugged. "What are you going to do? It's what the state cops said at the beginning, somebody who the victim knew."

"Still hard to believe."

"What do you want to do now?"

"We call those two shitheads, what else can we do?"

"They'll probably be happy."

"Well, it's not like the case is over. The girl says the victim was fine when she left her and went home in her boat, and then somebody else killed her afterward."

"Sure, she does, what do you expect her to say? But if she's got nothing to hide, why'd she lie about the whole thing in the first place? And she obviously knew the deceased had her car. She could've hit her friend over the head with an oar or something, dumped the body and come back and tied up at the dock, moved the car and then gone home in the boat. Not that many people actually knew about the car, and, remember, there were no unusual prints on it."

"Where were the girl's parents, for Christ's sake?"

"Out in Longmeadow. Her grandfather'd been taken to the hospital that day, and they'd gone out there. So she was home alone."

Mullally sighed. "You're starting to convince me."

"Kids do stupid things sometimes."

"Well, this is all up to our numb-nuts friends to figure out. All we're doing is giving them somebody with a motive, an opportunity and a means. At least that's a lot more than they had before today. They're the big time investigators, let them put the case together. Assuming there's a case."

The phone in Mullally's office had conference call and speaker phone capabilities but he'd never used either of them before because he had no idea how to do it. So, naturally, he put me in charge of dealing with the phone. I thought figuring out how the speaker phone worked would be easier than trying to sort out how to connect a call to another phone in the stationhouse, and we didn't want to be blabbing about this on a phone out in the common area anyway. To my surprise and relief, it turned out to be not all that difficult; all you had to do was push the button on the phone labelled "Speaker" and there was the dial tone. I dialed Balzano's cell phone, and we listened to it ring about six times before he finally picked up.

"It's Brian Bonner," I said at the phone in a loud voice. "Can you hear me? We're on the Chief's speaker phone."

"Jesus, you practically blew my eardrum out," he said. "For Christ's sake, you don't need to yell, I can hear you fine if you just talk in a normal voice."

"Is that better?"

"Yeah, but still too loud."

"Okay, how's that?"

"That's better. What's up?"

"I've got the Chief here with me."

"I figured. Hello, Chief."

"Hello," Mullally said. "We wanted to talk with you guys because we think maybe we have a breakthrough. Got a few minutes to talk or are you in the middle of something?"

"We've got a few minutes. We're in the car. What've you got?"

"I'll let Brian tell you about it." Mullally nodded at me.

I cleared my throat. "Okay, well, we've got a witness who's changed her story," I said. "Or at least she's telling us more than she did the first time around."

There was a silence on the line for a moment. Then, Balzano said, "Which witness?"

"Rongoni, the friend who loaned the victim her car."

There was another pause. Finally, Balzano said, "Okay, I take it you talked with her?"

"Yeah. I'd been thinking about the case and decided I'd go chat with her again."

"So what does she say now?"

"She's now owned up to the fact that she met up with the victim the night she disappeared. Sometime around midnight, she texted the victim on McGruder's boat that she needed to talk with her. The victim left the boat and went down to the Yacht Club and met up with Rongoni on the Yacht Club's dock that goes out into the Sound."

There was a pause. "Why out on the dock?"

"Because the victim had her car and Rongoni had come over from her house in a boat. Her family's got a Whaler, and she took the boat over, said it was a calm night."

"Interesting. Okay, what does she say happened on the dock?"

"The two of them had something like an argument. The victim told Rongoni she wasn't going to go to college and room with her, she was going to go to the University of South Carolina where McGruder goes. His old man was apparently going to get her in and get her a full ride scholarship. This apparently got Rongoni really upset, and she admitted to the victim she's gay and was in love with her."

There was another pause. Then, Balzano said, "Okay. So, what does she say happened then?"

"Rongoni says she got back into her boat and went home, leaving her friend standing there on the dock, and she supposedly never saw her friend again. Of course, neither did anybody else, as far as we know."

"Except the killer."

"Right. Unless Rongoni was the killer herself."

"Yeah, but why would she kill her best friend?"

"Maybe it was a crime of passion. The person she was in love with was dumping her for somebody else. They were alone there. In her emotional state, Rongoni could've easily whacked her over the head, put her in the boat, dumped her in the Sound, and then gone home."

"What about the plastic the victim was wrapped up in?"

"Who knows. Maybe she had it with her in the boat. And something to weigh the body down. Maybe the whole thing was premeditated."

"She would've had to've moved the car, too."

"Sure. To throw everybody off the track. She obviously knew the victim had her car and where it'd be parked. Most people, especially a stranger, wouldn't have known that, but she would've. So, after she dumped the victim's body she moved the car up by the bus station, walked back, and went home in the boat. That would explain why there were no unusual prints in the car. And why she didn't want to report her friend's disappearance to the police."

There was another silence on the line. "You still there?" I finally asked.

"Yeah, I was filling Jim in. We're talking. Give us a minute, I'm going to put you on hold."

"No problem," I said. "Do you want to call us back?"

"No, just hang on for a minute."

Mullally and I sat there staring at the phone. About three minutes went by, and then Balzano finally came back on. "Okay, like I said, this is all very interesting," he said, "but it's a little weird."

"How so?" I asked.

"Well, for one thing, high school girls don't usually kill their best friends. And they usually aren't clever enough to then cover up the crime the way the killer did here, either. And number two, people don't usually change their story all of a sudden to potentially incriminate themselves in a serious crime."

"I hear you," I said. "But as for your first point, these weren't your typical high school students, or maybe it'd be better to call them high school graduates. Rongoni was in love with the victim in a sexual way, and that kind of love has obviously been well known to cause somebody to murder somebody else. As for your second point, she didn't actually volunteer. Like I said, I went back and questioned her a second time. A third time actually because I'd also questioned her once before after you guys had talked to her."

"And she just told you all this? That's a little hard to believe, Brian. So, what'd you do to her? Slap her around?"

"Jesus, no, I didn't touch her, honest."

"That wasn't supposed to be serious. But I gotta' believe you did something to get her to talk some more, Brian. And I'm a little uneasy about what it was you did."

"Let's say I took a gamble."

"We don't like gambles," Balzano said.

"It wasn't much of a gamble, trust me. I just told her we had a witness who'd come forward since you interviewed her and who'd told us they'd seen her meet up with the victim that night over at the Yacht Club sometime around midnight."

"Do we have such a witness?"

"No."

"So you lied."

"Yeah, well, like I said it was a gamble. We did stuff like that in the Army all the time. Well, maybe not all the time, but at least a few times anyway. And it worked sometimes, like here. And it wasn't that big a gamble this time, really."

"Why not?"

"Well, I got to thinking about the victim telling the guys on the boat she was going to go somewhere and might or might not be back, and then she took off. So, I'm thinking, okay, somebody must've called her or texted her to get her to go somewhere, probably to meet up with them. Remember McGruder said he thought she'd gotten a text or something? And it must've been somebody she knew pretty well and who she would've felt safe meeting up with at that time of night. She supposedly didn't have a lot of friends at school, and it wasn't McGruder obviously, so who would be the most likely possibility? But I figured for them to meet up, the victim would've had to've driven back to Rongoni's house because she had Rongoni's car, which was one possibility. But then how did the car wind up at the bus station and Rongoni all the way back at her house? And I knew Rongoni had another means of transportation, her family has a Whaler, and it was a calm night and the Yacht Club is right there at the entrance to the harbor just down from McGruder's boat. So I took a gamble, and she talked."

"Interesting," Balzano said.

"Yeah, like I said, it was a gamble. But it worked, at least in getting a lot more out of her."

"More like a shot in the dark."

"Well, not quite but almost."

"Almost? The stuff about the victim getting a call or a text came from McGruder. He could've told us that to cover up for himself. Or for Dowling. Or the call or the text could've been completely innocent and nothing to do with her getting killed."

"Yeah, I hadn't thought about any of that. Maybe I was luckier than I thought."

"Okay, so you got lucky," Balzano said. "But she claims she left the victim on the dock and went home, and we don't have any evidence she didn't. So, where are we?"

Mullally jumped in before I could say anything. "Well, at least we've got somebody with a plausible motive, and the means and the opportunity. That's more than we had before this. Don't you guys at least want to do some follow-up? It seems like you have to."

"It sounds like you're telling us how to do our job," Balzano replied.

Mullally got red in the face. "Jesus, no, that's not what we're trying to do at all. This just seemed like a new development, that's all. That's why we called you."

There was a brief pause. Then, Balzano said, "Yeah, okay, I know you're trying to help. Let me talk to Jim here again for a minute."

We sat there in silence again for another forty seconds, and then Balzano came back on the line. "So, to make sure I've got this straight, what you're saying is this girl who's just graduated from high school kills her best friend who she was going to go off to college with because she's in love with her and finds out the friend is leaving her for somebody else. She dumps the body in the Sound, and then moves her own car that the friend had borrowed over by the bus station to throw everybody off, goes home in her boat, and then the next day goes driving around with somebody and, lo' and behold, they supposedly find the car where she'd actually left it herself the night before. She lies to us about not having seen her friend that night, and then when you make her think somebody saw her with her friend on the Yacht Club dock, she comes up with a new story and admits she actually did meet up with her friend on the dock that night but maintains after they'd had a conversation she left the friend alone on the dock and went home. Is that it?"

"Yeah, that's pretty much it," I said.

"Okay, based on that what're your thoughts on what we ought'a do next?"

"Can you get a search warrant based on this?" I asked.

"Maybe. It's a little thin, but this is a murder case so a judge may cut us some slack if it's not too broad. But looking for evidence a month after the crime has been committed isn't usually all that productive. You got something specific in mind?"

"What about a warrant to look at Rongoni's boat for forensics?"

There was a pause. "Let me talk to Jim for a minute. Hang on." We were on hold again for another minute. Then, Balzano came back on. "Yeah, that might work. I don't know what you'd find, though, especially where the boat's probably been outside all this time and been used at least a few times. Tough environment for the forensic guys to come up with anything you could link directly to this crime, but I suppose we need to cover that base. We'll get on it and keep you posted."

"Great," said Mullally . "We'll wait to hear from you."

"Probably be a couple days. That it for now?"

"I think so," Mullally said. "Good luck."

"We'll be talking," replied Balzano, and hung up.

I hit the speaker button on the phone again and the light went out. We sat there in silence for a minute, and then Mullally said angrily, "It sounds like you're telling us how to do our job. Well, somebody ought to, for Christ's sake. Jesus, how did we get those two fucking idiots."

I nodded. "Anyway, maybe something'll come of it. At least we've got grounds for a warrant. That's more than we've had up to this point."

"Yeah, a warrant for a forensics search outdoors a month after the crime. Great. If those two assholes had been doing their job, we would've had the warrant a long time ago and maybe an arrest. Now, who the fuck knows."

"Let's see what happens," I said.

That evening, I was scraping the remains of my frozen dinner into the garbage disposal when my cell phone vibrated. I looked at the number. It was her again. I ignored it and finished cleaning up. Then, I went into the bedroom, flopped on the bed, and played her voicemail.

"I assume you're avoiding me and don't intend to return my calls, so I'm going to stop. I'm not going to embarrass myself where you don't seem to have the decency to end things by telling me to my face. I'm not quite sure what I thought I saw in you, but you really shouldn't treat people this way. It's time you grew up. Have a nice life."

That's all I need right now, I thought to myself, and hit DELETE.

23

August 8, 2012 I was out in a cruiser when I got a call to come in to the stationhouse ASAP per the Chief's order. In four years, I'd never gotten a call like that before. It took me about ten minutes to get there with the blue lights and the siren on. Mullally was waiting for me in the common area. He didn't say anything but just motioned for me to follow him into his office. I went in and, out of reflex, closed the door behind me.

He sat down heavily in his chair and faced me. "The state cops are on their way here," he said flatly. "They said they want to talk to you about something."

"Any idea what?"

"I was going to ask you the same thing."

I shrugged and gave him a blank look. "Damned if I know."

"They were on the bridge when they called. Should be here any minute now. Sit down, we'll wait for them in here. Open the door so we can see them when they come in."

I opened the door and sat down. "They get the warrant?"

"They didn't say."

I nodded. We sat there in silence for about five minutes. The anxiety that had started to build up inside me after I'd gotten the radio call was excruciating, and I was afraid I was visibly shaking. Finally, after what had seemed like an eternity, I heard noise behind me. I turned around and saw Balzano and Cavanaugh coming through the outer door and through the office door Mullally waved them in. Of course, there weren't enough chairs, so I had to scramble back out into the common area and grab a chair, bring it in, and close the door again. Balzano and Cavanaugh were already seated. I wedged my chair in between them and sat down, trying to look as calm as I could.

"How you guys doin'?" Mullally asked.

"Okay, Chief," Balzano replied. "Been a busy couple of days. We've got some things to tell you, and then we've got some questions to ask Brian here."

"Floor is all yours," Mullally replied.

"We'll take this chronologically," Balzano said. "After we talked with you guys the other day, we talked with the D.A. and we were able to get a warrant to look at the friend's boat. Boat's a fourteen foot Whaler with an outboard, pretty standard. It has one of those slatted wooden floors you drop in. The first thing the forensic guys did was pull up the wooden floor and underneath they found a woman's earring. Silver. It's a match with the earing found on the victim's body when she was pulled out of the Sound. You may remember she was found with one earring missing."

Mullally leaned forward. "Jesus," he said.

"Yeah, pretty interesting. At that point, the forensic guys really went to work, went over the boat with a microscope, scraped off the surface material wherever there was the slightest discoloration, you name it. It all turned up blank except for the earring."

"So what do you make of it?" Mullally asked, still leaning forward on his desk.

Balzano and Cavanaugh exchanged glances. "Well," Balzano said, "it's pretty strong evidence the victim was in her friend's boat on the night in question. There's no evidence she was near the boat any time earlier that day, and, anyway, if she'd lost the earring sometime earlier in the day it's highly unlikely she'd still have been walking around at that hour of the night wearing only one earring. Maybe she got into the boat that night and then got back out and lost her earring in the process somehow, but that seems a little hard to imagine. She had pierced ears and those kind don't fall off that easily. So, like I said, it's an interesting piece of evidence. And the fact that it's the only evidence she was in the boat that night isn't all that surprising considering, as we talked about before, the boat's been outside for a month and probably been used at least a few times."

"Have we got enough to arrest the friend?" Mullally asked. "Sounds like it."

"Yeah, well, unfortunately it seems there's a bit of a problem on that end. That's why we need to talk to Brian here. I guess after she talked to Brian, she went home and told her parents, and her parents got her a lawyer. The lawyer's name is Lindsay Workman. She's from Boston. Used to be a prosecutor before she went over to the dark side to make some real money. Smart lady. She was present when we examined the boat and found the earring. She called the D.A. later in the day after she'd apparently talked with her client and told him we've got a problem with the warrant and the earring."

Mullally screwed up his face. "What kind of a problem?"

"According to Ms. Workman, when her client told the police about meeting with the victim on the dock that night and potentially incriminated herself, she'd been taken into custody but not informed of her of her rights, including particularly her right to remain silent and her right to consult with an attorney before answering any questions. Ms. Workman told the D.A. she's going to move immediately to have the warrant revoked and any evidence obtained under the warrant suppressed, and going forward she will vigorously fight any attempt to show that her client contacted the victim or was anywhere near her that night."

"What does the D.A. say?" Mullally asked, his voice rising. "Can she get away with that?"

"The D.A. didn't need to tell us anything we didn't already know, although he did anyway, probably because he's royally pissed. Yes, she can in all likelihood get away with that. And we're royally pissed, too. It's partly my fault. When we were on the phone the other day, I should've asked Brian more about how this all happened. Witnesses don't usually show up on your doorstep to incriminate themselves, and I think I said that at the time. I even joked about it, asked if he'd slapped her around or something. But I should've gotten the specifics of what happened before we went for the warrant and made sure we were on solid ground."

Mullally turned and faced me, his face beet red. "Brian, what the fuck did you do? You take her into custody before you talked to her?" He was spitting saliva all over the place.

All eyes were on me now. There was a silence for a moment. Finally, I said, "I may've fucked up."

Balzano stared at me. "So tell us, Brian, what'd you do?"

"Well, like I said, I put two and two together about Rongoni probably having been the one who contacted the victim to meet up with her, and when the victim left McGruder's boat it had to've been to go meet her friend somewhere, and she had Rongoni's car. So, Rongoni had to've come over in her boat. So, like I said, I lied a little bit and told her we had a witness that had the two of them together that night after the victim left McGruder's boat, and she believed me because she actually had met up with the victim that night."

Balzano frowned. "So where did this conversation with Rongoni take place, Brian?"

"In the cruiser. We were sitting in the cruiser when she told me."

"How did she wind up in the cruiser?"

"I stopped her on the road when she was on her way to work that morning."

"You pulled her over. Was she actually speeding or anything?"

"Maybe a little over the speed limit, I don't know."

"So you pulled her over, although you can't prove she was speeding. Did you put your blue lights on?" I nodded. "And you pulled in behind her? And then what happened?"

"I asked her to get out of the car."

"You asked her or you told her?"

"I think I said, 'please get out of the car and come with me.' Something like that."

Balzano nodded. "Then what happened?"

"She got out and followed me back to the cruiser, and that's where the conversation took place."

"Did you ask for her license and registration?"

"No. She asked me if I wanted them and I told her no, I just wanted to talk with her."

"So, you didn't cite her for any traffic violation?"

"No."

"And then you had this conversation where you told her you had a witness who'd seen her and her friend together that night? The night her friend was murdered?"

"Right."

"Which wasn't true."

"Right."

"Any emotional reaction on her part during all this?"

"Yeah, she was pretty nervous. She was shaking when she told me her story. And she cried at one point. She was pretty upset."

"You threaten her at all?"

"I told her lying to the police could get her into serious trouble. Maybe I mentioned jail time, I don't know. That was it."

"And what happened after she'd told you her story?"

"I think I told her at that point she could go and you'd probably want to talk to her again, but not to talk with anybody else about it except maybe her parents."

"No citation?"

"No."

"And this entire conversation took place while the two of you were in the car?"

"That's right."

"And at any time during this whole thing did you ever read her her rights?"

"No."

"Any reason why not?"

"I guess it never occurred to me."

Balzano looked at Cavanaugh, who had a grim expression on his face. Then, he turned to Mullally and said, "We're fucked."

Mullally nodded grimly and glared at me. "Brian, when you stopped her and had her get out of her car and get into the police cruiser, you took her into custody as a potential suspect. At that point, you needed to've read her her rights before you asked her anything about the case."

"Exactly," Balzano said. "If you'd cited her for a speeding violation or something, maybe we could've made a half-assed argument your questioning her was the result of your stopping her, but I doubt that would've gone anywhere anyway. And if this were to go to a hearing, you'd have to admit that, although you believed she was a suspect, you didn't read her her rights, you lied to her, you threatened her, and she was visibly upset, which is clear evidence of duress, and it was only at that point that she talked. The judge would be looking at us like we were the stupidest fucking idiots on the planet."

"What if I said I did read her her rights?" I said. "Maybe I actually did and I've just forgotten."

Balzano slowly shook his head. "We don't play games, Brian, particularly not in murder cases. There's only one way to do this job. My father and my uncle were both cops and they taught me early on you don't cut corners. Ever. We can't put the fucking toothpaste back in the tube, Brian." Out of the corner of my eye, I saw Cavanaugh nodding in agreement.

Mullally looked like he'd just swallowed a huge turd. "So, we know who did it and we won't be able to prove it. Is that it?"

"Well, we've got an idea who did it," Balzano said, "but the earring by itself isn't conclusive. I wouldn't want to go into the courtroom with just the earring and nothing else, but it is a pretty significant piece of evidence."

"So what are you going to do now?" Mullally asked.

"That's a good question. Jim and I need to talk about it some more and we need to talk with the D.A., find out exactly what the parameters of the investigation can be going forward. My first instinct is to go back over every detail of the case, the forensics, everything, and see if we can find another link between the suspect and the crime somewhere else. Maybe something will fall out, who knows. Like maybe the rope the victim was tied up with or something like that. We just have to keep digging."

"What do you want us to do in the meantime?"

"You guys stand down for the time being. Don't do anything until you hear from us." Balzano and Cavanaugh stood up.

Mullally nodded. "Okay." He stood up and I followed him up.

"We'll be in touch, Chief," Balzano said, opening the office door. No handshakes. Cavanaugh nodded to us as he followed Balzano out.

We watched them go through the common area and out the door. Then, I turned to Mullally, but it was as if he didn't want to look at me. I figured he was probably thinking about what he was going to have to tell the selectmen, and whatever he wound up telling them wasn't going to go down very well. He probably figured it wasn't worth chewing me out at that point. I didn't know what to say, and figured there probably wasn't anything I could say that would help. *Let it go*, I thought to myself. So, I picked up the chair I'd brought in and left him alone in his office.

It was obviously time for me to get the hell out of Dodge. I'd created the clear impression I was the world's biggest fuck-up and too stupid even to be a Cape Cod cop, and now the State Police were stuck with trying to come up with the goods on the prime suspect in the case with one hand tied behind their backs legally thanks to me. Mullally undoubtedly wanted me gone, and nothing would've make him happier than to have me resign so I wouldn't be around to remind him every day of how his department had royally screwed up the biggest case it'd ever had. So the timing of my departure would be perfect and not raise any suspicions, which was exactly what I'd hoped.

24

July 8, 2012 My knees and the palms of my hands were killing me from kneeling in the gravel behind the wall for so long, and I realized I'd been sweating heavily and my shirt was soaked. My back was starting to ache and I was dying to stand up, but I wanted to be absolutely sure they were gone. Finally, after a few more minutes had passed and it was still totally quiet, I slowly stood up and began to brush the dirt off my knees and hands. I was facing the dock and when I finally looked up, I found myself looking straight at Val, who was standing motionless on the dock staring out into the Sound with her back to me. Horrified, I froze.

I must have made some kind of a noise because suddenly she whirled around like she'd been struck by something from behind. "Who's that?" she said in a startled voice. "Oh, my God, Brian, what are you freakin' doing here?" Unable to speak or move, I just stood there. "Jesus Freakin' Christ, Brian, you've been stalking me, haven't you?" Her voice was now shrill. "I can't freakin' believe this. I've had a feeling you were following me around. And you're a freakin' cop, for God's sake. Really nice, Brian, way to go. I bet they'll love to hear about this down at the police station. You stay right where you are and don't you dare come near me, or I'm going to start screaming."

I took a deep breath and tried to think. Finally, I said, "Look, Val, I'm sorry. I was up by the park in my car trying to cool off from the heat, and I saw you get off the boat and come down here, and I was worried about you so I came down here after you, that's all."

"Sure, Brian, your police buddies'll definitely believe that one," she said, the contempt thick in her voice. "And that you're not a freakin' pervert. Sure, Brian, I'm sure you can explain it all. And then I'll tell them what I've got on you."

"Val, I'm not a fucking pervert, for Christ's sake, that's bullshit."

"Weirdo, pervert, stalker, whatever. All I know is, I don't ever want to see you again, ever. Now, I'm giving you exactly three seconds to disappear out of my life forever or I'm going to call the freakin' cops on my cell phone. And if I ever see your ugly face again, you're fucking toast, you understand? God, this is weirdo night for sure."

"Okay, Val, I get it, you don't have to call anybody. You'll never see me again ever, believe me. But I just want to ask you one question."

"Ask me what? You expect I'm going to stand out here all night playing stupid games with you?"

"The nights out in Hyannis, the inn, what was that all about?"

She laughed sarcastically. "Oh, Brian, you poor dumb schmuck. You still think that was real, don't you, you poor jerk." I stared at her blankly. "God, you men are so stupid. A woman lets you have a peek down her blouse and you immediately fall in love. Oh, my God. Do you have any idea how much I make in tips at the diner just acting sweet and showing off a little skin? Probably more than a cocktail waitress, and I'm just serving coffee, for Christ's sake. All those horny creeps that come in there and think I'm their girlfriend, they're so totally disgusting. And you fell for it like the rest of them."

"So it was all an act?"

"In your case it wasn't all an act. I needed you. Well, I didn't need you, I needed a driver. And a bodyguard. And you were perfect. I needed somebody to take me to some places in Hyannis I didn't want to go by myself. And there you were with all those muscles and a gun. And if things got hairy, a badge. All I had to do was get you to go with me, and that wasn't exactly hard."

"I still don't get it."

"You don't get it? You're a cop, Brian, for Christ's sake, figure it out. Somebody was paying me to go to those places and drop something off. Places where I didn't want to go alone."

"Drugs."

"That's the first intelligent thing you've said all night, Brian."

"Where'd you get the stuff? Who were you working for?"

"That's none of your freakin' business."

"What the hell were you doing in the drug business? There're a lot of bad people in that business. And you could've gotten caught, for Christ's sake."

"Why does anybody get into the drug business, for God's sake? For the money, you dumb shit. I needed money and that was the only way I was going to be able to get it. You don't really know what it's like to be poor, do you? I mean really poor, like you don't know what you're going to eat that night. Especially in a town like this with all those rich people around. I've been living that way all my life and I can't stand it anymore. People like you and everybody else around here would never understand, and I'm not going to try to explain it to you now."

"You were delivering drugs and you brought a cop?"

"Nobody was ever going to know you were a cop. Unless of course it was absolutely necessary. And you thought you were out on a freakin' date, for Christ's sake. I can't believe you never figured it out. I guess you were too in love."

"What if I'd figured it out? Weren't you afraid I'd turn you in?"

"Turn me in? Ha, that's a good one. What do you think I am, Brian, stupid? In the first place, you were too in love to turn me in. Here you were a cop with all those muscles and it turns out you were really just a little boy. I couldn't believe it, it was like you were still in the seventh grade and I was your very first heartthrob. It was actually embarrassing. And even if you hadn't been in love, you never would've turned me in anyway because if you'd tried, you were the one who would've gone down. You were my get-out-jail-free card."

"What the fuck is that supposed to mean?" I asked, coming slowly through the hedge to the walkway.

"Think about it, Stupid, you're a cop. Here's this poor eighteen year old girl who needs money to support her mother and go to college and who gets sweet talked into being a drug mule by a crooked cop who didn't want to get caught carrying the shit himself. So he drives her to the drop-offs and she does the dirty work. And he's forcing her to have sex with him on the side. So, maybe throw in a rape charge to go with the drugs. No, Brian, you weren't ever going to turn me in. Ever."

I stepped across the walkway and down onto the dock, and faced her. "So that's why you went to bed with me?"

"No, not entirely. I'll admit, the first time I thought I'd at least give it a try, see if I could get some fun out of it. You've got all those muscles and everything, and I was hoping they'd turn me on. So I picked a place I thought would maximize the pleasure part. A really nice place, the kind of place I'm going to be able to go on my own someday without having to fuck somebody. But you didn't rise to the occasion, Brian. Here I was, all sexed up and everything and ready to give you the freakin' time of your poor, dull life, and you freakin' passed out on me, for God's sake. I mean ice cold. Jesus, that was a first for me. I don't know whether it was the ecstasy and the booze, or whether you're just dysfunctional or something. Maybe I should've given you Cialis instead, like a major dose. And then when you finally woke up, you actually thought you'd gotten laid. Like in your dreams. But anyway, it got you to keep coming back for more."

I stared at her blankly.

"The main reason I did it, though, was to get a sample of your DNA to prove you'd raped me if I needed to, but that clearly wasn't going to happen that night. So I had to wait 'til the next time and do it the old fashioned way like in high school. But maybe you weren't that lucky in high school, maybe you had to do it yourself back then. You're probably still doing it yourself now. That is, if you can get it up, for God's sake. Of course, after I got some of your sperm, I didn't need to fake it any more, I knew you'd do what I wanted even if you woke up, which of course you never did. Then, I met somebody I figured had more potential and less risk than the drug business, which also meant I didn't need you. I thought I'd gotten rid of you, but I guess you didn't want to let go."

I shook my head. "You're really something."

She gave me a cruel smile. "Yes, Brian, I'm really something, and I'm going to get what I want and I'm almost there, and then I won't have to deal with losers like you anymore. So get out of my fucking life, Brian, I don't ever want to see you again, ever. Just stay far, far away from me or so help me God you'll regret it. Face it, Brian, you're just a dysfunctional loser and you always will be. Now, get the fuck out of here before I call your buddies down at the station."

I suddenly felt an uncontrollable rage come over me. It was like I went numb. I swung my right fist at her as hard as I could and hit her flush in the side of the face. The blow knocked her off her feet and down onto the dock. Her head hit something with the sound of a carton of eggs being dropped. She lay there motionless. I stood over her for a minute looking for some sign of life, and then I knelt down beside her. It was then I saw that her head must've hit one of the metal cleats on the edge of the dock, and I could see blood on the boards under her head. I rolled her partially over and checked her vital signs, although I'd seen enough combat casualties to know right away she was dead. I knelt there for a moment staring at her disfigured face. Then, I stood up. It was completely quiet with no sign anybody'd seen or heard anything. I looked out over the darkened Sound, and at that moment I had a flashback.

During the short time I was in New Hampshire before I moved to the Cape, I met a woman named Beth, who was a bartender at a place called The Growler a couple towns over from Lakeville, where I was on the local force. She was a cute, sexy creature with long dark hair, dark eyes, a slim, youthful body, and a large tattoo of a beautiful butterfly on the back of her left shoulder. She was a free spirit with a mischievous smile and had a popular following at the bar. I'd stop there a couple nights a week to have a beer and chat with her, and, as I gradually got to know her, found out she was single and lived alone. I would've loved to have asked her out, but I could never quite get up the courage, figuring I'd just bide my time and let things play out for a while, hoping maybe something might develop over time. I decided early on not to tell her I was a cop, figuring it might be a turnoff, so I told her I drove a truck for a company in Manchester. She was always friendly toward me and we seemed to get along great, and gradually over time I began to think of her as being like a girlfriend, although she obviously wasn't. But just back from Iraq and living in a place where I didn't have a lot of friends, I was probably drawn to her mainly because of her warmth and her femininity, something that had been missing in my life, and her flirtatious charm. In my mind, she was like the woman I'd always hoped I'd find during all those long, lonely nights in Iraq, although down deep I think I knew I was probably just kidding myself.

It was a Friday night, the last Friday of the month and The Growler was busier than usual so I hadn't had much chance to talk with her, although I was enjoying myself just sitting there watching her move around behind the bar in a tight pair of jeans and a sexy top as she waited on customers. Finally, when there was a lull she came over and we chatted for a few minutes. Then, she asked me if I wanted to join an after-hours poker game that night, something they apparently did on the last Friday of every month after everybody'd gotten paid. She said you needed $150 to play. I told her I wasn't much of a poker player and $150 was a lot of money, and I'd undoubtedly lose it all. She smiled and said the $150 was actually the entry fee with everybody then playing for a special grand prize. I told her it must be a pretty good prize. She smiled slyly and replied, yeah, it is, it's me. I looked at her blankly for a moment, at first not understanding what she meant. She chuckled at my seeming bewilderment. Yeah, she said, I make the winner's dreams come true in the men's room after the game's over. You interested in playing?

At first, I was too stunned to respond, but the look on my face must've said it all. The smile disappeared from her face, replaced by a hardened look I'd never seen before. I never thought you were like that, I said, but I guess appearances can be deceiving. I'm sorry if you're offended, she replied, dripping with sarcasm. If you don't like it here then get the fuck out. At that point, we were starting to cause a scene, and a couple burly guys standing nearby at the bar and overhearing our last exchange took a couple steps in my direction so that I was surrounded, and it looked like things might turn ugly in a hurry. I thought about the gun under my jacket and the badge in my pocket, but let it go. Thanks for the memories, I said. I tossed a ten dollar bill on the bar and walked out.

I sat in my car outside trying to clear my head. I realized then how much I had invested in her emotionally. *You stupid shit,* I thought to myself. Finally, I started the car up and headed for Lakeville, but half way there for some reason I turned around and went back. There was about an hour to go until closing time when I pulled back in. I sat there in a dark corner of the parking lot, waiting. Finally, a few customers came out and after they were gone the outside lights were turned off, although the lights were still on inside. I waited a few minutes, and then got out of the car and went over to a window on the side of the building and looked in. A large table had been set up in the middle of the room, and there were nine guys sitting around it with one guy dealing the cards. She was standing behind him leaning over his shoulder watching, a grin on her face like she was actually enjoying what was going on. *Hey,* I thought to myself, *she should, scoring a grand and a half for one trick, although she probably has to pay the owner of the bar something, too.*

They played eight hands with the guy with the worst hand eliminated each time until there was a winner, a fat guy with a beard who looked like he was in his forties and worked construction. There was a lot of loud swearing and insults that I could hear outside as he put down his winning hand. The winner stood up and looked at her, and I thought he was going to pull it out of his pants right there. She laughed when she saw who it was, and then beckoned to him as she started towards the men's room in the back swinging her hips for effect. Whatever she did for him didn't take long, and the two of them were treated to loud cheers when they reappeared after about ten minutes, all smiles. As the poker players all crowded around the winner, slapping him on the back, I saw her go to the bar and pour herself a glass of something and slug it down. *Probably to get rid of the taste,* I thought to myself, *and kill any bacteria.* Finally, things started to break up, and I walked quickly back to my car and got in. The guys came out in twos and threes, and got into their vehicles and drove off, leaving mine the only car left in the lot. *Her car must be around back,* I thought to myself.

I took my police flashlight and got out, and walked around to the rear of the building. Sure enough, there was a car parked there, a five year old Mazda SUV. I stood there in the dark a few feet from the car, waiting. After about ten minutes, the last lights inside were turned off and she came out. I watched her as she locked the door behind her and started for her car. I flipped on the flashlight, and her hand went up to shield her eyes. "Nice haul for fifteen minutes work," I said. "What'd you do for him?" I'd obviously startled her, but she quickly recovered.

"What the fuck are you doing here," she asked, her hand still shielding her eyes, "looking to get some without paying?" She slowly took her hand down, and I saw her slide it into her bag. *Mace*, I thought. *Or maybe something sharp.* We were about ten feet apart.

"No," I said, "I wouldn't want to catch anything."

"You better get the fuck out of here before I start screaming," she said.

"Go ahead if you think anybody can hear you," I told her. She pulled her hand back out of her bag, and I saw the eight inch switchblade snap open. "You won't need that," I said, "I'm a cop." I pulled my badge out and held it up in front of her, shining the flashlight on it.

She stared at it for a moment and then looked back at me. "Jesus Fucking Christ," she said, "and to think I once thought you were a nice guy. You going to arrest me? That'll be a hoot."

I shook my head. "No," I told her, "I just wanted to let you know you're going to be out of business after tonight."

I watched her slowly collapse the blade on the knife and put it back in her bag as a smile came over her face. "You shouldn't be too hasty," she said, "I bet we could work something out." She slowly took a couple steps forward until she was right in front of me. Then, she reached out and put her hand on my crotch. "Is there something you'd like that would make us friends again?"

At that moment, I lost it. It was like I blanked out. I swung my right hand around as hard as I could and smashed her on the side of the head with the flashlight, and she went down in a heap at my feet.

All this was racing through my mind as I stood there in the darkness staring down at Val's body lying crumpled on the dock at my feet. It was almost as if I'd been there before. *Why do I keep doing this, what's wrong with me?* My brain was working feverishly now. *Okay, you got out of it the last time, take your time and think it through.* Of course, it'd be pretty hard to claim it'd just been an accident where even the dumbest medical examiner on the planet could tell she'd been hit in the face before her head hit the metal cleat. And how was I going to explain being there in the first place? And then there was New Hampshire, too, if somebody started checking around. And I wasn't particularly excited about going to prison as an ex-cop. Standing there looking down at the lifeless form at my feet, I knew I was totally fucked and there was no way I could just turn myself in.

There are three possible ways to get away with killing somebody, or at least give yourself a fighting chance to get away with it: make the body and the fact of the crime disappear; make it look like somebody else did it; or, disappear yourself. I had to make a quick decision and standing there looking out at

Vineyard Sound in the dark, the first alternative seemed at that moment to be the best if I could pull it off. It was completely quiet with the humidity still blocking out the moon and the stars. I saw one lone boat light out on the Sound that looked like it was a couple miles away. Still no sign anybody had seen or heard anything. I looked at my watch; it was a little after 1:00 am. If McGruder or anybody was going to come looking for her, they probably would've showed up by now, although of course I couldn't be absolutely sure of that. The obvious solution was to dump her in the Sound in deep water, which meant I needed a boat, and it dawned on me I knew where I could get one.

I left the body on the dock and half jogged and half ran back up to the darkened Yacht Club, and went around to the inside dock where the Club's launch was tied up in its usual spot. I was praying the key for it was in its usual spot, hanging on the wall inside the door of the shed at the end of the dock. I went into the shed and in the darkness felt along the wall inside the doorframe. Presto, there was the key on a leather chord hanging on a hook just inside the door. I pulled the key off the hook. There was a small wooden block on the chord with the word "Launch" written on it with a black marker, just like when I'd driven it in the summer back in high school. I looked around and saw a big sheet of plastic bunched up on the floor in a corner of the shed and I grabbed that as well, thinking I'd wrap the body up in it. Somehow, I couldn't see just dropping her in the Sound without covering her up. Strange how the mind works sometimes.

I went back out onto the dock and put the plastic sheet into the launch, and then got in and started it up. The noise of the engine in the still night air had never seemed so loud. I backed the launch away from the dock as I'd done probably a thousand times before, swung it around and headed for the harbor entrance with the lights off and keeping the throttle as low as possible to try to minimize the noise. I went out through the channel and swung the launch around to the outside dock, where I got out and tied the launch up to one of the cleats, letting the engine idle. I spread the plastic sheet out on the dock. Then, I carried the lifeless body over and gently placed it on the sheet trying hard not to look at her face. After I put her down on the sheet, I felt in the front pocket of her jeans and pulled out her car keys. Then, I wrapped the plastic around her and placed her gently on the floor of the launch.

I needed something to weigh her down so she'd sink to the bottom, and I'd thought of that as well. There was a small anchor with a line on it that nobody ever used in a compartment tucked under the bow of the launch. It was supposedly there because of some safety regulation. I figured it'd be a long time before anybody noticed it was missing, and at that point it was unlikely anybody would ever connect it to her disappearance. I climbed into the launch, pulled the anchor out, and wrapped the plastic sheet tightly around her with the anchor line, leaving about six feet of slack between the anchor and the body. By now, I was totally drenched with sweat. I started to untie the launch and then stopped, thinking it'd probably be a good idea to take one last look around the dock to make sure I hadn't left anything behind. My eyes were well accustomed to the darkness by now, and I walked slowly around scanning the dock. It occurred to me that I should splash some water on the cleat she'd hit her head on and the boards around it to make sure nobody noticed any blood there the next day. Then, as I was about to get back into the launch, I saw a small shiny object on one of the boards of the dock giving off a faint gleam in the darkness. I bent over and picked it up. It was one of her earrings. I stuffed it into my pocket, figuring I'd slide it inside the plastic sheet when I dropped her in the water. I untied the launch and climbed in, and headed out into the Sound in the darkness. There were still no boat lights anywhere close by.

I figured about half a mile out was far enough. When I got out that far, I cut the engine and let it idle. The sea was still calm. I picked her up one last time and placed her in the water, and then stood there for a moment staring at the plastic sheet floating below me in the calm ocean. Finally, I picked up the anchor and slipped it over the side. In an instant, the plastic sheet disappeared out of sight. I stood there for another minute thinking about it all, but then I caught myself. I still had a lot to do.

I drove the launch back to the Yacht Club and tied it back up where I'd found it. It was now about 2:00 am. I put the key back on its hook in the shed and thought about what to do with her car. I didn't have a lot of options, but I wanted to at least get it away from the harbor so any later investigation wouldn't focus there. Making my way back up to the parking lot in the dark, I could see the lights were out on McGruder's boat, and there were no other lights anywhere except in the boatyard across the harbor. I went to the trunk of my car, where, like most cops, I kept a box of disposable plastic gloves. I put on a pair and got into her car and drove out. I knew I couldn't go very far because I'd have to walk back to get my own car. Parking her car near the bus station would at least take the focus away from the harbor and maybe create the impression she'd taken off somewhere on a bus. I knew there was a video cam in the bus station's parking lot, so I left the car on the street and then walked back to the harbor. I threw the plastic gloves in a dumpster I passed where there was some construction work going on. A couple cars passed me on the walk back but nobody paid any attention to me.

I got back to my car and drove home. I stripped off everything I had on, went over everything to make sure there was no blood anywhere, threw it all in the wash, and then jumped into the shower. After I got out of the shower, I figured I'd wait for my clothes to finish drying before I got into bed, hoping that by then my nerves would've calmed down a little. When the dryer finally stopped and I pulled the clothes out, I saw something shiny in the bottom of the dryer. I reached in and pulled out the earring, which I'd forgotten to get rid of when I'd disposed of the body. I stared at it for a moment. It was obviously an incriminating piece of evidence, and my immediate thought was to go dump it somewhere. But as I thought about it, it dawned on me maybe the earring might be useful someday, so I went outside with a flashlight and buried it against the foundation of the cottage. It stayed there until the night after we talked with Balzano and Cavanaugh about getting a warrant to search Rongoni's boat, when I dug it back up again.

Planting the earring in Rongoni's boat was easy. I waited until the deadest time of night, around 3:00 am. I put on a pair of black jeans, a black hoodie I'd purchased for the occasion, and a pair of black sneakers. I'd thought about painting my face black like we did for night exercises in the Army, but that shit is hard to get off and I figured it might be a little hard to explain if I unexpectedly ran into somebody along the way. I parked my car down the street from Val's mother's house where the road dead-ended at the marsh and put on a pair of plastic gloves just to make sure I didn't leave any prints anywhere. The neighborhood was completely quiet. My biggest worry was that somebody's stupid mutt would hear me and start barking, but my luck held. Val's house and the other houses on the street were all completely dark. The Rongonis' yard was wide open to the street, and I just went across the lawn and around to the back of the house where the Whaler was tied up to their dock. I walked out onto the dock, dropped the earring into the bottom of the boat, and quickly retraced my steps back to the car. Mission accomplished.

25

August 9, 2012 The next day, I went in and told Mullally I was resigning. I told him I was sorry I'd fucked things up so badly, and figured it'd be best for everybody if I left. I told him I'd been thinking about getting away from the Cape anyway, maybe going down to Florida and looking around for a job down there to give myself a fresh start. I thanked him for everything he'd done for me and told him I'd learned a lot from him, and maybe I'd see him in Florida after he retired. He didn't say much, just about what I was owed and that I needed to turn in the Glock and my badge, which I handed over to him. There was no handshake; he didn't even want to look at me. I just stood there for a minute, and then, after an embarrassing silence, I turned and walked out. A check was cut for me at the town hall, and I went from there to the bank and cashed it and cleaned out my modest savings account, and then went home to pack. That night, I told the couple I'd rented the cottage from I had to leave the next day because of a family emergency, and they could keep my deposit to cover any shortfall while they rented the place out again. They told me they were sorry to see me go as I'd been a good tenant, and they wished me luck with the family emergency.

I spent the evening cleaning out my stuff and packing. I wanted to travel light, with everything in one duffle bag. I put everything else, which wasn't much, in trash bags to be picked up in the morning by the trash truck. There was one item I'd kept in the bottom drawer of the dresser that I didn't know what to do with. When I was just about done packing, I pulled it out and set it down carefully on the bed. It was my bronze star and the citation for it that I'd had framed when I got back from Iraq. I stood there looking down at it and read the citation for the hundredth time.

March 22, 2007, Bagdad, Republic of Iraq. The First Platoon of the Military Police Company, Second Battalion, First Army Division was on a mission in the City

194

of Bagdad in the Republic of Iraq to provide backup support for another unit of the division that had come under intense enemy fire. En route to the scene, the High Mobility Multipurpose Wheeled Vehicle in which Corporal Brian Bonner and other members of his squad were riding detonated an explosive device that had been planted in the street. The explosion toppled the vehicle, throwing Corporal Bonner out onto the street where he sustained multiple fractures and other serious injuries. In the face of extreme danger and without regard to his own life, Corporal Bonner was able to crawl to the vehicle, which was overturned and in flames, and, one by one, managed to extricate two of his fellow squad members from the burning vehicle, both of whom were severely injured and one of whom was unconscious, while sustaining severe burn injuries himself to multiple parts of his body. Corporal Bonner's extraordinary courage on this occasion saved the lives of his two fellow squad members. His conduct was exemplary and in keeping with the highest standards of service to his country, and in recognition of his bravery Corporal Brian Bonner is awarded the Bronze Star Medal for Valor. Dated: April 16, 2007

When I'd had it framed, I figured it was maybe something I could show my grandkids, if I ever had any. I stared at it for another minute. It wasn't going to fit in the duffle bag and I couldn't see myself carrying it where I was going, so I finally stuffed it into one of the trash bags. Then, I took the trash out, came back in and went to bed.

Not wanting to leave anything to chance, I had a plan I'd been working on since the night I dropped her in the Sound, and that plan was, when the time was right, to disappear. Of course, I had no intention of going to Florida or anywhere near there. I'd spent a lot of time on the internet and my plan was to head in the opposite direction. If they ever came looking for me, I didn't know how much effort they'd put into it but I wasn't going to take any chances. I only wished I had more money, which would've made getting away a whole lot easier. I was going to drive to Canada and sell my car, which would've stuck out like a sore thumb with a Massachusetts plate on it. Then, I was going to use the money to buy a ticket, in cash, to go across Canada by rail to Vancouver, maybe get on and off a couple times along the way to hopefully confuse things. In Vancouver, I was hoping to pick up some menial job on a freighter headed south to Latin America that would hopefully get me out of Canada without having to show a passport. Then, I'd jump ship somewhere in Central America, maybe Panama, again hopefully without having to show a passport, assume a new identity, and find a job in some third world Central American country, maybe someplace at one of the beaches where they needed help who spoke English, and hopefully live the Margueritaville life for a while, maybe with a girlfriend, until I figured it was safe to go back to the States, although I knew I'd probably never go back to the Cape. The plan wasn't ideal, but it sure as hell beat going to prison if anybody ever got around to figuring the whole thing out, which was still a possibility.

In hindsight, maybe I should've taken off after I'd dropped her in the Sound, but I never thought the body would ever surface the way it did. Sure, I probably should've checked the anchor line more closely, but it was dark, and, anyway, I didn't exactly have a lot of spare rope lying around. When the body had turned up, I was afraid leaving then would've looked suspicious, so I decided to hang around and bide my time, and see where the investigation might lead. When Mullally had asked for a volunteer to work on the case, I'd jumped at it, figuring that was the best way to keep track of what was going on. At first, it didn't appear anybody could link me with Val, but once the drug thing with Marty Blair surfaced I couldn't take any chances. If they'd kept following the drug trail and talked to people at any of the places we'd gone together, they might've stumbled on the fact that Val had had an escort who looked like a body builder when she'd made some of her deliveries; and, of course, there also would've been a credit card record at the inn. So when the drug thing turned up, I figured I'd better move quickly. I'd known from the beginning I might need to try to set somebody up as the perpetrator if things started to get close to me, and Rongoni had seemed all along like the obvious choice, especially where she'd been stupid enough to lie the first time she was interviewed. At first, I'd stayed away from her, hoping the state cops would figure out she was the most likely person Val would've gone to meet up with that night, but after the Marty Blair thing surfaced I figured I had to force the issue. At that point, my plan had been to try to set it up so they were pretty sure it was her but couldn't prove it. And forgetting to get rid of the earring when I dumped the body had obviously turned out to be a stroke of good luck. Balzano and Cavanaugh weren't the brightest pair in the world, but, like I said, I wasn't about to take any chances. There were just a few too many loose ends I couldn't tie up. One thing I had going for me, though, was that I was a cop, which made me the last person anybody'd suspect of anything, something I'd learned long ago with the New Hampshire thing. And at least with that one, her body was never going to be found, I'd made sure of that.

Did I feel sorry for what I'd done? Yeah, sure, for what it'd done to my life, not that being a small town cop and living alone was much of a life. But now I was about to take off essentially on the run and with no money, and I'd pretty much fucked things up for myself, at least for a long time to come. Did I feel sorry about Val? Yeah, about the Val I'd fantasized about all those nights, but that hadn't been the real Val. No, the real Val had been a manipulative bitch who'd used a lot of people besides me, and it wasn't like she was now some kind of lost love or anything. After all the fantasizing I'd done about her, it'd turned out the real fantasy had been the notion she'd ever actually been attracted to me.

I had a few regrets about the high school guidance counselor and how that whole thing had ended, but what was I supposed to have done? She was the one who came onto me obviously with a long term relationship in mind, something I wanted no part of at that point, and with my academic record I couldn't really see myself hooking up long term with a high school teacher anyway, and the thing with her was never going anywhere as long as all this other shit was hanging over my head. And I'd long ago learned what's done is done, and you've got to move on. I had a long way to go and it was going to take my entire focus, and I didn't have the luxury of feeling a lot of remorse.

And then there were the thoughts that haunted my brain. What had I become? A serial killer? That's what it seemed like, but I couldn't bring myself to actually believe it. I'd killed two women, but it's not like I was some kind of predator or anything. Both times it was like they were the predators looking to take advantage of me and my stupidity. I liked to think it was the anger thing that Asian woman at the VA had warned me about that had just come out of nowhere, a brain disorder stemming from my time in Iraq and not my own natural state, a disorder that would resolve over time so I wouldn't always be this way and there was hope for the future if I could just get a chance to start over. I desperately wanted to have friends and someday find a simple woman who'd love and understand me, and help me get over the violent feelings that surfaced from somewhere inside me. I was hoping I could eventually find somebody like that and be able to lead a normal life. It was that hope that was my lifeline and was keeping me going.

26

August 10, 2012 I was anxious to get going, and didn't sleep very well, waking up repeatedly to look at the clock. Finally, daylight arrived. It was Saturday and it looked like it was going to be another beautiful Cape Cod day, and a nice day for traveling. I got up and showered, put on the travel clothes I'd laid out the night before, which were just a pair of blue jeans, a t-shirt and some sneakers. I needed to be fortified for the drive to Canada, which I figured would take about six to seven hours, so I made a pot of coffee and killed what was left of the last box of cereal in the cupboard. I loaded the dishwasher one last time, and took the last bag of trash with the coffee grounds and the other trash from breakfast out to the street and piled it with the others. I wanted to take one last look around to make sure I wasn't forgetting anything and that the place was in decent shape. My landlords had been good to me, and I owed it to them to leave the place at least neat if not perfectly clean.

I was in the bathroom taking one last piss before hitting the road when I heard a car pull into the driveway. The driveway was gravel, and it was pretty easy to hear when somebody drove in. I flushed the toilet, and went out into the little living room and peeped out through one of the windows at the driveway. A State Police cruiser had pulled in behind my car, and I watched as Balzano got out of the driver's side. Cavanaugh was sitting in the passenger seat, and he opened the door on his side but remained seated in the car. *Maybe they've got some last piece of the thing with Rongoni they want to go over with me*, I thought.

I opened the front door, waved, and called out, "Hey, good morning," as I walked down the steps toward their car. "What brings you guys out here at this hour in the morning? By the way, did you hear I quit?"

Balzano was all smiles as I approached. "Yeah, we heard that rumor."

"I'm on my way to Florida. I was just about to take off. You almost missed me."

"That would've been a shame," Balzano said, still smiling. "Glad we came early."

"What's up? You need something?"

"Yeah, Brian, we need you."

"For what? Something more on Gina Rongoni?"

"No. Actually, Brian, we're here to arrest you for the murder of Valerie Gray." I stared at him, dumbfounded. "Now, before you say or do anything," he said, "I just want to let you know we've got the street blocked off at both ends, and Jim here is sitting there in the car with a shotgun across his lap. Show him the shotgun, Jim." I glanced over at Cavanaugh, who flashed the barrel of the shotgun up so I could see it and then lowered it out of sight again. "Now, if I were you," Balzano continued, "I wouldn't fuck with Jim when he's got a shotgun. He's a range instructor at the State Police Academy, and at this distance he could probably put a couple rounds in your ear before you could even blink. But here, let me read you your rights first and get that out of the way. I don't want to forget because it might create problems later on, you know what I mean?"

He pulled a card out of the inside pocket of his suit jacket and began reading the standard warnings I never dreamed I'd ever hear being read to me. I stood there frozen, trying to figure it all out. *This must be a huge bluff,* I thought to myself, *they can't have anything on me. Maybe they figured out I lied about not having gone out with her, and they got wind I'd quit and was leaving, and this is their way of trying to keep me around while they see if they can come up with something on me because they can't prove a case against Rongoni. Just tough it out,* I told myself, *you know how the game is played. They want to see if they can get you to say something incriminating. Keep your cool, this is going nowhere.*

Finished reading, Balzano put the card back in his pocket and pulled a pair of handcuffs out from under his suit jacket. "You want to hold out your wrists?" he said, the smile gone now and his expression deadly serious.

I didn't hesitate. "Of course," I said, holding out my wrists. He clipped on the cuffs. Trying to look him straight in the eye, I said, "This is all bullshit. I know it and you know it, and it could have some very negative consequences for you guys down the road."

He let go of my wrists and let them drop. "Oh, really?" he said, raising his eyebrows. "Like what?"

"You've got no grounds to arrest me. You're making a huge fucking mistake doing this, and what goes around comes around. You guys better think this through pretty carefully before you go any further."

"Oh, we've thought it through, Brian, I can promise you that. Yeah, we've thought about it a lot. And you think this is the first time we've ever been threatened when we made an arrest? We get that shit all the time, mostly from people who're guilty. Like you, Brian."

I slowly shook my head. "I can't believe you're serious. Okay, you think you've got a case against me, go ahead and make it, I can't wait to hear what you've got."

Balzano smiled grimly. "Brian, you know we don't do that kind of thing, that's up to the D.A. You'll find out what the case against you is when the D.A. decides it's time."

I laughed. "Which means you don't have shit. It's up to the D.A.? That's bullshit and you know it. If you've got such a great case, you might as well tell me now. Somebody's going to have to lay it out for the judge when I'm arraigned anyway. That is, assuming this gets that far, so go ahead, I'm dying to hear what you've got. It should be entertaining."

"You don't think we're very smart, do you, Brian? We've gotten the clear impression you've thought that since day one."

"Well, I gotta' say, you haven't seemed all that smart, and now arresting me is about the stupidest fucking thing anybody could possibly come up with."

"Oh, really?" Balzano replied. "I'm sorry you think so."

"Yeah, I think so," I said. "Even Mullally thinks you're a couple of dumb fucks. And this little charade here this morning pretty much proves it."

Balzano shrugged and looked over at Cavanaugh, who nodded. Then, Balzano turned back to me. "So we're stupid, huh? Okay, we don't normally do this but seeing as how you're a cop, we're going to make a special exception. You want to hear it, Smart Ass? Okay, here goes. On the night of July 8th around midnight, you were down by the harbor somewhere in the vicinity of the McGruder boat spying on Valerie Gray, who you'd previously gone out with and who'd dumped you for McGruder. We expect there may be evidence you'd been stalking Ms. Gray for some time, and you were fixated on her and beside yourself because she'd ditched you. Sometime around midnight, Ms. Gray received a text message on her phone from her friend, Ms. Rongoni, who was down on the Yacht Club's outer dock, having arrived there in her boat. Ms. Rongoni was concerned that her friend had been avoiding her and felt they needed to talk. Ms. Gray texted her back saying she was on her way. You then followed Ms. Gray down to the dock and hid where you could hear their conversation. You heard Ms. Gray tell her friend her relationship with McGruder was serious, and she was planning to move to South Carolina to be with him and attend the University of South Carolina. This enraged you. You waited in hiding until you thought Ms.

Rongoni had left and gone home, and then you confronted Ms. Gray on the dock. In your rage, you assaulted her and killed her by smashing her head on one of the heavy metal cleats on the dock."

I stared at him. *Where the fuck did they get this from,* I thought to myself, trying not to let what I was thinking show.

Balzano continued. "You then went about attempting to dispose of the body. You went back up to the Yacht Club and got the Club's launch, which you'd driven for two summers while you were in high school. Knowing where the key to the launch was kept, you got the key and brought the launch around to the dock where you'd left Ms. Gray's body, wrapped it in a large piece of plastic you'd presumably found in the launch or in the shed where you'd gotten the key, and proceeded to take the launch somewhere off shore. There, you attached the launch's anchor to the body and dumped it in the Sound. You then returned the launch to its docking place, put the key back where you'd found it, and moved the car the victim had been driving to a spot across from the bus station hoping to confuse things and knowing to avoid the video cam that covered the bus station's parking lot. You didn't leave any fingerprints on the car; presumably, you were wearing gloves, and I'll bet we'll find a box of plastic gloves in the trunk of your car. You then walked back to your car and presumably went home. Then, when the anchor line failed and the body turned up, you volunteered to work on the investigation to try to make sure it never came close to you. To accomplish this, you attempted to frame Ms. Rongoni for the crime and planted evidence in her boat that could have only come from the real killer, you. What am I missing?"

"Nice story," I said, feigning a smile. "So, tell me, what happened to Marty Blair and whatever was going on between him and her, and the drug thing and the money in her bank account? I didn't hear a thing about any of that in your little story. How're you going to explain all that away?"

"Mr. Blair is not a suspect in the case because we believe we've found the perpetrator, which is you, Brian, although the State Police are still very interested in Mr. Blair's other business activities. But as far as this case is concerned, Mr. Blair has a very strong alibi for the night of July 8th, which we've known about for some time now. It seems he was in a late night poker game that night with a group of friends from town, one of whom is one of the town's selectmen. He was with those people for the whole evening until almost 2:00 am. From there, he went to the home of a female friend, where he remained for the rest of the night."

"Hey, that's really great. So let's assume for now that whole thing holds up and the girlfriend's not lying for him. Who knows, maybe she actually makes a good impression. So what about the money? Where'd she get the money if she wasn't in the drug business, did somebody just give it to her? She was obviously dealing drugs, which means she had to've been involved with some pretty bad people. And if she was trying to blackmail somebody, which was one of your own original theories, she was asking to get whacked."

Balzano shook his head. "Yeah, the money probably came from drugs, or like you said once, maybe she was a good saver. But the money didn't have anything to do with her death. No, Brian, you killed her because she ditched you and you couldn't handle it."

"Yeah, sure, I couldn't handle it. The only problem is your latest little theory seems pretty short on evidence just like all the rest of them, especially with all the stuff you're going to have to explain away at the same time."

Balzano smiled back. "Hey, Brian, for Christ's sake, give us a break for once, will you? We've got plenty of evidence."

"Sure you do. Like what?"

Balzano glanced at Cavanaugh, who nodded again. "Okay, you want evidence? Well, for starters we've got a witness who saw you on the Yacht Club's outer dock with the Club's launch on the night in question placing a large object in the launch and taking it out into the Sound."

I stared at him in disbelief. "You're shitting me. Don't tell me you guys are gonna' try to play the old 'we've got a witness' game to see if you can sucker me."

Balzano slowly shook his head. "We don't play games, Brian. Especially not in a case like this."

"So who's this star witness who was supposedly hiding out by the Yacht Club dock after midnight that night watching to make sure nobody got murdered? What, was there a submarine going by? You might as well tell me because if this witness is actually real, which I seriously doubt, you're going to have to disclose who it is once formal charges are filed against me. That is, if they ever are."

Balzano smiled grimly. "We have no problem telling you, Brian. I'm kinda' surprised you haven't figured it out already."

"So who is it?"

"Somebody who was sitting in a boat in the water about forty yards from the dock near the shore watching you put the body in the launch and take it out into the Sound."

"Who the fuck was that?"

"Ms. Rongoni."

You've got to be shitting me, I thought to myself. But then I said quickly, "Hold it a minute. I thought you said she left and went home. And that was her story when she talked to me in the cruiser. Don't tell me she's got another story now."

"No, I said *you thought* she'd left and gone home. She actually went about half way home, and then turned around and went back."

"Oh, great, and you're arresting me and not her? Guys, this is the third story she's told, for Christ's sake. You really think anybody's going to believe her? You're pinning your whole case on somebody who's told three different stories now, and who had the motive, the means, and the opportunity to commit the crime herself? Give me a fucking break."

"Actually, Brian, she's only told two stories. She only told you part of the second one in the car when she was scared shitless she was going to be your next victim."

"What does she say now? I can't wait to hear this."

Balzano continued, "Naturally, we considered her a potential suspect all along, but the story she eventually told us but never told you is perfectly consistent with all the other evidence we've found. It was really you who was pushing her as the perpetrator to try to point the finger at somebody else. Like I said, you even tried to plant evidence to incriminate her. By the way, as you've probably figured out already, that's an additional crime you're going to be charged with, planting evidence, which will also be evidence of premeditation." I stared at him blankly. "Anyway," Balzano continued, "here's what happened. You're right, the first time we talked to her the day after the body was found she told us she never saw her friend again after her friend had borrowed her car that night. That was what you read in the file. She later told us she said that because she was in shock over her friend's murder and didn't think her conversation with Ms. Gray that night, and particularly the part about her being gay, was anybody's business. At the same time, when she'd left Ms. Gray alone on the dock, Ms. Gray was obviously fine and intending to go back to McGruder's boat. Ms. Rongoni assumed her friend had then left and been murdered somewhere else after they found her car over by the bus station the next day. So, yes, she lied. I think it was you who said kids do stupid things sometimes.

"But it kept gnawing at her, the fact that her best friend and the woman she loved had been murdered, and that she'd lied about what'd actually happened that night. And she also began to wonder whether she'd in fact seen more than she'd originally thought. So, a while after that first interview she sat down with her parents and told them the whole story. They immediately decided they'd better get their daughter a lawyer, and they did, they hired a good one, Ms. Lindsay Workman. Ms. Workman's reaction after hearing Ms. Rongoni's story was that she should immediately come clean with the whole thing, and that indeed the young woman might've seen more than she'd originally thought. Ms. Workman called the D.A., who she apparently knows quite well, and told him she had a client who'd left a few things out of the client's original story in a very serious case, and would he agree not to prosecute the client if this person came forward. The D.A. said without any more information he of course couldn't make any promises, and a lot would depend on the circumstances of the witness and his or her level of cooperation going forward, but in a serious case if the perpetrator is ultimately brought to justice with the cooperation of a witness like that, very little thought is ever given after the fact to prosecuting the witness who ultimately cooperated and helped make the case. So, Ms. Workman told the D.A. to have us contact her, and the next day we met with Ms. Rongoni and Ms. Workman in her office.

"Ms. Rongoni told us about becoming distraught over her relationship with Ms. Gray, her boat ride that night over to the Yacht Club, her text to Ms. Gray, and their meeting on the dock. She then told us after she'd left Ms. Gray alone, or supposedly alone, on the dock and ridden off, on her way back home she'd become upset over their argument and some of the things she'd said to the woman with whom she was very much in love. She was about half way home when, on an impulse, she decided to turn around and go back to the dock, and, figuring her friend had probably gone back to McGruder's boat, she'd then text her to come back down to the dock again so she could apologize, and the two of them could go home together. The ocean was still calm, so she turned around and headed back to the dock, keeping close to the shore. Just as she got close to the mouth of the harbor, a boat came out through the channel without any lights on and swung around toward the Yacht Club outer dock. There was no sign whoever was driving the boat had seen or heard her over the sound of the other boat's engine, and there were no lights on the Whaler. Curious, Ms. Rongoni cut her engine and drifted in the direction of the shore, watching to see what was going on and figuring once the other boat had left she'd then pull in and text her friend. She didn't want to be seen because she didn't want to have to explain what she was doing was out there at that time of night, and she was also afraid she might be accused of trespassing on private Yacht Club property.

"The other boat, which was quite a bit bigger than hers, pulled up to the dock and the driver got off and tied it up with the motor still idling. At that point, she'd drifted closer to the dock and was tucked in by the shore. Her eyes were by now well accustomed to the darkness, and she could see the guy on the dock pretty well, although she didn't recognize him. He was wearing shorts and a t-shirt and was very muscular. She thought he might be somebody from the Yacht Club, or somebody who worked for the harbormaster. He fussed with something on the dock for a few minutes, but she couldn't see what it was because the boat tied to the dock partially blocked her view. Finally, he placed some fairly large object wrapped up in something into the boat, and then walked around the dock like he was inspecting it. It was then that she got a really good look at him. She held her breath hoping he wouldn't see her, but he was evidently focused on what he was doing and didn't look her way. At one point, she saw him bend down and pick something up. Then, he untied the boat and got into it, put it in gear, and headed out into the Sound still with no lights on. She waited until the sound of the boat's engine had receded in the distance before she started up the engine on her own boat. At that point, she was reluctant to try to tie up at the dock again for fear he might come back or somebody else might show up, and she wasn't sure where Ms. Gray was at that point given the amount of time that had passed, so she turned around again and went home, figuring she'd talk with her friend the next day."

"That's quite a story," I said. "Great case you've got there, Guys, good luck with it. But don't you think any half-assed lawyer could turn her into road kill on the witness stand?"

Balzano glanced at Cavanaugh, and then back to me again. "There you go again not giving us any credit, Brian. Like I said, we think Ms. Rongoni is going to be believed, not just because she's a sympathetic witness, but mainly because of the other stuff we've got that corroborates her story. Just be patient, Brian, there's more."

"I'm all ears," I told him. *Just tough it out,* I thought to myself, *they've got nothing so far.*

Balzano continued. "After hearing her story, we took Ms. Rongoni over to the harbor to see if she could identify the boat she saw that night. She picked out the Yacht Club launch as soon as she saw it. It's pretty distinctive looking, as you know, and you don't see many boats that're driven from the side. So, of course, we immediately had the forensic guys go over it with a fine tooth comb. They found small traces of blood on the floor of the launch that match Ms. Gray's blood type. They're currently being analyzed to see if the DNA matches as well. We're also analyzing some blood we found on the dock by one of the metal cleats. Of course, trying to find any kind of useful fingerprints on a boat like that that's been out in the open for a long time and carrying a ton of people back and forth is pretty unlikely, but we got lucky. There's a compartment tucked under the bow where the boat's anchor is supposed to be kept that has metal doors on it, and we got a couple of prints off those doors. They were the only prints on the doors, which means only one person had touched those doors in a long time. Also, the anchor was missing, which the Yacht Club people found to be very strange because supposedly it was never used and was only there because of some safety requirement. They were able, though, to identify the line the victim had been wrapped up with as the same type of line that had been on the anchor.

"Assuming the blood on the floor of the launch and on the dock would match the victim's and seeing the anchor was missing, we began to operate under the theory that the person Ms. Rongoni spotted driving the launch that night was probably the killer, who'd showed up on the dock after she'd left her friend there, smashed her friend's head on one of the metal cleats, and used the launch to dispose of the body, which he weighted down with the launch's anchor. But who was this guy?

"It was right at that moment that you stepped into the picture. Remember the afternoon you went over to the Rec Center to talk to Ms. Rongoni supposedly about traffic problems? Well, while we're waiting for an I.D. on the fingerprints to come back, she took one look at you when you showed up at the Rec Center that day and about wet her pants. She was sure you were the guy she saw that night. She could also tell right off we hadn't told you all she'd described to us about what she'd seen and done that night, so she wisely clammed up about it and stuck to her original story, figuring if you ever found out what she'd actually seen that night she'd probably wind up in the Sound like her friend."

I thought to myself, *no wonder she was so nervous when I talked to her that day. I thought it was because she was lying. I should've figured out something else was wrong.*

"As soon as you left," Balzano continued, "she called us. We could practically hear her shaking on the other end of the line. We were pretty surprised, but that's how these things go sometimes. So, we worked that whole weekend. Sure enough, the prints on the doors to the anchor locker on the launch matched the prints your department has on file for you in case they needed to identify your body someday and also the prints the Army has on you. And, lo' and behold, the Yacht Club's records showed you'd worked there for two summers driving the launch. So, at that point, we were pretty confident we had you, but we needed more evidence to nail it down.

"Remember I told you guys the first day we talked that where it's a woman it's usually somebody she's been in a relationship with? Well, of course, that was our first thought. So we went down to the diner and started interviewing people, and found out, sure enough, last spring you were in there chatting Ms. Gray up about five days a week. Sometimes you stayed for over an hour or more. You must've had to piss like a race horse some of those days after drinking all that coffee. Anyway, one woman who worked there said there was one night when Ms. Gray got pretty dolled up after work like she was going out. Curious, when she left the woman watched her out a back window walk across the parking lot and get into a car with some guy who was waiting for her, and the two of them drove off together. She couldn't see who the guy was, but the car was the same make and color as yours. Of course, we're going to go over your car and see if there's anything there that can prove she was ever in it. Maybe a stray blond hair or something, who knows.

"Anyway, then all of a sudden you stopped showing up at the Diner. Right around the time the Cape Cod League started up. At that point, we wanted to see what you'd say about your relationship with Ms. Gray, so we confronted you in Mullally 's office about whether you'd known Ms. Gray. Naturally, you lied out your ass.

"So, now we were pretty sure we had you as a former boyfriend who she'd dumped for a rich baseball player. Hey, remember you were the one who told us this was a crime of passion? Little did you know we'd already figured that out. And of course that's why you were out on the dock that night. You couldn't possibly have been there by accident, you had to've been stalking her. You'd most likely been spying on McGruder's boat, and when you saw her leave you went after her in a rage because you knew she'd ditched you for McGruder. You followed her down to the dock and who's there but Ms. Rongoni. So, you hide until Ms. Rongoni's gone, or you think she's gone, and then when you think you're alone you kill her. And then you very cleverly dispose of the body, and you might've actually gotten away with it if you hadn't fucked up and the body hadn't surfaced. Like we said at the beginning, an amateur mistake. Then, you went back up and moved Ms. Rongoni's car, and parked it up by the bus station to throw everybody off while of course avoiding the video cam in the parking lot. You left the keys under the seat so everybody would think Ms. Gray had taken off somewhere, leaving the keys behind for her friend. All in all, a clear case of premeditated murder, Brian, and you're going away for a long, long time."

"Of course, none of this is in the file."

"It's not in the stuff we sent you, no. That'd be pretty stupid, wouldn't it? No, the actual file is sealed. It was sealed the day Ms. Rongoni saw you at the Rec Center. Standard procedure when a police officer is under investigation. Avoids the possibility of a leak. Nobody knows about any of this except our superiors and the D.A."

"I assume you've told Mullally all this shit," I said.

"We haven't told him anything yet. Not even when he called to tell us you'd quit and somebody else was taking your place in the investigation. As far as Mullally 's concerned, we're still looking for evidence on Ms. Rongoni. Like I said, we can't have any possibility of a leak in a case like this, not even from somebody's body language. Only people who have a need to know have access, and Mullally's not one of them. Hey, Brian, there's more. You want to hear it? I don't want to leave anything out."

"More of this bullshit?"

"Yeah, right, this is all bullshit. Okay, so at this point we've got a pretty decent circumstantial case, but one that's not exactly foolproof given, like you say, all the stuff we'd have to explain away. Then, you come along and make another amateur mistake. Let's talk about the famous earring, Brian. Naturally, when Ms. Rongoni came to us with her complete story, we of course wanted to look at her boat. Like I said, she was a possible suspect at that point and we needed to cover all the bases. She and her attorney readily consented. So, our guys went over the boat in microscopic detail. Nothing, although a long time had gone by and somebody could easily make the argument that a search that turned up negative after that amount of time didn't really mean anything. Okay, so then we get to the point where you got Ms. Rongoni to admit to what had happened between her and Ms. Gray on the dock that night, which you of course couldn't have done if you hadn't been there yourself. Oh, and not giving her the warnings was a nice touch, by the way. But of course, she obviously wasn't going to tell you about her return trip back to the dock, figuring if she did, she probably wouldn't have made it out of that police car alive. Then, you and Mullally call us and tell us Ms. Rongoni's changed her story. Okay, we'll play along, see what the fuck you're up to now.

"You proceed to tell us you think we ought to get a warrant to search Rongoni's boat and of course alarm bells immediately start to go off. And we no sooner get off the phone with you than we get a call from Ms. Workman screaming at us to keep you away from her client, who's now scared shitless you're onto her and you're stalking her now. We tell Ms. Workman to just sit tight, we think we're almost there. So, with her permission we go over the boat again to make sure it was clean as a whistle. Then, we put a surveillance team with cameras on the second floor of the Rongonis' house in the bedroom closest to their dock, and we put the Rongonis up in a motel for a couple nights. Sure enough, the first night who comes hip-hopping along like the fucking Easter Bunny but you all dressed in black like that was going to make you invisible or something, and with plastic gloves on again to make sure you didn't leave any prints anywhere. Of course, we had you covered from the minute you turned onto their street. There were troopers all over the neighborhood that night in camouflage gear. You wouldn't believe how many night vision sniper-scopes were trained on you the whole time. We've got all kinds of video and still shots of you going into their yard and dropping something into their boat. We've also got plenty of shots of your car parked down the street, and you getting into it and driving off after you'd planted the earring. As soon as the word went out you were gone, we looked in the boat again, and, surprise, surprise, there's Ms. Gray's missing earring in the bottom of the boat. We got the whole thing on film, Brian. Don't worry, you'll get to watch it someday. In the courtroom.

"So now the case isn't so circumstantial any more. We were kind of waiting around to see if you'd make any more stupid mistakes, but when Mullally called and told us you'd quit we figured we'd better not fool around any longer. We had plenty of evidence, and we didn't want to have to chase after you somewhere, which probably wasn't going to be Florida.

"Oh, yeah, there's one other thing we haven't quite figured out yet. See if this makes any sense to you. So, it's our first day on the case, and we're at Ms. Gray's house going through the stuff in her room. Naturally, in the course of the search we flip her mattress over to see if there's anything under it, and there under her mattress we find a plastic freezer bag with some crumpled up tissues in it. Now that's strange. So we take the bag back to the lab and have what's in it analyzed. Turns out it's a couple tissues with somebody's sperm on them. That's kinda' odd, don't you think? Was this a memento from the first time she got laid, or from some unforgettable night of passion? Or was she holding onto this little sperm sample to maybe someday use it against somebody? Like maybe for blackmail? Or maybe to prove something against somebody, like maybe rape or something? Who knows. Anyway, we're going to be taking a sample of your DNA, and it'll be interesting to see if it matches. Maybe you killed her because she was blackmailing you, I don't know. But at the very least, if nothing else, if it's yours it'll prove you had a sexual relationship with her, which you then lied about. Probably won't be able to do much more with it than that, but you never know. So, Brian, what do you think? Still think this is all bullshit?"

I stared at him, not knowing what to say. He smiled. "So, what's your story going to be, Brian? That you met her on the Yacht Club dock in the middle of the night by coincidence, just happened to bump into her there? Or, maybe the two of you were getting back together? And she accidently slipped and hit her head on both sides at the same time, breaking her jaw on one side and suffering a fatal blow on the other? And instead of calling for help—you're a cop for Christ's sake—you stole a boat and dumped her in the Sound, and were part of the investigation into her death and tried to pin it on somebody else by planting evidence? Brian, think about it, Old Buddy, you're fucked. Backward, forward, and sideways."

At this point, I was staring at the ground, my mind a blank. It was like somebody had hit me in the stomach and I was having trouble breathing. I just kept telling myself, *shut up, shut up, they just want you to say something they can use.* "Hey, Brian," Balzano said, now smirking, "there's something else we wanted to ask you about. Of course, you don't have to answer if you don't want to, but it seems another question's come up. While you were working up there in New Hampshire in your previous job, did you ever know a woman named Beth LeDuque?" I kept my eyes on the ground, not moving. "Well, okay," Balzano continued, "like I said, you don't have to say anything if you don't want to, but we wanted to let you know in checking on you we talked to the folks up there in New Hampshire where you used to work. They said you were a good cop, but you left kind of abruptly, and they didn't know why. I guess you told them you didn't like the winters up there. Anyway, in talking with them we told them about this case, and at that point some bells started to go off in somebody's head about a woman from one of the towns around there who disappeared right around the time you left New Hampshire. She was a local prostitute named Beth LeDuque, who apparently vanished one night after she closed down the bar she worked at. According to the New Hampshire cops, her car was found behind the bar but nobody's heard from her since. I guess our telling them about this case piqued their interest, so they showed your picture around the bar and, sure enough, some people recognized you as having hung around there, although they apparently had no idea you were a cop. Anyway, there's a couple guys coming down from New Hampshire to talk to the D.A. and I guess they want to take a look at your car, too. Just thought we'd let you know so you're not surprised."

He paused and looked at me. "You all right, Brian? You don't look so good." I shook my head slightly, still staring down at the ground. "You know, Brian, things could be worse," he said. "You're lucky it's not my father or my uncle making this arrest back in the old days. One thing they didn't like was a dishonest cop. Somebody like you, before they took him in they would've beaten the shit out of him. Any broken bones, they would've said he fell down the stairs or something. Old school. We don't do that kind of shit any more. Like I said, things could be worse."

Balzano motioned to Cavanaugh, who got out of the car holding the shotgun and came over to where Balzano and I were standing. They each took one of my arms and led me to the car and put me in the back seat, Balzano putting his hand on my head as I got in to see I didn't bump my head. Then, they got in, and Balzano backed the car down the driveway and out into the street, and turned on the blue lights.

27

May 14, 2013 Carmen Belafontaine was sitting at her anchor desk in one of her striking outfits, her hair as usual perfectly coiffed. Her face held a serious expression as the camera zoomed in on her. *Good evening. We begin tonight with a report on a story we've been following since it first broke approximately ten months ago. In a surprise development today, former New Salisbury police officer Brian Bonner pleaded guilty to manslaughter in Barnstable Superior Court on Cape Cod two weeks before his trial on a charge of first degree murder for the death of Valerie Jean Gray was about to begin. Bonner has been held without bail since his arrest last August. In court today, under a plea agreement that had received court approval, in exchange for his guilty plea Bonner was immediately sentenced to twenty years in prison. If he'd been convicted of first degree murder, Bonner would have received an automatic sentence of life imprisonment without the possibility of parole. With the sentence he received today, Bonner will become eligible for parole in ten years.*

You'll remember that Valerie Jean Gray was a nineteen-year-old New Salisbury resident who was brutally beaten to death in July of last year just weeks after she'd graduated from high school. Her body was discovered in Vineyard Sound a week after she disappeared. A brief clip then appeared on the screen of Bonner being led out of the courthouse in handcuffs and put in a State Police cruiser, as Carmen continued her narrative. *Interviewed on the courthouse steps following the sentencing, Barnstable County District Attorney Wallace Neery said that Bonner's guilty plea "ends a long ordeal" and "dispenses justice for a brutal crime." He refused to comment on why the prosecution had agreed to a plea bargain, although it is generally assumed the prosecution likely felt there was a risk a jury could find the victim's death had been accidental and return a verdict of manslaughter, which would carry a significantly lesser sentence than murder. Bonner's defense attorney, Steven Hoffman, declined to comment following the sentencing.*

The camera went back to Carmen. *Bonner's guilty plea closes the books on the most sordid crime in the Town of New Salisbury's history. It was a story that captured wide attention both in the press and in social media.* The victim's graduation photo appeared on the screen. *The victim, a beautiful young woman who is described as having had fashion model looks, had just graduated from New Salisbury High School and was on her way to college. She had apparently dated Bonner, who was considerably older, over a period of several months, and then apparently broke off the relationship. It was alleged that Bonner had become obsessed with the young woman, and following their breakup had repeatedly stalked her. Finally, late on the night of July 8, 2012, he allegedly attacked her when she was alone on the dock of a local yacht club and killed her by smashing her head in. He then allegedly disposed of her body in Vineyard Sound, and, to attempt to cover up his role in the crime, Bonner then allegedly volunteered to be part of the police team charged with investigating the young woman's death in hopes of deflecting the investigation away from himself. He was eventually apprehended when he allegedly attempted to plant evidence to try to implicate a former friend of the victim's as the perpetrator.*

The camera went back to Carmen again. *The victim had lived alone with her disabled mother, who she had helped support by working part-time while she was in high school. Visibly shaken, her mother appeared in court for the sentencing today but declined to comment afterward. Reached for comment in Florida, where he is now retired, former New Salisbury Police Chief Thomas Mullally said that, "Bonner had us fooled for a while, but in the end good police work was responsible for apprehending him." It had been rumored that Mullally was forced to resign from his position with the New Salisbury police force following Bonner's arrest.*

A high school drop-out, prior to being hired by the Town of New Salisbury Bonner had served as a military policeman in the Army, including a tour of duty in Iraq. A picture of Bonner in his Army uniform flashed on the screen. *He was honorably discharged in 2008, and hired as a police officer by a town in New Hampshire, and then moved to Cape Cod and was hired by the Town of New Salisbury. He lived by himself and is described by sources as being a "loner." Following his arrest, he was ordered to undergo a psychiatric evaluation, which had determined he was competent to stand trial, although it was believed that the defense was contemplating an insanity defense, possibly relating to Bonner's service in Iraq, had the case gone to trial. His parents, who live on Cape Cod, have avoided the media since his arrest and were unavailable for comment.*

The camera went back to Carmen once again. *The case has also been colored by rumors that the victim may have been involved in the drug business, but a source close to the prosecution has told us that drugs played no part in this crime, which was apparently simply a case of love gone bad. Now, it's finally over. This station has also learned that Bonner may be under investigation by New Hampshire authorities in connection with the disappearance of a young woman in a town in that state close to where Bonner had worked as a policeman before coming to New Salisbury. We will keep you updated with any further information that comes out of that investigation.*

Carmen feigned glancing at down her notes, and then looked back up at the camera. *In other news tonight....*

ACKNOWLEDGEMENTS

Thanks to my dear friends Russell Kelley, Al Larkin and Tamara Smith Holtslag for their support and helpful comments, and thanks most of all to Kathy, my partner in all things, whose love and encouragement made this book possible.

CPSIA information can be obtained
at www.ICGtesting.com
Printed in the USA
BVOW04s1929010617

485803BV00001B/57/P